This
Year's
Model

Also by Carol Alt

EATING IN THE RAW: A BEGINNER'S GUIDE TO GETTING
SLIMMER, FEELING HEALTHIER, AND LOOKING YOUNGER
THE RAW-FOOD WAY

THE RAW 50: 10 AMAZING BREAKFASTS, LUNCHES, DINNERS,
SNACKS, AND DRINKS FOR YOUR RAW-FOOD LIFESTYLE

This Year's Model

CAROL ALT

A V O N

An Imprint of HarperCollinsPublishers

HarperCollins books may be purchased for educational, business, or sales promotional use. For information please write: Special Markets Department, HarperCollins Publishers, 10 East 53rd Street, New York, NY 10022.

FIRST EDITION

Designed by Elizabeth M. Glover

Library of Congress Cataloging-in-Publication Data
Alt, Carol, 1960–
   This year's model / Carol Alt.—1st ed.
      p. cm.
ISBN 978-0-06-136624-6
1. Models (Persons)—Fiction. I. Title.
PS3601.L73T47   2008
813'.6—dc22   2008006890

08 09 10 11 12   OV/RRD   10 9 8 7 6 5 4 3 2 1

Prologue

I thought I was safe a minute ago when I literally sprinted past Cinnabon, but an empty stomach can really play tricks on the brain. Only now there's a whole procession of chocolate, peanuts, licorice, and assorted Gummies leaping onto the counter to slink and sashay and *sell it, sell it, sell it.* Call it candy bar couture. Unfortunately, food is my nemesis, and the one thing you cannot escape—it's everywhere! Tearing my eyes from the evil array of temptation at Hudson News, I stride toward the puzzle books—I don't need sugar; I need some sudoku to occupy my mind—and nearly collide with this kid. Tall for her age, but still a baby. She stares at me and it's as though my Puma tracksuit has been stripped away and I'm standing there in that gilded Oasis bikini, the one they let me keep.

"Oh . . . my . . . God!"

Reflexively, I look over my shoulder, sure she has spotted a terrorist in the act of setting off a shoe bomb, when I realize *I'm* the one who has caused her to shriek with what sounds like genuine excitement.

"Hi, Mac!"

She says my name with such familiarity that I look at her for a long moment. Then, embarrassed that I don't recognize her, I ask, "Do I know you?"

"Know me? God, no—why in the world would *you* know *me*?"

I blink, then realize that I'm having that moment. The one in which you find yourself confronted with celebrity and are about to make an absolute fool of yourself in the name of getting an autograph. Except in this case, *I'm* the celebrity. I glance down at my sweat suit. I suppose I could be better dressed for it.

"I cannot believe you're even talking to me," the girl chatters on. "I can't believe *Mac Croft* is even standing in front of me! You are absolutely my favorite model! I know everything about you. And you know what? You're so much prettier in person."

"Thank you. That's sweet of you to say." I'm not sure this is a compliment since my business is taking pictures. Shifting my crammed carryon from my right to my left shoulder, I assess her like I've come to do with any female over age twelve. Occupational hazard. "You're really pretty too."

"Oh, thank you! You are *so* nice. My brother would die—he thinks you're incredibly hot. Ha on him! I was bugging him, so he gave me money to buy magazines for the plane. I told him he should come with me!" She beams at me. "Hey, where are you going? If it's okay to ask."

Good question. Where *am* I going? "Sure, it's okay," I say, stalling. These last two months I've been on a plane twenty-nine times; I feel like I'm aiming to get into *Guinness*. It takes me a moment, but I finally remember. "Montana. I'm going to Montana."

"Really? Montana? We're going to California—we have a week off from school. Montana doesn't sound very glamorous, if you don't mind me saying."

Glamorous? Maybe not—but it's a big job, the kind you might go to Siberia for if that's what the client requested; an exclusive for Mountain, the new Calvin Klein perfume. It's the kind of job I'd never refuse, though I suppose there are better ways to spend Valentine's Day. Six hours from now I'll be bareback on a horse, in a man's arms—Ivan Gladst, I think that's who they booked—surrounded by snow and braving the kind of windchill factor that puts icicles on your eyelashes. I'll be freezing—not that you'll be able to tell in the final pictures—but I suppose I'll thaw out when they cut that check for $100K.

"Hey, can I ask you a question?" My fan—I'm still getting used to the idea that I *have* a fan—is wearing a bad Burberry knockoff over pajama bottoms shoved into soiled Uggs, a look so very, sadly wrong and yet so darling I want to pat her on the head. "Do you think I could model? Tell me honestly."

"Sure," I say. "You've got great bones, great hair. How old are you?"

"Thirteen. I'm already five eight—and still growing."

"I bet we'll be working together soon." The funny thing is I'm not lying. In fact she kind of looks like the girl who beat me out for that Juicy Couture ad. "What's your name?"

"*Uck*, Shyla." She shakes her head and puts on an air of sophistication that doesn't fit. "What *were* my parents thinking? I intend to change it eventually."

"Why? Unique names are all the rage in the business," I say.

She smiles, becoming a kid again. "Hey, can I get your autograph, Mac? Because I've got the *Sports Illustrated* right here."

And there I am, in all my glory—artfully airbrushed tan, which has made even the scar on my right forearm disappear, my hair a mass of choreographed tangles, the Oasis bikini clinging wetly to every curve. "Wow, Shyla, you know what? I haven't even seen it myself yet," I admit. "I just flew in from Europe and—"

"I can't *stand* it. You're on the cover and you're so fabulous you haven't even *seen* it." Shyla absorbs the unbelievable truth. "I'm so glad they put you on the cover instead of some cheesy celebrity, like Beyonce or whoever. You're a supermodel. And you have the best body—*ooh*, sorry, I don't mean that in a gay way. Wait, here's a Sharpie. God, this is going to be such a collector's item."

I move a bit farther into the corner, trying not to take over the store with my first random celebrity moment. "So, Shyla—that's S-H-Y-L-A?" I take the pen. "You want to hear something ironic? When I was your age I was seriously into tennis. I even dreamed I'd be in *Sports Illustrated*—but I never thought it would be *this* way."

"Really? You mean you didn't always want to model? That is *so* interesting. Oh, I wish you were on our plane to L.A. Then we could sit together and you could tell me all about Fashion Week and the European collections." Shyla sighs. "But then you probably fly first class."

Today I am in first, courtesy of Calvin Klein. But I worked my way up to flying first class. Wouldn't she be shocked to learn it isn't always like this for every model and that even now, after months of struggling and starving and pounding the pavement in search of the next job, I still find myself in coach when the client can't afford to upgrade the ticket. If the job is prestigious enough, I would allow them to shove me into the overhead compartment if it meant the difference between getting the job and not. Handing her back the magazine and marker, I glance around, trying to get my bearings, trying to remember what gate I'm going through and wondering if I'll even be able to grab a puzzle book before they announce pre-boarding for first class customers.

"Mac, thank you, thank you so much." Shyla studies my signature, clasps the *S.I.* to her chest. "You are just so unbelievably nice. Can I ask you one more question?"

Yes, please, let it be the last one. I hate to be rude, but I'm already understanding why most celebrities travel incognito. If I hang around too much longer, I won't even be flying coach as I may miss my flight altogether.

"What's the best part of being a supermodel?"

"*Hmm* . . . wow . . . it's hard to say." And I mean it; meteoric rise and all that, I'm still so new to the game. Of course, months can be like years in modeling. I glance at Shyla. The kid looks at me as though I'm about to impart the secret meaning of the universe. "The truth is it's just like any other job," I tell her. "It all comes down to the people. . . ."

One

MORRISTOWN, NEW JERSEY
Eight months earlier . . .

"Welcome to the Porter House, sir. I'm Melody Ann, and I'll be your server this evening." Lucky me: middle-aged guy, nicely dressed, dining alone— maybe he'll even order a bottle of wine, really run up the bill. I'm already calculating the tip.

"No . . . ," he says.

"*No*?" What does he mean? It's not like he gets to pick. If you're seated at table eight on a Wednesday evening, you get me.

"That apron, it's not some fetishistic trompe l'oeil diversion?" My table for one removes his sunglasses and looks at me so strangely, I suddenly feel self-conscious. It's almost as if he's . . . weighing me, wondering what I cost per pound. "Miu Miu isn't reinventing black-and-white polyester this season?"

I don't even understand what he's saying. Maybe I'm not so lucky—maybe I've got a crazy at table eight. Crazies aren't necessarily bad tippers, but they really make you earn it. "Excuse me?"

"Goddamn it, if I didn't know we were in some burb an hour outside of Manhattan, I would swear you were walking a Bryant Park runway right now. In fact, you're pretty graceful for a girl your height. Most models are gawky until they learn how to walk," he says. "So you really are a waitress?"

I smile, still trying to humor him. "Must have been all those ballet lessons my mother took me to as a kid. I'll send on your compliments. In the meantime, yes, I really am a waitress, though actually we prefer the non-gender-specific 'server.' It's more professional, don't you think? May I bring you a beverage?"

"What I think is your smile is dazzling, simply dazzling. And, sure, I'll have a beer."

"On tap we have Amstel, Beck's—"

"Surprise me—I trust you. And listen, I'm not kidding, you really are a beauty."

"Thank you. I'll be right back with your beer."

I hustle to place his drink order. What do I know about beer? I've tasted it twice, and once was enough. Charlie, the bartender, is cool; he commiserates when I moan about table eight.

"He says I should surprise him."

Charlie laughs, pulls the tap. "Well, I could spit in it if you like. Bet that'd be a surprise."

After I decline Charlie's offer, I start back with the beer, hurrying past the party of five at table six. It's a family—must be a special occasion. Morristown isn't a fancy town; the Porter House is not the best restaurant we've got, but it's affordable for a family. Any cheaper is a drive-thru. Two of the kids are fighting over who has more French fries. As I go by, the dad asks me for steak sauce, and I tell him it's coming right up.

Back at table eight, Mr. Cuckoo says, "So . . . ah . . . Mela-nie, is it?"

"Actually, it's Melody, Melody Ann. Our specials this evening—"

"You're what's special."

He thinks he's so clever, so what's the word . . . *suave*. This is going to be a long night.

"I've been watching you, the way you move. Those ballet classes paid off. You've really got presence."

"Well . . . *sir* . . . I'm not on the menu. But we do have a wonderful New England clam chowder. I highly recommend it—it's yummy," I recite. "As an appetizer we have stuffed mushrooms, and the catch of the day is mahi-mahi, grilled with a citrus glaze."

"How could I not have the clam chowder with your en-dorsement?" He ogles me, slowly and serenely. " 'Yummy,' you said."

Uck, I think.

"And bring me the filet mignon, medium."

"Will do."

It's a madhouse in the kitchen, a madhouse in hell—flames leaping from the grill, sauces trying to escape sauté pans, cooks sniping at servers, the kitchen manager reading the sous-chef the riot act. I wish for the thousandth time that I'd tied my hair back before I got here but my ponytail thingie was so stretched out, the elastic was shot, and it broke. My hair is my best feature, I think, but it's hell to live with. The only reason I wear it long is so I don't have to *do* anything to it; girls with shorter hair are always pumping on product and endlessly blow-drying. All I commit to is conditioner.

Shampoo is whatever I can find in the shower. Usually soap, ~~i~~ my brothers always use up the good stuff. My hair is so low-maintenance I can't even remember to buy ponytail thingies. Maybe they've got a regular rubber band in the office or at the cash register. . . .

I swing out with table seven's orders; they need extra sour cream, they need more bread, they need soda refills. Yes yes yes. Minimum wage at some store in the mall is looking *so* good to me right now. Better push that thought from my mind; at least as a server I earn tips, and where I'm going I'm going to need some real money. It's a miracle I got this job, with no experience. But if I didn't have a miracle, I had one thing better: a connection. The restaurant owner remembered when my firefighter dad rescued his family's puppy. There'd been a blaze at his home—luckily, there wasn't much damage, but when Dad found the little dog cowering under the sofa, he became an instant hero . . . and I found myself employed. I shouldn't complain about the work. It's only been two weeks; I'll get the hang of it. I swing back into the inferno to see if the order for table eight is up and it is.

Plate in hand, I make my way over to my least favorite table tonight. "Your steak, sir."

"Stop with the 'sir'—makes me feel old," table eight grumbles. "I'm Jonathan Novak. Ever hear of me?"

Jonathan Novak? I look at him, really look at him, for the first time. Our eyes meet, and after a moment he's the one who looks away.

"You probably think I'm some sleazy stalker."

He sounds so humble all of a sudden. "Oh no, I wouldn't think that . . . well, maybe for a second."

"I'm not a stalker—I'm a photographer. Only reason I'm

siting family in Cleveland, but you know: can-
al car. Thought I'd make it back to civilization
, till the hunger pangs hit."

Civilization? Do I look like Pebbles Flintstone? "You came to the right place, then," I say haughtily. "The Porter House is a fine dining experience to savor. Enjoy your meal." I go back to work.

The kitchen closes at ten. I'm not wearing a watch—I just don't feel comfortable with jewelry on—but my body clock is telling me it's getting to be that time. I'm eager to get home, take a shower, and curl up in bed with my phone. Eric's supposed to call tonight. Ever since my boyfriend left for his first year at Notre Dame last fall, we've been really good about talking regularly. But with finals coming up for him and my new waitressing job, it's been nearly a week since we've spoken.

Fortunately the Porter House empties out; most people around here eat early. But table eight is lingering, talking on his cell phone. Finally, when the busboy attends to his water glass, Jonathan Novak waves the plate away dismissively. He's eaten maybe a third of his steak, and he doesn't want to take the leftovers with him. Much as I'd like him out of here, our final exchange as server and diner is a crucial one—if I want my nice fat tip, that is.

"May I show you our dessert platter?"

"Oh God, I'm dying here." He slaps the tablecloth.

"I wish you wouldn't—it would be bad for business."

"Gorgeous *and* funny! What a combination." I don't even notice his hand slide across the cloth until his fingers reach for the scalloped edge of my apron. The hem of my skirt is about an inch below. I take a step back, a small step but a firm one. "No no no—it's just killing me to see you wasting away in this . . . this beef brothel," Jonathan Novak says with an exaggerated sigh. "I mean it—you should be a model. You *must* be a model."

Oh, please. Am I supposed to be flattered? He's saying that because I'm tall. And from what I understand, most models are tall. Aside from that there's nothing model-like about me. I'm not skinny, I don't wear makeup, and I wouldn't know a . . . a Miu Miu from a Yoo-hoo. I've had enough of this guy, but he's been sitting here all night, taking up the table so that I've had no turnover. Since he's going to be my only tip on table eight tonight, I'm not about to blow it now. "No thanks, not me," I tell him lightly. "I'm starting college in the fall. University of Pennsylvania, premed. I'm going to be a doctor . . . or maybe a nutritionist." He probably thinks I'm some bimbo—I'm tempted to add that I'm up for a scholarship. Of course it's a huge enough deal that I was even accepted to a prestigious school like Penn. My mother has her associate's degree from the community college, and my father joined the fire department straight out of high school.

"Nutritionist my left nut," Jonathan Novak says. "Look, I'm going to give you my card—but don't call me. I'd rather you call the agencies directly and use my name. Let me write some numbers on the back, bookers at the top agencies. Let's see . . . Karen at Elite, definitely . . . and Francesca at Delicious, she'll devour . . . I mean, *adore* you. Oh, and Carlos at Ford. Now I expect you to contact these people first thing tomorrow, and I know I'll be seeing you in my studio very soon."

I just love it when perfect strangers think they know what's best for me. But I hold my tongue behind my smile and I give Jonathan Novak his check and I tell him, with as much charm as I can muster, "Well, that's really nice of you, but I wouldn't hold my breath—unless Miu Miu or whoever starts designing scrubs . . ."

Two

I'm running up Eighth Avenue in sling backs, no easy feat, considering that it's 9:54 a.m. on a Wednesday morning and everyone is on the streets, rushing to offices that are, apparently, in the opposite direction from the way I'm going.

"Excuse me," I say, for about the sixteenth time in ten minutes as I almost collide with yet another suit who has little tolerance for a nearly six-foot-tall girl doing a half marathon in a jersey-knit dress that feels a size too small and probably a year too late, fashionwise.

The dress was Liza's idea. "Your boobs look amazing in that dress," my best friend advised me when I told her I had bitten the bullet and called one of those phone numbers that Jonathan Novak, aka the nutjob from table eight, had scribbled on the back of his card. Apparently, he isn't such a nutjob because all I had to do was utter his name to land an interview with the first agency I called. An interview I'm about to blow if I don't make it to the offices of Dalton-McGill in T-minus six minutes.

"Ouch!" I stop to adjust the strap on my shoe, which has been digging into my heel since I got off the train at Penn Station.

The shoes were my mother's idea.

"Well, if you're serious about this, you can wear my good heels," she said, as she stood in the doorway of my bedroom last night, a wary expression on her face.

"Are you sure?" I replied, taking the box she held out to me. The shoes are a designer pair she splurged on last year to wear to the Morristown Fire Department's Annual Christmas Dinner. Being close in size and the only women in a houseful of men—I have two older brothers—my mother and I sometimes share clothes. That is, when my mother actually purchases something cool enough for me to covet. The shoes, which are not only gorgeous, but right on trend, are just such an item. Except that up until now, my mother refused to hand them over, saying that she wanted to save them for special occasions. That she is lending them to me today is a tentative endorsement of my plan to spend the summer making as much money as possible.

At least, that's the plan as I related it to dear Mom and Dad.

"I can't count on that scholarship to come through for me," I explained to my parents, after I announced that I was going into the city for the interview. True, of course, but that isn't my only reason for pursuing the career that Jonathan Novak insisted I "must" do.

My more pressing motive has to do with the fact that Eric will be home from school any day now. And I definitely do *not* want to be sitting around Morristown all summer like some kind of lame-ass when my loser ex-boyfriend gets back to town.

The boyfriend who swore, before he headed off to Notre

Dame, that the distance would only make us stronger. The boyfriend who decided, not two weeks before he was about to come home, that maybe it was time we see other people. What a waste of a year!

Just the thought of him makes me run faster, despite my blister having broken two blocks ago. I glance down at the cell phone I'm clutching in one hand: 9:57. Three minutes to make it another ten blocks. I should take a cab. Except I'm already down twenty-one dollars for my round-trip train ticket, and since every dollar spent on what my dad calls "this farce" is less money I'll have for college in the fall, I need to watch my expenses.

"Come on, come on," I mutter, maneuvering around a woman who has stopped, mid-sidewalk, to carry on an argument on her cell phone.

"Fired? What do you mean, *fired*?" the woman practically screams, sending a chill ominously up my spine.

I stop in my tracks, knowing I need to do something but not knowing what. Then, like a prince on a white charger though not half as charming, I see a bus ambling up the avenue toward me. Yes! I race to meet it at the stop one block ahead, breathing a sigh of relief when the doors open easily to admit me.

"Hi, I'm Melody Ann. Melody Ann Croft. I have an appointment at ten? I'm sorry I'm late. I didn't figure on how long it would take to get here from Penn Station and then the bus dropped me off two blocks away and I had to run. And I really wasn't sure where I was going or even how far your office was from the train . . ."

I know I'm babbling, my eager apologies echoing baldly around the pure white, minimally furnished reception area of Delicious Models, but somehow I can't stop myself. I hate being late. . . .

The receptionist, who with her sleekly styled platinum-blond hair and pale features, might just be a piece of the pallid furnishings herself, blinks at me.

I'm suddenly aware that I'm sweating, and most likely flushed from my mini-marathon up Eighth Avenue.

Blondie doesn't notice, or doesn't care. Her face is completely devoid of expression. It's as if she's waiting for me to self-destruct.

Which I seem to be on the verge of doing. "Anyway, I'm here to see Francesca DeLongue and I realize I'm ten minutes late but I'm hoping she can still see me. If she's already moved on to her next appointment, I can wait. Or I could come back later—"

"Don't move."

At first, I think Blondie has a talent for throwing her voice. But then I realize the throaty command is coming from a well-heeled brunette who has stopped in the midst of that white-walled splendor to stare at me.

Blondie finally does open her mouth—to introduce me? I don't know—because the brunette holds up a hand to quiet her as she steps carefully toward me, like a sleek cat approaching its prey. She stops, folds her arms, dark eyes gleaming as a smile lights up her features, which I realize, despite her ravenous gaze, are quite pretty.

"Well, well, well . . . ," she says, almost to herself. Then, to the receptionist: "Sloane, cancel the rest of my appointments."

I feel a prickle move through the room, the sound of bubbles bursting as the six women seated in the waiting area look up, shift restlessly. Irrationally, I feel protective of my fellow interviewees. "And you are?" I ask.

Her smile widens. "Francesca DeLongue. Your new best friend."

Then her expression becomes businesslike. "Come with me," she insists, leading me into her office, which is dominated by a large desk covered in what looks like trash. Upon closer inspection, I realize what's littering the desk, the floor, and even the chair she motions me to sit in, are pages torn from magazines, photographs, and even, in one case, a line drawing—all of young women. Models.

"Now," she says, smiling graciously at me once I'm seated. "May I see your book."

"My book?"

"Yes, your photographs. Your *book*," she repeats, clearly struggling to remain patient with me.

"I don't have a book, but I did bring some photos." I quickly pull the envelope out and dump the pictures into my palm. "They're from our family vacation this past spring break," I say, handing them over.

Francesca takes them and begins flipping through quickly. "Oh! . . . Okay. Well, I see. You went to Downingtown, Pennsylvania, on vaykay?"

"Sure did. We even went to Hershey Park. It was the best week *ever.*"

"*Umm*, right." She picks up the receiver on her phone. "Excuse me a moment, would you?"

At my nod, she presses a button on her phone. "Renee, there is someone you must meet." She puts a hand over the receiver, and looks at me. "Do you have a moment to wait?"

"Of course I do—well I mean, I have a meeting with Ford's in about an hour. If I hurry, I think I can probably still make it—"

"Yes, Renee, she'll wait for you."

I look at her with alarm.

"You're canceling your meeting with Ford's," she replies in a voice that says she will accept no arguments.

Within a few minutes I'm standing before Renee Kitaen, president of Delicious Models and second-in-command to Paul Anders, who owns the agency. Even if I hadn't done my homework on Delicious before I came, I would know Renee, who was a supermodel in the eighties, when being a supermodel really meant something, before celebrities usurped models' supreme reign over magazine covers. Renee made it through some turbulent times relatively unscathed, but she saw it all, toiling with all her era's infamous train wrecks. Gia. Janice. So one must pay homage.

And I do. In fact, I've just begun to gush to her about how my mother, in an uncharacteristic act of vanity, actually tossed her tweezers back in the day in an attempt to mimic Renee's famously lush brows, when Renee raises a hand to silence me.

Turning to Francesca, she asks, "Will you step out into the hallway with me?"

"Where did you say she was from?" I hear Renee ask in a loud whisper once they are outside.

"God knows. Somewhere in New Jersey. She went to Downingtown, PA, for vaykay, for crying out loud."

I can hear them speak about me. Do they think I'm deaf? It's almost as if I don't exist and it makes me uncomfortable—especially when I hear them laugh. Still, I smile at Renee when she reenters the room, and she smiles back. I can see that she's still quite beautiful, though there are parts of her face that appear to be . . . frozen.

"I don't mean to be rude, but I'm supposed to be at a casting call at Ford in—" I glance at my cell phone— "twenty minutes."

"Casting call?" Renee says with surprise. "Is that what they called it? They meant a 'cattle call'! Darling, don't worry, you aren't missing anything." Then, to Francesca, she says, "Chain this one to the desk! She's ours!" She turns to me once more. "You do like to travel, don't you?"

""Yeah, well, I guess so. Depends on where, I suppose."

"Everywhere! We will have you going everywhere, Melody Ann Croft! Everywhere!"

I smile back at her. "That's great. But I probably can only travel in the summer. I'm going to the University of Pennsylvania in the fall—"

"Of course you are, darling!" Then, with a wink to Francesca, she says, "Start making phone calls." She looks at me. "What cover would you like to do?"

"Well, I only really know *Cosmo*." I smile. "My dad accidentally bought my mom one on vacation last year and when she tossed it, I got it. So . . . maybe *Cosmo*?"

"*Cosmo*? Please! What about *Vogue, Elle, Harper's* . . . ?" She shakes her head. "You leave it up to us. We'll have you working in no time! You do want to work, don't you?"

I nod my head vigorously. "Yes, Ms. Kitaen. I do!"

"Nothing truly good ever comes easy." This, my father's response to Francesca DeLongue's not only wanting to sign me immediately, but having already called me the very next day with an interview, or as she referred to it, a "go-see," at *Teen*

Vogue. It seems one of the editors there needs to find a brunette ASAP for a story she is shooting.

"Natalie Portman is on this month's cover," I said to my father last night, tossing out a name that might be recognizable to Dad, who is a big *Star Wars* fan, and hoping this might show how big a deal getting this job would be.

He rolled his eyes at my mother, who shot me a nervous smile.

What I didn't tell them was that it's a go-see for an editorial job, which, as Francesca warned me, would mean more prestige than money. "And perhaps some photographs for your book," she'd added.

The photographs I required were another thing I didn't tell my parents about.

According to Francesca, no one in the business would take me seriously until I had a book of photos to bring to the various editors, photographers, and ad agencies. Then she gave me the card of a photographer I could see, rattling off a price that was easily half my tuition for my first semester at Penn. She must have seen my expression because she suddenly backtracked, offering to look into test shoots, which meant that I could essentially work for a photographer in exchange for free photos.

A no-money-down approach to this business is what I'm banking on, that and the hope of getting this job today.

Now as I make my way down to Shatterbox Studios via the subway, a route I'd carefully mapped out the night before, I'm calculating my odds. According to Francesca, it isn't usual for a go-see to take place during a shoot, but apparently Jesalyn Rivers, editor at *Teen Vogue*, is desperate. Francesca seems to think this makes me a shoo-in for the job. That and my "great hair and great bones." Excitement bubbles through me when I remember Francesca's enthusiasm. "I can't *wait* until Paul meets you," she said, referring to Paul Anders, owner of the agency. Then she sighed, eyes moving over me dreamily, as if she were responsible for my very creation. "It's not every day a girl who's got 'it' walks into my office. And mark my words, Melody Ann Croft, you've got 'it.'"

Whatever "it" means.

"Are you *it*?" Jesalyn Rivers demands when she finally arrives at the studio, a full forty-five minutes late for her own shoot. "Isn't Delicious sending anyone else?"

The smile on my face freezes in place.

"Jesalyn, please," comes a voice, faintly British in accent. I turn to see a reed-thin, bespectacled man come up behind her, his mossy green gaze running over me in that assessing way I'm still getting used to. "She'll do."

"Bird, are you insane? Look at her . . . she's . . . *fat*! And who the hell plucks her eyebrows—Edward Scissorhands? Helen Keller? And that hair is *awful*."

Bird places a hand over his mouth to cover his smile. "Oh, stop it Jesalyn, so she is a bit . . . big. She'll work in the Luellas, and damn it, she's here! Please *do* make an executive decision whilst I'm still in relatively good humor."

"This is madness," Jesalyn mutters. "If ever I needed a miracle worker in makeup, it's today." Then she lets out an angry sigh. "Sit over there and we'll see if we can get to you. I may not even need you!"

I follow her orders, though what I want to do is leave. Francesca already called me twice this morning, wondering what was taking so long. I had five other go-sees today—two of which she had to cancel because I was still here—and the editor wasn't.

Though the way I feel now, my next go-see may need to be with a shrink!

Though I'm still reeling under the weight of Jesalyn's insults, once I'm called from my corner and ushered into a director's chair next to the blond glamazon who is now my colleague, I feel like one of the chosen.

I smile at her in the bank of mirrors facing us. This girl must have just popped out that way, pink and white, wide-eyed and lush-lashed. And that cap of silky curls. When babies are born with hair, it's usually dark and matted, like an old man's wet toupee. Not this corona of fluffy pale gold.

"Go ahead, blame my mother," she says. "I do . . . for virtually everything. Only kidding. Really. I don't believe in blame, or guilt, or any of that muck. Of course, that's because I'm entirely amoral. Jade Bishop, by the way. Bishop. As in two steps down from the pope."

And then she flashes a smile. Have you ever felt you could trip on a smile, fall into it like a trap? That's how I feel when Jade turns her smile on me. That smile could sell *buzz* to bees. Unlike the other two models, at least she's being nice. A relief, since I *so* do not belong here—in a SoHo photo studio, about to strut my stuff in dresses by Luella Bartley (whoever she is). Carrying platters I can handle, no problem. But posing in designer clothes? I'll give it my best shot, sure, but let's just say I'm not turning in my Porter House uniform yet. The way Jade picks up on my nerves, you'd think I'm actually still wearing that uniform.

"What are you, a virgin?"

At first I take the question literally, and it startles me—who would dare ask that? Jade Bishop, that's who, in a tough New York accent that sounds like she eats pulverized cement for breakfast. I glance at the others who are being professionally primped around me: a redhead having her braids undone for a zigzag effect, and a cocoa-skinned, angular girl with nothing but peach fuzz on her head. The way they ignore me is an art form.

"First time on a shoot?" Jade clarifies.

"Oh . . . yes." My breath still hasn't quite returned to me. "I can't believe this is even happening. Two weeks ago, modeling was the farthest thing from my mind. Even after that photographer gave me contact info for all the agencies."

"Photog? Who?"

"Jonathan Novak. Have you ever—"

"*Pfft!*" Jade scoffs. "I'm amazed anyone even saw you, coming from that loser."

A short guy with an ornate beard and mustache steps behind my chair, and grabs fistfuls of my hair. "Well, you know what I did with his card?" I smile up at the man, now elbows deep in my mane. "Hi, I'm Melody Ann. You can just call me Melody, though."

"Charmed," he says. "I'm Arturo."

"Hi, Arturo. Nice to meet you." I look back at Jade's reflection. "Stuffed it in the pocket of my apron, never thought about it twice. It even went through the wash."

Expertly, moving only her eyeballs—which are translucent amber, so unusual with her pale blond locks—Jade shifts her gaze to meet mine. "Yet here you are today," she says, her voice making a seamless transition from guttersnipe to socialite. "To what do we owe the pleasure?"

Maybe it's my not knowing her that suddenly gives me the freedom to bare my soul. Kind of like you feel when you're in the beautician's chair, which, technically, I am. I've hardly even had a chance to talk to my best friend about my breakup with Eric and yet here I am suddenly gushing to a stranger about the heartbreak that had me falling asleep in tears last night.

"Can you believe he ended a relationship that's been going on long distance for nine months right before he was planning on coming home? I thought we had something real. It was the whole reason I agreed to remain exclusive with him, despite that he decided on a college in the Midwest. Now just when we have a chance to be together again, *really* be together, he suddenly decides it would be 'healthier' for us if we saw other people. Translation? He wants to sleep around. So what was I supposed to do? Hang out in Morristown, feeling like a fool while he dated all the new graduates from our high school? My best friend has a boyfriend, so there's no way I was third-wheeling around with them—"

"*Whoa*, Mac—you mind if I call you Mac?" Jade interrupts, and I realize I've been spewing like a lunatic.

"*Um*, sure . . . I guess so. But I already have a nickname. I used to play tennis and in sports, everyone has a nickname—"

"I'm sure you do. But I like Mac," she says. "Anyway, this guy, this *Eric*." Jade coughs up his name like phlegm. "You let him live?"

I laugh. I laugh so hard and so long that Arturo has to stand back. It might be the first time I've laughed since Eric dumped me.

"I take that as a yes," Jade says. "Most benevolent of you." She flickers her eyes closed so the makeup artist can line them with an infinitesimally fine brush, then snaps them wide again. "Don't worry," she says. "You'll learn."

I'm not sure what she means by that, and I can't ask, since Arturo has swept my hair completely in front of my face, curtaining me off from the rest of the world, leaving me completely in the dark.

Three

Melody Ann Croft no longer exists. At least, by the time she steps in front of the cameras, she's been transformed.

Into Mac, I think, grasping onto the only reality I have available to me at the moment.

My hair teased to gargantuan proportions, eyes done smoky and lips nude matte, I'm swathed in this sweeping Luella Bartley caftan with about thirty pounds of beads roped around my throat—more jewelry than I've worn in my lifetime, much less all at once.

Britpop pumps through the speakers, some band with a touch of reggae, and Bird, a big-time British photographer, according to Jade, urges us to pick up on the exoticism of tabla and sitars. "You're in Bollywood, my babies!" he cries. "It's your last mad dance before the funeral pyre. I want frenzy! I want pure, unadulterated, maniacal bliss!"

I glance over at Jade, who is wearing the kind of clunky platforms more suited to clog dancing than belly dancing, but she's managing to look ethereal, sensual. Lacey Alvin, the red-headed model I said hello to earlier only to receive in return the cold recitation of her name (as if I should have known who she was), is waving her arms as if dementedly hailing a cab. At least Lindsey Burton, the stunning African American model who received my overtures with only slightly more warmth than Lacey, looks like she's dancing, though from the blankness in her expression I have to wonder if she's enjoying it.

I know I am. Which surprises me. But as I flow with the music, improvising poses, I realize this is more fun than I ever expected. I glance at Jade, wondering if she still takes pleasure in posing—I learned in makeup, that she's been at this fifteen years, having been a child model. But whatever she's feeling is carefully shielded behind what I can only describe as a "model" face. Jade's look? Innocent-angelic, though something about the way she sways her hips tells me she's anything but.

"Wait!" shrieks Jesalyn, and everyone comes to a halt, including Bird, who joins her behind the computer monitor. She points at the screen. "You see what's happening? We can't have *that* going on in every frame."

"No . . . ," he says, his expression thoughtful.

I realize that Jesalyn is reviewing every shot on that computer she's parked herself in front of. And judging by the expression on her face, she's not happy with what she sees.

Bird is now looking up at us. Or I should say, up at *me*.

Uh-oh.

"Muriel!" he yells.

For a moment, I think he's forgotten my name. Until I realize that Muriel is his gamine assistant, who scurries soundlessly over to the computer to check what's causing such offense, then runs to the set, wordlessly moving a ladder and reaching high above my head to adjust a light.

Whew.

And suddenly the show is on again. Stepping into character with new confidence, I strut, stretch, and slither into pose after pose, trying not to notice that Lacey is practically doing a strip-tease (is that allowed?), Lindsey is now writhing on the floor, and Jade has taken on the ecstatically slow, blissed-out move-ment of a heroin addict.

"Got it! Gorgeous!" screams Bird, who flicks us off to change for the next setup. I smile with relief when Jesalyn disappears from the set—the way she watches that monitor stresses me out. Looking to Jade to commiserate—Lindsay and Lacey, after all, have already glided over to the stylists and are slipping out of their clothes—I see that she has detoured to the table of food for a doughnut.

Lindsey glares at her upon her return and when Jade sticks her tongue out at her through the doughnut hole by way of reply, her glare grows radioactive. "What? It's not my problem your ass is the size of Indiana," Jade says.

"No, it's not," Lindsey says icily. "You have so *many* prob-lems, Jade, I don't think you could handle another."

Far from being offended, Jade begins to lick at the frosting, eyes closing as she savors the sweetness.

I smile at her antics. "The only problem I can see is that Jade's headed for a crash."

Jade's eyes flicker open, her amber orbs now focused on me, and not in a friendly way.

"From the sugar," I say, realizing she's taken what I've said in the *entirely* wrong light. "No matter what your metabolism is like, there's no escaping the crash from all that sugar. I'm sorry, it's just that I'm going into nutritional medicine," I say. "If you want something sweet, you're better off with fruit; at least it has vitamins and fiber." I smile again, but clearly I've just joined Lacey and Lindsay on the list of people Jade could live without.

She gives me a glacial smile. "What can I say, sucrose is my life." Then she shrugs, her eyes roaming over me as if she's deciding whether or not I'm worth the effort of shaming. "But they do have some melon and berries at the catering table. You ought to eat some—keep up your strength. You're going to need it."

Before I have time to consider that, Sophie, one of the stylists, pulls me out of the Luella Bartley under which I wear not a stitch, and before I know it I'm stark naked in front of Jade's gleaming gaze, feeling suddenly fat in the face of her rail skinniness, and more vulnerable than I have since the night Eric broke my heart.

"Do you think I'm doing okay?" I ask Sophie, a few hours later. I'm not sure why I'm asking her this question. Maybe it's because she's yanked me out of my clothes no less than six times, creating a sense of intimacy I would not otherwise have with someone I've only known a few hours. Or maybe it's because Jade has barely spared me a glance since our last exchange, and Jesalyn stopped the last shot three times on account of me. Granted, one time was because Arturo had to fix my hair, but if I heard Jesalyn yell at me one more time to "stay within the frame!" I was going to march right out the door.

Okay, not really. I'm still having fun. But I'm tired, so tired. And hungry, since I never did get a chance to hit the catering table.

"It's just that I was never fond of taking pictures," I continue. "Not even on family vacations. My mom says I always make a face."

Sophie smiles at me as she cinches a belt around my waist so tight, I'm suddenly glad my stomach is empty. "You're doing fine," she says.

I smile with relief. It's all I need to get me through for now.

"Let's go, move it!" One of Bird's covey of assistants bustles in, and we're shepherded back to the set before I can even grab a piece of fruit.

Thought is the enemy. If I think about what I'm doing, or how I look, or how hungry I am—focus in any way on myself—I'm doomed. Instead, I put everything out there and just react. There's the camera, there's Bird, the other models, and ultimately all the girls who read *Teen Vogue*. My concentration is on them, what they want and need from me. And I give it. It was the same with tennis, especially when I competed; I was a machine. With modeling, I can't shelve my humanity; if I'm going to be good at this, my soul has to shine through—that's what reaches people. So here I am, dressed in these amazing clothes but in a weird way baring myself to the world. A simple thing like having Sophie's nod of approval helps. Mostly because it seems like she's been doing this awhile.

"Lacey, you wear the Heatherette, huh, sweetie? You'll look so hot in sequins." Jade prods the stylist holding a skimpy outfit toward Lacey as we prep for our seventh and, thank goodness, final setup.

"*Hmm?*" Lacey sighs vacantly. "All right, whatever."

"Ooh, please, Jade—no," Sophie, the stylist, gets hesitantly assertive. "Jesalyn really wants you in the Heatherette."

"That's because Jesalyn doesn't know shit from Shalimar. I was Viv's muse for this collection." Jade hustles over to some slashed minis on a rack, picks one, and holds it against her.

"Amy's certainly aware that Viv and I are tight as toes in a Christian Louboutin."

She's spitting out names faster than a ball shooter gone haywire, but it has the desired affect. Sophie caves, lets Jade wear what she wants. But Viv, Amy, Christian—who are these people? I pick one. "Who's Amy?" I ask. Let Jade think I'm clueless; you don't ask, you don't learn, and I'm a quick study.

"Amy Astley, head honcho at *Teen Vogue*." Jade seems pleased that I'm not up on all things fashion. If anything, my ignorance appears to smooth over whatever tension our last exchange caused. "Former beauty editor of *Hag Vogue*," she explains, warming to the role of mentor. "Still dresses like a schoolgirl, even though she must be my mother's age. But God, if you want to talk relic, talk Vivienne Westwood. Positively ancient. Yet still cool, an icon—she designed for the Sex Pistols."

My brain catalogues every bit of information Jade offers as Arturo steers me toward a chair. "Do you really know her?"

"Sure, I saw her a bunch of times when I was squatting at my father's place in London. She lives in his neighborhood." Jade slaps at Sophie's fingers and ties herself into the dress that looks like it ought to come with an instruction manual.

"Your dad's English?"

"No, but when he's in his clammy phase he likes writing there. The dampness gets his juices flowing."

"Oh, a writer!" I'm about to go off about how English was always my worst subject, but I check myself. "That's cool," I say evenly as Arturo begins sculpting my hair, which already has so much mousse in it, I'll need a few cycles in the Maytag to get it all out. "I admire people who can put thoughts on paper in a coherent way."

Jade emits her syllable of scorn. "*Coherent* is the last thing

I'd call my father," she says cryptically. Closing her eyes, she accepts a spritz of Evian from an aerosol can.

Before I can ask her what she means, we're being hustled off to the set again.

I have no idea what time it is. The studio's shut off from the world, I haven't looked out a window since I got here, and I am *starving*! I wonder how I will get through the next shot. Somehow, though, back on set, with the whir of the camera and Bird's unceasing commands, I forget everything else and turn it on again and again, until at last we wrap.

"You should take those," Lindsey comments as we're getting undressed.

"Excuse me?" I'm shocked—she's actually speaking to me.

"Those shoes," she says. "They're cute."

They *are* cute—for medieval torture traps. "Are we allowed to?" I ask.

Lindsey and Lacey titter. "*Allowed?*" asks Lindsey. "You don't understand anything, do you? This is your first shoot, you *have* to take something."

"*Mmm*," murmurs Lacey. "You have to 'shootlift.' It's a rite of message."

"Rite of *passage*," corrects Lindsey.

Everybody's packing up. Now that we're done for the day, we might as well be invisible to the stylists who attended to us so fastidiously. No one would notice if I did walk out with the cruel suede stilettos. "But they don't belong to me."

Lacey and Lindsey crack up again.

"Ignore those polyps," Jade says. Nice of her to stand up for me, but I notice she hasn't bothered to remove her intricate Vivienne Westwood number yet. And to my astonishment, she grabs her bag and brushes past. "Don't forget to have your voucher signed," she reminds me. "Crucial, if you want to get paid."

I already have. And I'm still blown away by the amount of money I've made today. Six hundred dollars. For one day's work! My head fuzzy from lack of food, it almost feels like a dream. As if I might wake up tomorrow and discover I've imagined everything.

Including the sight of Jade stepping onto the elevator in the Vivienne Westwood.

"You took that dress!" I whisper incredulously.

"And you, hon-bun, have a flair for the obvious," she retorts. "Personally, I don't believe in possession—unless of course it's demonic. Ownership? Obsolete! There are simply . . . things . . . afloat in the universe."

Lindsey and Lacey exchange a smile, clearly pleased with Jade's interpretation.

Out on the street it's a warm, dreamy dusk. Lights and music from SoHo's bars and restaurants beckon, and passersby amble in and out, laughing and gesturing. Tired as I am, I have an urge to link arms with my companions and join in the merriment.

Of course, companions might be too strong a word for the girls I worked with today.

"Well, it's been a real thrill," Jade says, raising a hand to the air to hail a cab as Lacey and Lindsey kiss—one cheek, two cheeks, back to cheek one—then head off in opposite directions.

Jade looks at me, eyes narrowing. "You do know how to get back to—where did you say you lived?"

"Morristown," I supply, though my hometown clearly doesn't

register with Jade. "I know where I'm going, I just . . . I'm going to walk for a bit."

"Suit yourself," she says, then slides into the cab that pulls up beside her.

And then she's gone, leaving me to shuffle along Broadway, alone.

The moment I sit down on the train home, exhaustion hits. As does a searing loneliness I haven't felt since those first weeks after Eric left for school.

I pull my cell phone out of my bag and dial my best friend.

"Hey, how'd it go?" Liza says upon answering.

"It went," I say. "I showed up for the go-see and they put me right into the shoot."

"And?"

"I'm exhausted." Then, realizing I'm depriving my BFF all the juicy details I know she's dying to hear I say, "Pick me up at the train in an hour and I'll tell you everything."

"Oh my *God*! You look *amazing!*"

It's only when I see Liza's face, gawking at me as I slide into the passenger seat of her Honda, that I remember that I'm still in full hair and makeup. No wonder everyone was staring at me on the train. I pull down the mirrored sun visor in front of me, marveling at my hair, which is still falling in artfully tousled waves around my face, my eyes smoky and even more mysterious in the darkness of the car. I would have washed everything off at the studio except the sink in the bathroom was so tiny I drenched myself every time I tried to even wash my hands. And the thought of applying that cream remover the makeup artist used on me during the three makeup changes grossed me out. My skin actually hurts from all it had to endure today.

Turning in my seat to face Liza, I run a hand through my hair—unsuccessfully, due to the amount of product. I laugh self-consciously. "I look weird, right?"

"Weird?" Liza's eyes widen in disbelief. "You look like . . . like a celebrity!" Then her eyes light up mischievously. "We should drive by the park—the guys are playing touch football—and let Eric get a look at you."

"Eric's *home*?"

Liza bites her lip. "Since last weekend."

I absorb this news, surprised at the fresh hurt I feel. I mean, I know we broke up, but the fact that he's home—that I haven't even seen him, that he hasn't even told me he's back—stings anew.

"Forget about him," Liza says, shaking me out of my stupor. "Just look at you." She flops the visor down again. "You are sooo going to be a supermodel!"

My family, unfortunately, isn't as starstruck as Liza.

"They paid you *how much*?" my father said.

"Six hundred bucks," I say, glad my father has finally recovered enough from the shock of seeing his "little girl" transformed into a sultry siren to ask questions about my day.

"For one day's work?"

I nod, still unable to believe it myself. In fact, I'm not sure it'll feel real to me until I receive the actual check.

"Are you sure what you did today was . . . legal?" my father asks, scrutinizing me again.

"Sam!" My mother admonishes him. Then she smiles at me, her eyes a little misty. "I'm proud of you, honey."

"I'm proud of you, too," my brother Richie chimes in from where he's parked, lounging on the couch. "In fact, so proud that I'm going to let you buy me new rims for my car."

"Don't hold your breath," I tease back.

The steps to the upstairs creak, and suddenly my own breath is backing up in my throat. "Teddy," I yell in surprise at the sight of my oldest brother, whom I haven't seen since he came home from school on Christmas break. "I thought you weren't coming home until next weekend."

"I heard someone has to keep an eye on you," he says, opening up for a hug. Though Ted has three years on me to Richie's one, we've always been closer. Mostly because of our shared love of sports.

Leaning back from the hug, I smile up at him. "I've missed you," I say. It's the sort of thing I can't say to Richie, who would tease me mercilessly.

He waggles his eyebrows. "And I don't even recognize you. Though you look somewhat like my baby sister except . . . all grown up."

It's clear from his expression that something about this bothers him, but whatever he's thinking disappears behind his smile. "And with that hair, I think you've gained a few inches," he says, straightening to his full six-foot-two height and staring down at me.

I smile wider, so glad to be home.

"Bet you still can't beat me in a game of one-on-one, little sister."

His words send a surge of adrenaline through my otherwise aching limbs. "You're on."

And within moments, I'm a kid again, out on the make-shift basketball court that is our front driveway, weaving and jumping with my big brother. Despite how tired I am, it's all I need. This reminder that no matter who I became today in that studio, I'll always be Melody Ann Croft. Teddy's little sister. The fire chief's only daughter. My mom's rival for the shoe closet.

And . . . I leap, sending the ball into the air, laughing at Teddy's expression as it sails through the hoop.

Queen of the home court, apparently.

Four

Ever been so tired that sleep is a fantasy, an aching, impossible need an inch out of reach? That's me, working the four-to-midnight shift at the Porter House the day after my first shoot.

When I woke up this morning, not sure if the soreness that penetrated my body was from late-night basketball or all those weird poses I struck at Bird's command, I was tempted to call in. But if anything, coming home after the shoot reminded me that what happened in the studio yesterday wasn't reality. In fact, it might even have been a fluke, if Jesalyn's initial objections to me are any indication of things to come. So for now it's back to serving up sirloin, all in the name of college in the fall. Even if I get that scholarship—and that's a big *if*—it's only going to go so far.

Still, it's a lot easier reciting specials and recommending the soup, ad infinitum, knowing I've already got six hundred dollars coming my way. Six hundred dollars for one day's work. It's almost too good to be true.

As is the phone call I receive Monday morning.

"Melody? It's Francesca. You're coming into the city today. We have much to discuss."

What I'm discovering about Francesca DeLongue is that,

despite treating me with the kind of confidentiality and affection she would a best friend, she has a way of issuing orders that sound like invitations you simply can't refuse.

"Of course," I reply automatically.

"Paul will be in today, and he really wants to meet you."

"He does?" I hadn't expected to meet the owner of the agency so soon, swathed in mystery as Paul Anders is, commanding Delicious from his windowed corner office when he's in town, which isn't often from what I understand.

"He sure does. Especially when I told him that Amy Astley over at *Teen Vogue* e-mailed me immediately after seeing the results of your session, quite impressed with Delish's latest acquisition."

I let the word *acquisition* slide. "She *is*?" I smile to myself. *Take that, Jesalyn!*

"Of course," she says, as though she had predicted this outcome. "So you'll be here by three p.m."

"Okay," I reply, though it wasn't really a question.

Francesca greets me in the reception area, looking so happy to see me I think she's going to hug me.

But she doesn't, instead roaming an eye over me as if making sure I'm still the same girl she met last week. Something firms in her expression, as if she's made some sort of decision, though it's not clear whether it's in my favor.

I don't have time to wonder. Grabbing my hand, Francesca leads me past the receptionist, who I mouth a hello to, only to receive a surprised stare in return.

"We want to catch Paul before he leaves," Francesca says, as if to explain why she's practically running down the hall. "He's having lunch at three with Ron Perelman at Revlon."

Who has lunch at three o'clock? But this isn't the question I ask, instead going for a more pertinent one: "Do I look okay?"

Francesca slows down, her expression softening, as if she just remembered she's hauling human cargo. Squeezing my hand gently, she lets it go as she takes in my outfit, a fitted pantsuit with a cropped jacket and funky, wide-legged trousers that I got on sale at the mall three weeks ago.

"Honey, only you could make polyester look that good."

My eyes widen and I start to protest—it's a rayon blend, after all—but then suddenly I'm smiling, realizing that my "good bones and great hair" have earned me the kind of unconditional adoration from Francesca that one usually only gets from a mother.

And, much like a mother, she turns to me once she reaches Paul's door, to give me some last-minute advice. "Try not to fall in love."

For the first few moments after Francesca graciously introduces me, then disappears, I have no idea what she's talking about. Fall in love?

From the sumptuous leather guest chair where I'm sitting, it seems as though Paul Anders is gay.

That's my initial thought, anyway. Perhaps it's his perfectly tweezed brows and well-pampered skin. Maybe it's the beige linen suit and loafers-without-socks ensemble. Or maybe it's because his hair is an assortment of browns and golds that could not have come from nature. He's older—probably in his early forties—and not what you'd call a traditionally handsome man, yet he looks like a model, from the way he leans his lanky body back in his chair to regard me from wide, pale gray eyes to the way his long, tanned fingers move thoughtfully to his impeccably groomed goatee.

But soon enough I understand what Francesca meant.

Soon enough, I am seduced.

There's something about his voice, the smooth modulated tones, like a DJ on a smooth jazz station. And the way he focuses all his attention on me, as if I was the only woman in his life.

Though if nothing else, it's clear to me I'm *not* the only woman in Paul Anders's life. Behind him, the walls are covered with photographs, some of the images black-and-whites, some of them autographed with scrawled words of affection. All of them women. All of them beautiful. Models, of course. Delicious Models. I recognize some of them, stars of yesteryear like Paulina, Christie, and Cindy, and newer faces I see staring out at me every day from magazine spreads and billboards: Heidi, Giselle, Karolina.

Suddenly I want to be one of Paul's girls.

And it's clear to me, Paul wants me, too.

All this time—really only about seven minutes, because that's all he has to give me before lunch—he's been selling me on the idea of building my career with Delicious.

As if he had to.

Now he smiles, standing up, which lets me know that our time together is over.

"I hope to see more of you, Melody," he says, his gaze so intent on mine I practically lean in for a kiss.

"Forget it, he's married," Francesca tells me when I appear in the doorway of her office, dreamy-eyed.

But the dream doesn't last long. Because if it was Paul's job to be the good cop, it's Francesca's duty to be the bad cop.

"Obviously, we're all very excited about your potential," Francesca says, once we are seated across from one another. "But we are all in agreement about one thing. What happened with *Teen Vogue* was a fluke."

I stiffen, as if my entire body has been sprayed with Aqua Net.

"Do you know why you wore only Luellas on that shoot?" she asks, artfully shaped eyebrows rising. "Because as luck would have it, Luella's doing voluminous this season. The truth is . . . ," she continues, leaning in as if she's about to tell me something of great import, " . . . you're much too . . . *big* to do fashion."

And there it is. The reality that has plagued me ever since seventh grade, when I sprouted three inches in a year, making me a full six inches taller than all of the girls at Morristown Junior High—and most of the boys. I'm a freak. Always have been.

Apparently always will be.

"Don't grimace, Melody, you'll get frown lines." Then, grabbing my hand in what I'm discovering is a habitual gesture, she continues, "There is hope. Your hair is a Fructis commercial waiting to happen, your eyelids were made for makeup, and there's something about you—the way you don't hold back—that's very appealing. In fact, I know Albert Lazar would go crazy for you; he's big on bouncy enthusiasm.

"So, here's what's going to occur," she went on. "I'll send you out for beauty. If you're lucky you'll get some editorial—it doesn't pay, but it is prestige. If you're very lucky you'll get advertising, that's where the money is. But honey, you must lose weight; that is nonnegotiable—I can't even send you out for catalogues, much less real fashion . . ."

"Oh . . ." The word sputters out of my mouth. Is that what she meant by "big?" Here I thought I needed to be amputated at the knee. "But I play sports. I'm more muscle than fat. My body is athletic—"

"'Athletic' doesn't work in fashion. You need to lose fifteen pounds minimum. And I suggest you lose it fast. Do as I say and Renee will introduce you to Albert. He'll want you to walk, I can virtually guarantee it—and when Albert wants you, everyone else will come begging. Next season will belong to Albert Lazar, and if you cut out the corn dogs and the Taco Bell, it will belong to you as well."

Then she smiles. "Make sense?"

Blindsided, I give the only acceptable answer. "Yes . . ." Then, remembering myself, I add, "But—"

Francesca looks up from her computer, where she's already turned and started to type, no doubt scheduling my next week. "But?" She blinks. Clearly she has never heard a "but" before.

I smile, then gird myself to remind Francesca of the truth, as I know it. "Everyone at Delicious has been so great; I just don't want to misrepresent myself. The thing is I've been accepted to Penn. . . ." Warmth suffuses me as I remember this simple fact, how much pride I'd felt when I received the acceptance letter. "I'm even up for a scholarship, and they don't grow on trees. So modeling can only be a summer job and—"

I stop when I see the expression of dismay on Francesca's face, which she quickly shifts into a somewhat patronizing smile.

"Look, I respect your desire to get an education. I went to Fordham myself. But the truth is, college doesn't mean anything unless you use your common sense. Once you start earning money, you'll be able to buy and sell Penn many times over. Your plans will change."

This time, Francesca doesn't wait for my usual acquiescence and I don't give it. Because if there's one thing I know for sure, my plans won't change. Not these plans anyway, which I've been harboring ever since I took my first health class in junior high. I've always seen myself working in health care, either in sports medicine or nutrition. Lovely as Ms. DeLongue is, she can't just sweep my dreams under her Louis Vuitton desk set. As far as the fall is concerned, I'm going to Penn, collections be damned.

But I'll lose the weight. If that's what's going to get me six-hundred-dollar-a-day jobs, I'll starve if necessary. Actually, maybe that won't be necessary. True, I've never had to lose quite so much weight before, but surely with all the sports training I've done, it should be a piece of cake.

A rice cake, that is.

If getting the job on my first go-see wasn't a fluke, it certainly was a stroke of very good luck. For the next two weeks, it's go-see after go-see, with Francesca sometimes calling me as I race from one to another, seeing if I can squeeze in another editor, another casting agent.

The cool thing is that Francesca gave me three hundred bucks to use for cabs—and even suggested I buy myself some jeans and a white tee for go-sees! Which was pretty nice of her. At my first opportunity, I headed straight for the big, beautiful Anthropologie store I discovered in Rockefeller Center and got the perfect jeans and a cute new tee.

Still, go-sees feel like a grind. Other girls eyeing you suspiciously, or being bitchy by intonation; they'll say, "Oh, hi, I can't believe *you're* here for this," as if the editor or creative director would have to be blind to hire you. Some of the girls are nice, even showing me their books. I cannot believe how some of these girls look when photographed! Even the girls I wouldn't consider very attractive in person look amazing with the benefit of lights and makeup and hair. It's intimidating, as I'm not sure I'll ever look as good as some of them, and I do get jealous, I'll admit. I'd show them my book except I don't have one yet. At this rate, it seems like I'll never get any pictures beyond the ones I did for *Teen Vogue*.

Sometimes I wonder if half of the go-sees aren't bogus— like the felonious ad exec I met on the train one morning on my way into the city for go-sees. I went to school with his son, so when he asked me what I was doing this summer and then if I would come to his studio to fit some jeans, I felt comfortable going. I didn't bother to tell the agency. Just went to his office straight from the train station.

It seemed like a totally cool situation—until he grabbed my crotch to see if the jeans "fit." I grabbed my clothes and ran, still in the jeans, which I later threw out just because the memory was so skeevy.

No wonder the agency tells us to always call them. You can't trust anyone—not even the father of a school chum!

Despite the setbacks, I continue to beat the pavement in evil shoes. Every single toe has a Band-Aid on it right now, a rubbed-raw blister crying beneath.

Today I'm vying for a campaign featuring a new brand of women's razors. "They've already got their ethnic type and their blonde; they're looking for a blue-eyed brunette, so you're a shoo-in," Francesca tells me. "Just don't go in too elegant; be sure to look sporty, and show lots of leg."

Got it! I gather my hair in a high ponytail, sweep a bit of bronzer onto my cheekbones, put on running shorts, and—

how's this for a shoo-in—slide into this trashed, beat-up pair of Reeboks that I should have retired years ago but hold onto for sentimental reasons (I won three tennis championships in those sneakers). I even wear the little sport socks with the pom-pom at the heel.

So up I trot, and what do I see? Fifteen replicas of me. All with brown hair and blue eyes. All with flawless fake tans and perky ponytails. All affecting that girl-next-door archetype in shorts and casual tees and ratty running shoes they must have resuscitated from some dark corner of the closet. It's like being in a carnival hall of mirrors. Except creepier.

The first six pounds come off fairly easily, if only because Francesca keeps me running so much, I barely have time to drink water, much less eat! Twenty six go-sees later, I head into Delicious, which is where I hang out on the rare occasions I have some time to kill. At first, I felt stupid, but really, I didn't have anywhere to go between meetings. So I started bringing in snacks for everyone, which made me popular pretty fast. This time I'm bearing a box of Krispy Kremes. Sloane's usually inanimate face lights up at the sight of me.

Clearly the way to the receptionist's heart is through her sweet tooth.

"Oh, you're here! Francesca's been looking for you . . ." She presses the intercom button on her phone as I flip open the box of doughnuts before her. "I shouldn't," she says.

Of course she does, grabbing a chocolate glaze, my favorite, too. I'm tempting my own fate by bringing doughnuts. Sloane's not the only one with a weakness for sugar. And I haven't had so much as an apple since 8:00 a.m.

"Mac is here!" she announces, almost joyfully, once Francesca answers.

Now suddenly everyone is calling me by my new nickname. Somehow it fits. At least it fits when I'm pounding the pavement, looking for jobs in New York City. It makes me feel powerful. Unstoppable. Kind of like a Mack truck, only prettier.

I smile to myself. Next time I see Jade—if I ever see her again—I'll have to thank her for the inspiration.

That's another thing about these past couple of weeks that gets to me—besides starvation. I didn't realize there are so many models. It seems I rarely see the same girls twice. I would have liked at least to see Jade again. She seems fun. And she's about the only person in this business so far who's even made a stab at being friendly.

I mean, besides Sloane, whose affection for me is directly related to the contents of the bakery box I'm carrying.

And Francesca, who actually hugs me this time when she sees me, though from the briskness of it, I'm wondering if she's merely checking my body mass index.

"Good news," she says. "I found you a test."

"Oh, Francesca, you're the best!" Free photos! And not a moment too soon. The thought of going to another go-see without pictures is almost too daunting to contemplate. According to Francesca, "tears"—that's pictures torn from magazines—are the only thing that matters in this business. They prove you've done work. But since I won't have tears from *Teen Vogue* for another month and a half, test photos are the next best thing. Besides, Francesca says it's better to have as many different looks in your book as possible.

"It's an up-and-coming photographer," Francesca continues,

"But hot, definitely hot. They're staging a shoot at Frank Lindo's place in East Hampton. Lindo is an exec at BBD and O, so it'll be good for you to make the contact. Especially since Lindo is probably going to be choosing the new model for the Guess campaign in the coming month." She gives me a meaningful look.

She doesn't need to elaborate. I know by now that an advertising contract is the crème de la crème of modeling contracts, outside of Victoria's Secret, which is the Holy Grail in terms of money earners. If I could land Guess—a big *if*, but still—I could probably pay cash for my education at Penn. After all, Guess was the campaign that launched Claudia Schiffer.

"You shoot this weekend, and you'll have pictures for your book by next week. Lindo's even offered to put up the models—"

"This weekend?" I say, all excitement draining out of me. "I have to work this weekend. At the Porter House."

"Mel-o-dy *Ann*," Francesca says, resorting to my real name and enunciating each syllable, much as my mother might if I suggested doing something that was beyond her reason. And missing this test shoot obviously falls in that category. "An opportunity for free photos does *not* come along every day. I worked very hard to get you this shoot—without even so much as a photo to send to Frank, who is trusting my judgment. You simply *can't* afford to miss this for the sake of catering to the cholesterol crisis in this country. And for what—a few dollars here and there? Once you start getting jobs, you stand to earn so much *more*."

If I start getting jobs. I look at Francesca, this woman I've come to trust in a few short weeks. I feel bad that she's been working so hard and now I can't come through for her. But I've been working hard, too, and with nothing to show for it. I've probably eaten away a good portion of my waitress tips on train and subway fares and snacks for my newfound family at Delicious. Now she's asking me to give up two weekend shifts—that is, if I *could* get them off, without losing my job altogether—for the sake of photos, which I desperately need but which may or may not get me another job.

It's a gamble.

Francesca sighs, turning to her computer and clicking through some files. "I suppose I could find someone else. Let's see, who do I have going already . . . Lacey . . ."

I smile, mostly at the novelty of potentially working with the same model twice.

"Elana, Mariah, Jessica . . ."

"Jessica Holloway?" I say with surprise. Jessica Holloway, I knew, just got her first cover. *Harper's Bazaar.* I don't know her, but I read an interview with her on the Internet, and she seems pretty cool. "Why would Jessica Holloway still be doing tests if she just got a cover?"

Francesca looks at me. "Newer models never turn down opportunities for photos. That is, if they want to get anywhere," she adds.

I look at her, hearing the challenge in her voice. Maybe it's all those years of tennis that taught me to never back down from a challenge. Or maybe the lack of food has finally gone to my brain. But I find myself agreeing to the impossible.

Though my choice made Francesca gleeful, my parents . . . not so much.

"There is no way in *hell* you're going to stay at some stranger's house this weekend." My father is so confident of this fact that he doesn't even bother to lever himself off his La-Z-Boy to make this declaration.

My mother, however, is a bundle of nerves. "What about your job at the Porter House? You can't leave them short-handed at the last minute."

"I've already spoken to them. As long as I can get someone to cover me, it's okay. And Becca Hanson has already agreed—"

Now my father does stand. "I said you're not—"

"I'm eighteen, Daddy. You can't tell me what to do anymore!"

My mother's face looks stricken. My father's face goes from furious to something even worse . . . cool resolve.

"Well, Melody Ann, if you don't want to live by my rules, then maybe you'd like to live somewhere else."

"Sam!" My mother actually yells, which is uncharacteristic for her. Then, more gently, she says, "Look, Melody, your father and I are just worried. We don't know who these people are."

"For all we know, you could be making a porn flick!"

"That's crazy!" I cry, incredulous. "I can't believe you think I'm capable of—"

My mother intervenes again. "We're not saying you would *willingly* do something like that, but how do we know these people are legitimate? Maybe if we could . . . meet them somehow."

That ought to go over big. *Mr. Lindo, I'm here about the job. Don't mind my parents. They just want to make sure you're not a perv.* "Mom, it just doesn't work that way."

"Then you're not going to work at all!" my father declares.

Until now, the only time I have gone against my parents' consent was when I was fifteen and I told them I was going roller skating when I was, in fact, going to a party at Binky Freeman's house, an event my parents hadn't endorsed, mostly because they knew Binky's parents were out of town. Of course, when my ride got too drunk to drive me home and I was forced to call my parents to pick me up, I had to endure not only a lecture, but being grounded for a whole month.

Now that I'm legally an adult, my parents could only silently fume while I packed my bags. Their other option—short of throwing me out, which my father couldn't bring himself to do, thank *God*—was to refuse to lend me a car. So now I'm shuffling a duffel bag from New Jersey via Penn Station and the Long Island Railroad to the Hamptons—a three-and-a-half-hour trip, all in the name of what my father refers to as "this foolish business."

Truth be told, by the time I board train number two, I'm starting to have my own misgivings.

"It's just nerves," Liza assures me when I call her from my cell phone as the train whizzes past town after unfamiliar town. "Your agent wouldn't send you to this if it wasn't legit," she reminds me.

I know she's right. Maybe it's knowing that my parents aren't on my side that makes the whole thing seem scarier. That and the fact that Liza isn't even going to be around to call this weekend. Bright and early tomorrow morning, she and her family are heading to some beyond-the-cell-phone-range campground in New Jersey for a weekend getaway.

So here I am, heading out to God knows where in Long Island without a soul to call.

It has all the hallmarks of a horror movie.

Okay, not really. I *am* going to the Hamptons, after all.

Five

When the car service sedan pulls up in front of what looks like a small country road, I suspect the driver that Frank sent to pick me up has gotten lost and given up, deciding instead to drop me in the middle of nowhere. But then the car turns down a gravel drive I had not seen at first and I realize we have arrived—or, more precisely, *I* have arrived.

"Wow," I say, leaning out of the window to get a glimpse. And what a glimpse it is. At the end of the drive sits an ultra-modern house that appears, in the late afternoon sunlight, to be all glass.

When we pull closer, I realize that this is just an illusion created by the large, luminous windows overlooking the lush grounds. Still, it's a pretty magnificent house.

As is the lineup of cars parked in the front—a Porsche, an Escalade, a Mercedes convertible, and even a Hummer.

"You can let me out here," I say, then slip out of the car with my duffel bag, butterflies fluttering in my belly, temporarily keeping my now-constant hunger pangs at bay.

When no one answers the front door, I follow the slate foot-path into the yard, where I discover there's a party going on.

The sounds of a smooth and mellow reggae song drift through the air. A sandy-haired man in his mid-forties leans up against the outdoor bar, talking to a bikini-clad blonde whom I don't recognize but I can only assume is a model, if the way she has propped herself next to him, as if a camera might turn her way at any moment, is any indication.

But there is no camera in sight, though there should be. The backyard looks like a spread from *House Beautiful*, with artful shrubbery, a patio as big as a soccer field, and an Olympic-sized pool glittering like a jewel smack dab in the middle.

Beside the pool is a redhead in an emerald bikini, lounging on a recliner beneath the adoring gaze of a balding guy probably twice her age. Lacey Alvin, I realize, watching her release a peal of tinkling laughter. I almost didn't recognize her with a personality.

And, cutting through the clear blue surface at the deep end of the pool is a dark-haired dream I recognize as Wade Loden, the model-turned-photographer whom Francesca—and all the websites I'd found gossiping about him—have declared hot. They weren't kidding.

"Well, well, well, and who do we have here?" I turn and find myself gazing down at a man who is about a foot shorter than I am.

"Hi," I say, gamely reaching out a hand. "Mac Croft. I'm looking for Mr. Lindo—"

"Johnny Matarazzo," he says. "Senior VP at BBD and O and Frankie's right-hand man." Latching on to my outstretched palm, he reels me in close to him. "Welcome," he whispers, a little too close to my ear.

Reflexively, I yank myself back and he releases me, smiling

wider as he yells over his left shoulder, "Hey, Frankie! We got a live one!"

I smile back, though what I want to do is pound him even closer to the pavement than he already is. But if he really is Frank's right-hand man, I'd do well not to offend him. That is, if I hope to even have a shot at the Guess campaign. And I do hope.

Frank Lindo, or the man I assume is Frank Lindo, comes out of the house carrying a pitcher of margaritas. Spotting us, he puts the tray down on a table and heads over, blue eyes crinkling merrily at the corners as he grins at me. "You must be Mac."

I beam him back a smile. "Very nice to meet you, Mr. Lindo."

"Please, call me Frank," he says, holding my hand between his two larger ones. I decide that I like him. Something about his demeanor makes me feel safe; at least compared to his pal Johnny, over here.

"Thank you, Frank," I reply. "I'm really happy to meet you. And I can't wait to meet your wife, too," I say, referring to Caroline Gregory, a big supermodel in the eighties until she married Frank and settled down to a quieter life. "I've always been a fan of hers."

He smiles, letting go of my hand. "You mean my ex-wife."

Oops. Suddenly, I feel stupid. I'm just about to scrape together an apology when Frank, who doesn't seem the least bit bothered by my gaffe, sweeps a hand toward his model-strewn surroundings and says, "Welcome to my fantasy."

I'm not ready to say my father was right, but when my new best friend, Johnny Matarazzo, suggests that I'm overdressed,

I start to worry that I'm in a bit over my head. But I play along, donning a pair of shorts and a T-shirt—it is, after all, 5:30, and what kind of sun exposure are these women really hoping for?—joining my companions for the weekend in the yard.

My first surprise of the evening is learning that Jessica Holloway is not, in fact, coming, as she was called away at the last minute for a paid shoot in Palm Beach, or so I am told. In her place is Sandrine, a doe-eyed, pixie-haired waif I've never met before. Not that that's saying much. I haven't met Elana or Mariah before, either, and when I say hello to Lacey, she acts as if she's never seen me in her life, tittering with laughter when I point out that we worked together not three weeks earlier. Where this laugh came from I have no idea. I suspect it's Lacey's way of flirting, which she's doing a lot of tonight.

That's the other alarming thing about this weekend. I notice that there are exactly five men—and five models.

I have a feeling this is not a coincidence.

"Who wants to go for a swim?" Thad, a sandy-haired sales rep for Lucky Brand jeans and, apparently, a good friend of Frank's, suggests after the lavish dinner Frank had brought in and I couldn't eat is cleared away.

"But we already took off our bathing suits!" Elana cries, gesturing to the filmy little minidress she put on just before dinner.

"Who needs bathing suits?" Cliff, Lacey's bald paramour replies, waggling his eyebrows at Lacey.

"I'm going to bed." I stand up, trying not to notice Johnny practically choking on the olive in his martini.

"So early?" Frank stands with me, ever the host. I smile at him. Of all the men here, I actually like him the most. Not that I plan on doing anything about it. He's old enough to be my father. "I'm tired from traveling today and I want to be fresh for the shoot in the morning." I say this last bit hopefully. Because even though I've been playing along with this whole party scene, if I don't wake up to stylists and a makeup artist on board, photographer notwithstanding, I'm outta here.

Still, I accept Frank's kiss on my cheek, waving to everyone as I quickly make my escape.

Once I get to the second floor, where Frank said I was to choose any bedroom, I notice that there are only five.

Okay, Daddy, maybe you were right. Not that I'll ever admit it to you.

I consider locking myself into one of the bedrooms, but then realize I might be forcing one of my fellow models into the uncomfortable position of sharing a bed with more than one partner. Though all of them were looking a little *too* comfortable down there.

With a sigh, I slip into one of the beds, though I have a feeling I'll be sleeping with one eye on the door.

When I wake up in the morning in bed, alone, I breathe a sigh of relief. When I go downstairs and find a stylist and a makeup artist picking at the assortment of fruits and pastries laid out on the kitchen island, I want to smother both of them with kisses.

It seems there *are* going to be some pictures taken today—and clothed, if the trunk the stylist is unpacking is any indication. *Whew!*

Grabbing a slice of cantaloupe, I introduce myself. "Mac Croft. And boy, am I ever glad to see you two."

* * *

The shoot takes place on a deserted stretch of beach a short distance from the house, and I'm grateful to see that outside of the stylist and makeup artist, our hottie photographer and his assistant, it's just me and the other models.

Everyone looks pretty perky, even though Sandrine claims, with a somewhat mysterious smile, that she didn't get to bed until close to 2:00 a.m. It's hard to tell who she shacked up with—if anyone—but if I were to put money on any pairing, I'd have to say Elana and Mariah shared *something* last night, from the way they keep huddling together, whispering and laughing.

Maybe it's my imagination, but it seems everyone is a little friendlier with everyone else this morning. Except me, that is.

I came here to get pictures, I remind myself, focusing on Wade, who seems to be the only one interested in my presence this morning. If anything, he gives me a little extra attention, asking me to do a series of photos standing alone on one of the jetties.

Of course, this only isolates me further from my fellow models. At one point, I even hear Lacey telling Elana that I'm a "suck-up."

I want to protest but a sense of pride, and professionalism, keeps me silent; that and the fact that Wade is moving us into the next setup.

He's different from the last photographer, Bird. For one thing, he likes us to stay still longer while he moves around stealthily, capturing angles. It's not easy, remaining motionless for so long. I find myself staring out at the ocean, trying to focus my attention in a meditation of sorts, and it is mesmerizing, until I remember that the last time I was at the beach was at the Jersey shore. With Eric. The thought only makes me feel lonelier.

"Beautiful look on your face." Wade's voice cuts into my memories. "Keep that look—it's so sexy."

Here I thought I looked sad, not sexy.

Back at the house, Frank greets us with *mojitos*. As usual, I take a pass, though I'm tempted after the day I've had.

It seems the party is in full swing again. In fact, if anything, Frank's backyard is even more of a scene than it was last night. Thievery Corporation pumps through the speakers. On the patio, Thad passes a blunt back and forth with two men I've never seen before.

It's not the sight of the pot that does me in—I never touch the stuff—but the food. It's everywhere, and it looks incredible, especially since I haven't eaten since this morning's sliver of cantaloupe.

The aroma from the barbecue is making me weak, so I go up to one of the bars to get a bottle of water. Flat water, of course; bubbly causes stomach distention. Why do I *know* this? Why do I care? Why can't I just belly up to the grill and get a plate full of grease with extra cheese?

"Hey, you look hot," Johnny says as I sidle past.

"*Umm*, thanks," I say, sidestepping his groping hands.

That's when I decide to keep moving like a fish in a tank, swimming constantly to avoid being eaten by bigger, meaner fish, insatiable fish with too many teeth.

"Hey, baby—," says one of the new guys, following Johnny's lead and grazing my bare leg with his hand.

I make it to the bar, help myself to a bottle of water, and wonder how long I have to socialize here before I can escape to my room, unnoticed. I realize my moment may have arrived when Elana and Mariah, encouraged by a few tokes off the blunt, have decided to perform a striptease together.

The moment Elana's top hits the floor, I dash from the yard.

All I need to do is make it to the bedroom, I tell myself, wishing I'd at least grabbed some of the tomatoes garnishing the steak platter, before I left.

I'm halfway through the kitchen when I'm stopped in my tracks. A dark tower compels me toward it. It stands in the center of a table, and it's made of my personal kryptonite, irresistible and deadly: brownies. A big, gooey stack of them reaching toward the sky. I can't help myself. I sneak up, grab three—they're small after all—and dart for the stairs and my room.

The most evil thing I've had in ages has been half a chocolate chip cookie during a weak moment nearly six days ago, so I aim to savor my purloined treats slowly. Sitting on the center of my bed, I take a small bite, expecting heaven to melt away inside my mouth. Only these brownies are different—sweet, yes, chocolaty, yes, but chewier in texture than good old Duncan Hines. That's cool; maybe they'll last longer, maybe I'll come to my senses before I devour its napkin-wrapped sisters in my lap. I take another nibble, and another. God, it's good.

I'm licking the sticky remnants of the second brownie off my fingers when Sandrine bursts through the door, startling me. A man's shirt is tied around her waist, and she's got one flip-flop on her foot, the other in her hand.

"Hiiiii!" she says. "This isn't Cliff's room," she says confused.

I'm confused, too. All this time I thought Lacey and Cliff were an item. I guess Sandrine has moved in on Lacey's turf. My, how quickly the tide turns.

"Sorry. I'm a little lost."

I smile at her—she looks more than lost, she looks out of it.

She giggles, and burps. "Oh God, I'm such a pig—excuse me."

Instead of agreeing with her, I ask, "Party still going strong out there?"

"Yeeaaaah," she says dreamily, looking like she is going to collapse on the carpet before me. "How come you're not out there? We're all going swimming! I just came up to . . ." She suddenly looks confused, as if she can't remember what she came up her for. Then she tugs at the shirt around her waist. "Maybe I was going to change?" Then she shrugs, emitting another belch, followed by a giggle. "You coming down?"

"Oh, well, I, uh, I'm not much of a swimmer," I say, glancing down at my remaining brownie and realizing it is getting stuck to the napkin and rapidly becoming inedible. Waste not, want not, my mom always says, so I unwrap it completely and dig in.

"*Whoa!*" says Sandrine, apparently my new best friend, despite my outcast status this afternoon. "Those brownies are killer!"

Like I need her to tell me that. "I know," I say guiltily. "They must have about a thousand calories apiece."

"Calories!" She squeals out a laugh. "Who's talking about calories? What do you think got me so trashed?"

Abruptly, I stop chewing and stare at her, openmouthed.

"There must be a quarter ounce of hash in each one."

Forget good manners, I spit the mushy mess back into the

napkin. "Hash!" I blurt with a gag. "You're kidding me; please say you're kidding me—I've already eaten two!"

"Wow! I've only had one, and man, I'm blitzed." Sandrine giggles, then sees through her haze that I really am upset. "Oh, come on, don't worry. It's not like it's bad for you or anything. At least, it doesn't feel bad." She smiles dreamily. "Wait about half an hour, you'll see . . ." Then, dropping her bathing suit onto the floor, she turns on her bare foot and skips out of the room.

I look for the nearest bathroom and lean over the toilet, all those articles on bulimia I've read in women's magazines suddenly coming in handy. But my attempts to vomit out the brownies are to no avail. Just as Sandrine predicted, within a half-hour, I'm bouncing between giggling fits and abject paranoia.

Feeling vulnerable, I lock the bathroom door behind me. Then I bolt for the shower—a kind of weaving bolt, and I giggle in spite of myself—I'm a lightning bolt. My face in the bathroom mirror looks so strange. Oh God, am I growing a mustache? Francesca will murder me! Hurriedly I undress, turn on the water. The echo of the rushing spray on the tile sounds like a million pygmies drumming . . . or something. Glancing down at my naked body, I'm horrified. *Uck*, everyone is right—I *am* fat, I'm disgusting, my gut is bulging, my thighs, they're like twin giant Redwoods with dimpled knees.

Icy cold, at first the shower is shocking, stinging me, striking me. Then—I'd say against my will, but it's like I have no will—I start getting into it, turning the tap from cold to hot, hot to cold to hot again. Soap is so . . . soapy! Shampoo, *ah*, the smell, divine. So this is what it is to be high. Well, now I know. I'll be more careful about anything I eat at a party, that's for damn sure. Only maybe it's good in a way; if I ever encounter a truly wasted person, at least I'll know what they're going through. I'll never understand why they do it, though—buy drugs, get high on purpose, day after day, night after night. Being out of control of your thoughts, your sensations, it's insanity. *Go away, go away, go away*, I repeat to myself like a mantra, willing the feeling down the drain. *Go away, go away, go away*.

Maybe if I exercise. I can work this out of my system. Though once I have my sneakers on, I realize I may have to tour all the Hamptons by foot before I feel right again. . .

The next morning I have only one thing on my agenda. Getting as far away from Frank Lindo's House of Fantasy as soon as possible. I can't even trust the food here! If I can get out of here today without insulting anyone and still get my photos from yesterday, then I think the beach shots Wade captured should be enough to satisfy both Francesca and Frank—that is, if he really is looking for someone for the Guess jeans campaign.

So who can I call? Everyone I know is hours away from here. Then I remember that I do have a friend who lives on Long Island. Sayville or Bayville or something like that. Well, not a friend exactly; an ex-boyfriend. Billy Hutchinson and I were an item sophomore year. Mostly because Billy had sprouted to nearly his full six-foot-two height by then and was one of the few guys an amazon like me could date in high school. We stayed friends afterward, despite that Billy wanted us to be more. In fact, he wasn't too happy when Eric and I got together, and he made a point of letting me know, which was uncomfortable. I was kind of relieved when he and his family moved to Long Island last year.

Come to think of it, maybe he isn't the guy to call. The last thing I need is an enraged ex-boyfriend making a scene in Frank's swanky East Hampton home.

But calling my parents is not an option. After the fight I had with them to let me come here, if I go home early they'll know something is up and they'll do everything in their power to keep me from ever going on a test shoot or any sort of agency-endorsed trip again. I consider calling one of my brothers, but it will take them hours to get here and then home again and I know that luring Richie away from his regular Sunday softball game will require retribution, and Teddy . . . well, as much as Teddy's my ally, he's also my big brother. If I told him why I wanted out of here so fast, I wouldn't make it out of here without him paying some retribution, too. And much as I don't want to be part of Frank Lindo's fantasy, I still don't want to lose the contact. This is delicate.

It has to be Billy. At least he'll be able to get here the fastest.

Then I realize that I don't even know *where* to tell him to come, since I got here via Frank's driver.

I'll have to ask Frank. I mean, I have to wait until he gets up anyway. There's no way I can get out of here without getting the address and providing a compelling excuse for why I'm in such a hurry to leave. The last thing I want to do is insult an exec at BBD and O.

"Going somewhere?" Startled, I nearly drop my duffel in the front foyer at the sight of Frank, looking almost fatherly in a navy Ralph Lauren robe and matching pajamas. I hadn't expected him to be up yet—it sounded like the revelries had gone on quite late last night. And I haven't even prepared my excuse yet!

"Oh! Frank . . . hi . . . I hope I didn't wake you. . . ."

He raises an eyebrow at me.

"That is, my phone. It must have rung about seven a.m. *Um, uh* . . . my grandmother died." Not exactly a lie, my grandmother did die—about eight months ago.

"How awful for you, dear. I'm so sorry," Frank replies, his face crumpling with sympathy.

His kind response only makes me feel worse.

"Thanks, Frank. *Umm,* I'm just wondering if you can give me your address. I need to call my, *um,* brother and give it to him."

"Of course," he says, and I realize that he's waiting for me to make the call, so I pull out my phone, relieved to find Billy's cell phone number is still in my list of contacts.

When he answers, I say quickly, "Hi, Billy, it's Melody. I'm ready for you to come get me." I look up at Frank, who is hovering over me. I start to cough uncontrollably. "*Um,* could you—*cough, cough*—get me some water, please, Frank?"

He disappears, giving me a momentary reprieve. "Listen, Billy, I'm in trouble and you have to come get me *now.* Just take down this address I'm going to give you. I'll explain everything when I see you. . . ."

One hour later, everyone is up and asking me questions and offering condolences on the death of my grandmother. I think I am going to faint from nerves before Billy gets here, and I almost do, when I hear the wheels of a car crunching on the gravel outside. "That must be my brother!" I exclaim, waving good-byes at everyone. Then, I quickly rush over to Frank, who has stood up from the couch.

"Mac, I'm sorry you have to leave like this, but I want you to know it's been a pleasure working with you." He smiles, then leans in and gives me a sloppy wet kiss on the lips that I have to fight not to wipe off. "Maybe we'll meet again someday."

"I certainly hope so," I say, beaming him a smile that I hope screams Guess jeans.

Then I bolt for the front door as quickly as I can without looking like I'm running away, turning one last time to wave before I make my escape.

And not a moment too soon. Billy is already out of the car and sauntering over to the door.

I smile, so happy to see him I could kiss him.

Billy must be feeling the same thing because before I know it, he's picking me up in his arms and planting one right on me.

"Billy!" I say, struggling out of his arms. Glancing behind me, I discover that Frank has not only followed me to the door, but is standing on the front porch.

"Well, Mac, I'd hoped I'd get a chance to meet your *brother*," he says, one eyebrow raised. "But I see I'm mistaken."

"We're a very close family," I offer feebly as I jump in the car and make my narrow escape.

Well, I may not ever see another job with BBD and O, but at least I still have my self-respect.

Either Frank Lindo believed my reason for my early escape from his fantasy weekend, or he was impressed by my subterfuge, because the following week he actually requested me for one of his clients. Granted, it wasn't the Guess campaign, but an ad for Aveeno body lotion, which isn't too shabby.

"Advertising is where the money is," Francesca reminds me. The look on her face is the classic "I told you so." Of course, I didn't tell her about the fiasco at Frank's and I realize now that it was the best decision.

She's clearly pleased with me, and not just because I'm a full ten pounds trimmer than the first time I walked into Delicious. It seems everyone is digging me these days. Over the next two weeks, I actually get bookings! Saks Fifth Avenue requests me for their catalogue and a couple of small editorial pieces come in, one of them for *Teen Vogue*, at the request of Amy Astley, who remembered me from my first shoot. Nothing huge, but decent. And it's a good thing, too. Because when my first check shows up for 180 dollars instead of the expected 600, I start to wonder if I'm in the middle of some sort of a con.

True, I'd forgotten that the agency gets 20 percent. But if I'd known that three hundred dollars Francesca had handed me from petty cash, encouraging me to take cabs and buy an outfit, was going to be docked from my pay, I'd have stuck to my old clothes and taken the subway! All this time I thought Francesca was giving me money as some sort of investment in me and my future. As it turns out, *I'm* the only one taking the financial risk.

"You have to think of the *big picture*," Francesca says to me when I complain. Well, not complain, exactly. I did plop a papaya mango smoothie from Jamba Juice on her desk before I brought up my diminished paycheck. Smoothies are Francesca's weakness. She doesn't eat the bagels, donuts or chocolates I bring in for the rest of the office—unlike Sloane, Francesca at least pretends to watch her weight. Of course, I don't tell her that her smoothie has more calories than most cookies and probably about twice the insulin jolt.

After all, I'm discovering a woman does need some illusions in this business.

I sigh, and don't argue with her. I'm too tired to argue. Between running from shoots to go-sees during the week, and long Porter House shifts on weekends, I'm exhausted.

I wilt visibly in Francesca's guest chair. As if in response, Francesca stands up. "I've got something to cheer you up."

She reaches under her desk to a pile of books and pulling one up, she hands the book to me with a big smile, watching my expression.

Delicious Models is inscribed in gold on the front. At first, I think I'm going to be asked to read and memorize the company history. But when I open to the first page and see myself—or someone resembling me—I realize it's *my* history—as Mac Croft, Delicious Model. A short history—flipping through quickly, I notice only the first few pages are full—but a history nonetheless. I have a book!

I turn back to page one and there I am, against the exotic tableau that Bird had set up for the *Teen Vogue* shoot, my hair a disheveled mane rushing over my bare shoulders, my eyes standing out indigo blue against a matte palette of browns and greens and pinks.

"Oh my *God!*" I say. It's about all I can manage at the moment. I look amazing.

"Amy sent over an early copy of the mag. It's a great picture, right? That's why I put it first," Francesca says with satisfaction.

In the next one I'm bending over in a short swingy dress, tending to the strap on my stiletto, my gaze forward, as if caught in the act. "My legs look like they're a mile long!" I say with surprise. I'd never thought of my legs as anything but athletic.

"I'd say two miles." Francesca smiles, then runs a finger along the faint shadow along my thigh. "As you can see here, they Photoshopped your legs thinner. So don't be too pleased with yourself. You still have a ways to go."

"Oh," I say, running a hand down my thigh self-consciously.

"Don't worry. Your Photoshop days are almost over. Remember, you were eight pounds heavier on this shoot."

"Actually it was ten," I remind her, moving on to the pictures from the test shoot. It's true that I'm visibly slimmer in these pictures, and thank God for that; in one I'm standing in the surf in nothing more than two scraps of turquoise that Calvin Klein is passing off as a bikini, in another, I'm propped up on a rock barrier in an itty-bitty white tank and a filmy Donna Karan sarong. Next, I'm tossing a beach ball in a frilly red-checked Shoshanna one-piece, the expression on my face one of pure joy. Funny how photos lie. Wade Loden somehow managed to make Frank's House of Fantasy look like an innocent frolic among teenage girls.

"You did have more pictures than I put in the book, but the triples with other girls had to be cast out. And there were one or two where I didn't like the angle. We need to pick only the best photos, even if that means some have to be discarded."

Nodding, I close the book, admiring again the cover, the gold lettering of the agency name—my agency. Warmth suffuses me at the sense of belonging this brings. I look up at Francesca. "Thank you for this," I say.

"Don't thank me yet. We've only just begun to fill this book." Then she smiles, that familiar gleam visible in her dark eyes. "If I have my way, pretty soon editors and designers around the world will want Mac Croft."

Six

As it turns out, Francesca isn't kidding. By the time I come into the office the following week, there is a buzz in the air. It starts with the Escada catalogue booking, a coup in itself, in which I wow the photographer by what he calls my mix of "grace and effervescence." Apparently not all girls are graceful. So this is a plus for me! Then Saks Fifth Avenue actually requests me for a second catalogue shoot, Cathy, the woman who hired me the first time, asking Francesca if I'm "still available."

Cha-ching! Of course, I'm available! If I keep going at this rate, I might be able to pay cash for my first year at Penn!

Then there's the L'Oréal advertisement with Sandrine of the hash-brownie fame. Of course, we both conveniently forget about *that* incident, though it's not clear whether Sandrine's amnesia is actually authentic. And then there is a test shoot with none other than my "old friend" Bird, who not only requested me for the test, but is clearly delighted with my trimmer self.

"Mac, Francesca is looking for you. She has a go-see that she wants to talk to you about ASAP," Sloane says when I head into the agency after completing the half-day shoot for the Saks catalogue.

"Sure thing," I say, exuberant. I liked going back to do the same catalogue twice, seeing the same people. And I like Cathy, the casting agent for Saks. We click. And there are so few people I really click with in this business. So far, anyway.

Switching tracks, I head to Francesca's office, nearly slamming into a short blonde I hadn't noticed when I'd come in.

Marcy Golden, the commercial agent for Delicious. "Sorry," I say, about to duck out of her way, when she stops me.

"You're Mac Croft, right?"

I nod, surprise filling me. I didn't realize Marcy even knew I existed, much less my name.

"I've been meaning to talk to you about a spot I may have. Do you have a minute?"

I freeze, torn, but my loyalty to Francesca wins out. "Actually, I don't have time now, but I could come back later—"

Her eyes narrow. "Never mind." Then, just when I think I've lost my golden opportunity to win Ms. Golden over and get a high-paying job doing a TV commercial, she says, "I'll just talk to Francesca."

"Great," I say to her, retreating back, watching in amazement as she marches into her office.

"You *do* know *who* that is, don't you?"

I look up, startled to discover none other than Jade Bishop, draped over one of the white sofas in the waiting area. "Hey, Jade! It's so great to see you!" I step toward her, with some idea of throwing my arms around her in a hug, but I sense Jade is *not* as glad to see me.

At least, that's my initial thought. But whatever menace I may have glimpsed in her expression suddenly vanishes, replaced by that impish smile, at once innocent and sensual.

I smile back. "I'd love to catch up with you—it's been like, *forever."* It's only been a month and half, but if *feels* like forever since I'd seen the only model to ever show me any sort of camaraderie. "I have to run right now but—"

"Yes, I heard," she replies, amber eyes glowing mysteriously. "Clearly we *do* have a lot to catch up on."

"Here's my modus operandi," Jade explains as we stride down Madison Avenue toward *Glamour* magazine, hot on the scent of a hair shoot. "When I've had enough of my mother, I live with my father, and vice versa—or I tell one I'm living with the other and instead squat with friends. Male friends mostly— I'm a friend with incomparable benefits."

I smile, reveling in her openness. In fact, I'm downright delighted to be going on a go-see with Jade. This trekking around town after jobs is not only tiring, it's lonesome. So when I came out of Francesca's office and discovered we were lined up to see the same editor, I was thrilled.

Jade seems thrilled, too. Apparently while I was talking to Francesca, she'd gotten an earful from Sloane about what kind of jobs I've been doing lately. In fact, the moment we were out of the agency, all Jade did was question me about how the L'Oréal ad had come up, or who I met at the Saks shoot. At first, I felt embarrassed by all the praise she was heaping on me after every tale I told about a job landed or an editor I'd impressed.

But then Jade became . . . Jade again. That sharp-talking, wiser-than-her-years girlfriend I'd been longing for. So much so that I confided in her how exhausted I am, asking how she managed to stay so perky. Lucky her, she lives right in NYC. With her mother, too, but at least her mom sounds cool whereas mine . . . every time I come home these days it's an interrogation. Mom and Dad are none too happy with the hours I've been keeping, but the truth is, if an editor at *Harper's Bazaar* can only see me at 8:00 p.m., I go.

Stares laser us as we stand on a corner in Times Square, waiting for the light, stares from males of every description—suits, skateboarders, bicycle messengers, geezers, teenagers, college students, dads. It's warm and humid, and I am sweating and worrying about it because we have to look cute for the editor at *Glamour*. Still, I wish I'd worn more than these Rag and Bone shorts and Gap tank. I feel half naked. Jade, however, could care less. Her Alice + Olivia sundress is insanely short, her sweat only adding to the allure, and something about the way she walks makes me wonder if she's going commando underneath. Trying not to look at the men looking at us, I can imagine how passionately they'd like to be Jade's beneficent friend.

"Anyway, my early teens were a tour of duty with Daddy. Greece, Turkey, the whole Mediterranean affair," she goes on. "But he's all about extremes, so once he got sick of sunshine and olive oil, it was back to London, and when that wasn't dreary enough, Finland. Ghastly. So now I'm with my mother in TriBeCa. You've got to come over, Mac, meet Tom Jones. He's the cutest."

"Who?" I say, trying not to show too much surprise at this unexpected invitation.

She slaps my arm. "My kitten. I just got her. Well, I mean I thought she was a he when I named her. I found her in an alley after shooting a Dillard's ad. I took it as a good omen." Then Jade tells me about some '70s sex-symbol singer who always wore a tuxedo with a ruffled white shirt. "And my Tom Jones has the exact same outfit." As she details her antics—the way she attacks her toes, likes to nap in the bathroom sink, chases after her shadow—it strikes me as sweet. Here's this girl who's been everywhere and done everything, head over heels for an alley cat.

I decide to tell her about the fiasco at Frank Lindo's. Exposing myself to Jade feels easy, safe, since she's so open with me. Only I leave out the part about the brownies. No use coming off like a total loser.

"Sounds like a typical 'garmento' gathering," she says.

"Garmento?"

"A person in the rag trade."

"Rag trade?"

"Garment business. Gee-zus, Mac, we *are* in the garment business, you know. Should I get you a cheat sheet?" She puts on an accent, not unlike the ones I heard at Lindo's, for a little comic relief. "No, seriously, hon-bun, next time you should *call* me if you think you might be entering a down-market den of iniquity."

"Well, thanks. I'd like that," I say, grateful for the offer. "I guess at the time I thought I knew what I was doing. I mean, the agency encouraged me to go, so I thought it was legit. Though to be honest, the whole thing felt off from the get-go."

"How would the agency know? I mean, they sit behind desks while we go out and brave the world. They can't possibly know what it's like to be us. And I'm the queen of acting against my better judgment. Like I get a sense that something's fucked-up, but I go for it anyway. . . ."

Jade understands, maybe a bit too much. That's when it occurs to me what targets we are. A regular girl, sure, she has temptations, creeps who want to take advantage, but a model faces so much more. We actually have to walk into strange offices and studios and dark elevators at night; there is corruption around every corner, shark-infested waters in every puddle. That's why at the very least I make sure the agency always knows where I am. Even if they send me into those shark-infested waters, they have an account of my whereabouts, in case anything happens—and things happen all the time.

Even yesterday, I was walking on the street with my book under my arm and a man approached me asking if I was a model. I suppose the book is a dead giveaway—it's a pretty big portfolio. Almost a giant calling card for creeps to approach. Pretending to be in the market for a model like me to shoot the cover of a "famous" book, he invited me up to his studio. At least I was smart enough to tell him I was on the way to an appointment (I wasn't) but that if he called my agency, I would make sure they were expecting him and they would give him special treatment. My thinking was that if he was legit, I wouldn't lose the job opportunity. If he wasn't, well, then I saved myself from a potentially dangerous situation.

Having friends as back up wouldn't hurt either.

"Next time, I will call you," I say, pulling out my cell phone to program in Jade's number as Jade does the same. It's nice to know that there's someone I can reach out to who actually has a clue. "Maybe your take will save me from the road to ruin."

Jade nudges me in the ribs. "You better call," she says. "Of course, I may just want to ride shotgun."

Turns out Jade and I both snag the *Glamour* booking—"Good Hair for Bad Girls"—and I meet her at her apartment before the shoot, happy not to have to sit around the agency between appointments for a change. Why they scheduled me a go-see at 8:00 in the morning knowing full well that I'm not due at *Glamour* until 1:00 p.m. is beyond me. I'm starting to think they are liking the treats I bring to the office a little too much, even strategizing so that I show up with more! Don't get me wrong. I like Francesca and Sloane and the rest. But Francesca has a tendency to fret over my eyebrows mid-conversation. And Sloane, well, Sloane isn't much of a conversationalist, unless you count the sighs of delight she utters upon eating whatever confection I plop before her. Too, sometimes I wonder if they are even capable of understanding the business from the model side of things.

It feels good to have someone to commiserate with.

Especially someone like Jade, who not only has seen it all and done it all, but apparently, has it all.

For starters, she has an amazing apartment—huge, with wide windows overlooking the Hudson. The decor is minimalist—nothing like my house, cluttered with family heirlooms and, well, crap—but I can't tell if this is an aesthetic decision or if Jade and her mother just haven't gotten around to buying much furniture.

Sitting on a sumptuous leather sofa, I watch Jade devour a takeout container of spicy Thai shrimp, trying not to be taken in by the aroma. It amazes me that Jade would eat an hour before a shoot. My last meal was four hours ago and calling a snack baggie full of celery and carrots a meal is a bit of a stretch.

"Where is your mother?" I ask.

"Who knows?" she says. "Our paths don't cross much."

Tom Jones is very interested in the Thai takeout. Jade licks the spicy sauce off a shrimp and flips it to her. She sniffs, whiskers twitching madly. "Eat it, Tom-Tom—don't use it as a hockey puck," she warns, all strict, then says to me, "The last thing you want is to step on a cold, dusty crustacean in your bare feet." The kitten hunkers down to her treat, purring appreciatively. "I'm spoiling her so bad, but I can't help it. It's like I have 'sucker' tattooed to my forehead."

"I know, animals can really work you," I say. Don't think I missed how Jade changed the subject. Family doesn't seem to be her favorite subject, and I feel a little sorry for her, all alone in this rambling loft. "Anyway, I do hope to meet her one day," I say, changing the subject back. "Your mother, I mean."

"If you settle for a reasonable facsimile, you can meet her right now."

I must look at her funny; she mimics my expression. Then she grabs a plastic fork, stands up, and leads me to a locked door that she easily jimmies with to-go cutlery. There's a bed on a platform in the center of the room, some doors I assume lead to closets, and hanging on all four walls, enormous paintings—each by a different artist, each of a nude. "You could say my mother has an advanced degree in 'egonomics,'" Jade says. "This one's pretty cool though." She walks toward an impressionist-style piece, all soft strokes and watery colors conveying the image of a pale, lean woman with a cascade of platinum hair, much like Jade's own. "Mac Croft," she says, looking at the painting, not at me, "meet Leonora Paige Anderly Bishop."

My own mother is waiting for me on the front porch when I get home that night. Or, I should say, early the next day. In fact, I'm so surprised anyone is still awake, I nearly shriek when I see her shadowy form standing there.

"Melody Ann Croft, do you know what time it is?"

"Mom you scared me, what are you doing waiting in the shadows?" I hedge.

"Don't change the subject. I asked you if you know what time it is?" The anger in her voice is mixed with relief.

"Twelve thirty?" I reply, knowing full well it's later than that.

"It's one fifteen, and you'd better be glad your father isn't awake. What kind of *job* could keep you out until the wee hours of the morning?"

I wouldn't classify this as the wee hours of the morning, but since I'm standing on my mother's stoop, still gussied up in my bad-girl hair and makeup, I'm in no position to argue. "I'm sorry, Mom, I had a last-minute go-see for TV I couldn't turn down."

Mom is in no mood to hear my good news—that Marcy Golden had gotten me an opportunity to meet with the casting director for a Neutrogena commercial. Of course, I didn't feel a need to mention that I got the call while I was out with Jade for celebratory cocktails after our successful shoot—a Pellegrino for me, though Jade had a full-fledged martini. How could I not go out, when Jade and I had had such a blast together, mugging for the camera in miniskirts, over-the-knee boots, and rock-star hair? And I'm glad now I did agree to go, tired as I was. Otherwise, I would have been sailing home on NJ Transit when Francesca called my cell to tell me that Ogilvy & Mather were willing to look at a new girl for the Neutrogena spot, but only if I could go immediately. Of course, I hadn't realized I would have to sit around a half-empty TV studio for what felt like an eternity. Apparently Barbara Mintz, the casting director, likes to keep late hours and I wasn't the only new girl she'd agreed to see that night. I was there an hour longer than I thought I'd be!

My mother is shaking her head at me. "Melody, I know you're an adult, but that doesn't mean I don't worry about you."

"I know," I say, noticing for the first time, the grayish shadows under her eyes. "But it's only until the fall. And if I get this TV ad, well, I might not even need that scholarship."

My mother looks more worried than impressed. I think of Jade's mom, the sultry nude pictured on the walls of a TriBeCa loft, and wish, for a moment, that I had been born to another life. A more glamorous one.

I'm finally getting a taste. And, much to my surprise, I'm hungering for more.

Seven

"They fired me!" I wail to Jade on my cell phone, striding up Fifth Avenue on the way to yet another go-see.

"Who?"

"Who do you think? My waitress job! Can you believe it? I've never been fired before!"

"So you're finished at the Slaughter House. Big deal."

"It's the *Porter* House, Jade!"

"I stand corrected. So what?"

"It's just so . . . final. I feel like a failure—and just when I was getting the hang of it, too! Not that I blame them for giving me the ax; I was skipping and swapping shifts like crazy, just for go-sees."

"*Just* go-sees? Mac, wake up and smell the sizzle: you're a model now," she replies. "Not a model-waitress. You battled the bulge valiantly and now you're green lit for fashion. You've got two catalogue shoots coming up. You had a go-see for a television commercial, you polyp!"

"Yeah, but I didn't get it," I say, practically whining now as I remember the late-night lecture I'd had to endure from my mother last week. All for nothing.

"Yes, but you're on the radar, hon-bun. I'm surprised Francesca hasn't moved you up to Delicious on Demand yet," she adds, naming the next, higher level a model goes to at Delicious if she makes a name for herself as a newbie. Jade moved up to Delicious on Demand after six months, but she swears it's going to happen much more quickly for me. "You've got buzz, hon-bon," she's always saying, leaning into me like she's hoping to catch some of the vibration.

I sigh. "I know, you're right, it's probably for the best I got canned. The truth is the commute to the city alone is killing me. In fact, I was going to ask Francesca for some downtime between bookings. I'm fried."

Jade makes a *pffft* sound. "Be happy you have no downtime. Most girls are clawing to get go-sees and you have too many. Show a little more respect for the go-see, hon-bon. It's a wonder Francesca doesn't have you sleeping on the couch in her office just so she can keep her greedy little eye on you. At the rate you're booking these days, it's only a matter of time until you hit."

Francesca doesn't exactly offer me her couch, though she does have a plan for me.

"Oh, Melody, shame on me for being so insensitive. It's just that I've been focused on getting you go-sees and jobs—by the way, I'm thrilled about how things are going for you," she begins with her usual two scoops of charm, some sympathy syrup on top. "I guess I haven't thought about your commute. But never fear, I have the *perfect* solution for you. You can live at the Valencia! It's this fabulous hotel in a really great neighborhood—the agency keeps several suites there for girls in your situation. It's like a college dorm, only *très* chic."

Sounds a lot better than tromping through Penn Station every other day. "A hotel. With maid service and everything?"

"Of course, and cable, and Wi-Fi, and a spa on premises."

Sounds good. Too good. As was all that car service and cab fare Francesca offered—and docked me for. Wiser now, I say, "It must be expensive. Who pays for it?"

"Well, ultimately, you do—but it's a pittance compared to any other Manhattan accommodations; Delicious gets a discount, since we keep so many rooms." Francesca looks mildly injured. "Really, Mac, I wouldn't suggest it if I didn't think it was a good idea."

Though the Valencia turns out to be more *shabby* chic than *très* chic, I need something to make life easier, so I'm not completely turned off. And while it's true that Times Square is no longer the peep-show mecca it once was, I'm pretty sure not even the savviest NY real estate broker would classify this neighborhood as "great," the way Francesca had.

Still, the hotel itself is pretty serene. Or, at least, it is on the Tuesday afternoon I finally have a moment to make a visit. Doormen and desk clerks stand about in uniform, looking bored; the lobby is dowdy-posh and the adjoining bar is as quiet as a mausoleum. The suites are fairly tidy, the atmosphere tinged with the scent of disinfectant.

The biggest obstacle I face will be convincing my parents to let me stay there.

"I don't know, Melody . . . you're only eighteen—," my mother begins when I bring up the subject over dinner.

"Mom, I'm only going to stay in the city on the nights when I'm working late. I'm thinking of you, too—I don't want you waiting up on the porch for me to get home at all hours of the night. Besides, I'm going to college in the fall. It'll be just like me staying in a dorm, only closer."

"The difference is the University of Pennsylvania isn't in Times Square," my father says.

"Hey, Teddy," Richie chimes in between mouthfuls of pot roast, "isn't that where you and the guys took Buddy Robertson for his first, *uh*, experience with a . . . a woman?"

Teddy glances at me. "From what I understand, Giuliani cleared out all the prostitutes."

"Prostitutes!" Mom says, eyes widening.

"Mom, there haven't been prostitutes in Times Square in almost a decade. It's a *great* neighborhood, right in the heart of the Theater District!" I argue. "If anything, I'm more likely to run into the bad element traveling on the subway late at night."

"I thought you told us you didn't take the subway late at night?" Dad says, eyes narrowing at me.

Oops. "I meant the train."

"Last I checked, there weren't any vagrants on New Jersey Transit," Richie adds, barely containing his smile.

Though I feel like clubbing my brother, instead I opt to ignore him. "Wouldn't you feel better knowing that on a late night, I only have to get in a cab and go to a doorman-attended hotel room with a bunch of other girls my age under the watchful eye of the agency? Girls from all over the country stay there—some go to school during the day and do go-sees after they get out of class. Some of them even have their mothers staying there with them."

Mom sighs, clearly bending. I know she's remembering those sleepless nights when I came home much later than expected. She looks at my father.

Dad looks at me. "You're only going to stay there on late nights then?"

I nod.

"And you agree to come home every night you're not working . . ."

"I will—"

"Then I guess it'll be okay." He looks at my mother and she nods at me.

"If this is what you want, Melody."

"I do."

Then my father gives me a stern look. "But there is one thing you absolutely must promise: no matter what happens, if you are ever in any sort of trouble, you always call home. Understand?"

I stare at him and it's as if he had spies planted at Frank Lindo's house, seeing it for the dirty old man fest that it was.

"Of course."

Two nights later, it's not my father I'm dialing from the Valencia at midnight, but Jade. And not just because I know she's more likely to be awake.

"Jade, these girls are animals!" I whisper, huddled in the hall outside the room with my cell phone.

"You're exaggerating, Mac," she says. "You're just homesick or something."

"If I'm sick it's because one of these psychos poisoned my green tea!" Then I tell her what a dump the hotel is turning out to be. It's as if the whole place transforms after 8:00 p.m. The lobby, and most especially, the room, bears little resemblance to the seemingly innocuous hotel I saw on my one and only visit a week earlier. And the smell! It's no wonder they douse this place with disinfectant.

"Do you know they are piling ten of us to a room? They've got us sleeping on cots!" I say. "Worse, there've been, like, a dozen 'visitors' since I got here. One girl was just making out with a guy right on her cot in the middle of the room, in front of everybody! Someone else plugged in an iPod and is blasting music, another girl has a TV turned up high. There are half-eaten bags of chips and empty Häagen-Dazs cartons on the floor. And I think someone is now smoking pot in the bathroom. The whole place stinks!"

"Sounds like my kind of scene. I'll be right over."

Twenty minutes later, Jade enters the suite, where I've now huddled on the bed, pretending to be asleep.

When I see her slender statuesque frame slip into the room, I leap up, grab her hand, and yank her into a corner between the wall and the bureau. "I had a hundred-dollar bill tucked into a compartment of my wallet, and now it's gone. Plus . . ." I pull her closer, gesturing with a tilt of my head. "That one, the one spilling out of her bra . . . I could be wrong . . . and not that I have anything against gay people but . . . I think she hit on me."

She follows my gaze. "Possibly," she nods knowingly. "That's Tess O'Dair, equal opportunity slut."

I hug my elbows. "Of course I'm telling my parents everything's fine, but—"

"But you're anything but," she replies, glancing around. Her eyes widen at the sight of a waifish girl clearly trying to vomit up whatever she might have in her stomach into the trash can beside her bed. "You know, I'm all for a party, but this is pathetic." She wrinkles her nose, grabbing my hand. "Let's get out of here."

We wind up back at Jade's apartment, after I convince Jade that it's too late to go out for a nightcap. "We both have go-sees early in the morning," I argue, uncertain where she gets her energy until we enter her lavish TriBeCa loft and encounter Leonora Paige Anderly Bishop herself, aka Jade's mother, wide awake and lounging on the sofa.

I barely recognize her with her clothes on. In fact, Mrs. Bishop almost has too many clothes on for one o'clock in the morning. I'm not sure if she's coming or going, but either way, I can't think of anywhere *my* mother would have to go on a Tuesday night wearing a silver minidress and glittery earrings dangling well below her chin-length Victoria Beckham bob.

"Jade," she says, eyebrows rising in surprise when it appears her daughter is about to march off to her bedroom without even acknowledging her. "Aren't you going to introduce me to your new friend?"

Jade stops, and I catch an eye roll before she turns and says, almost mechanically, "Mac Croft, meet Leonora Bishop."

"Mac, how charming." She extends a hand, though she doesn't exactly smile.

"Good evening, Mrs. Bishop." I get this sudden urge to curtsy. "Or maybe I should say good morning!" With a self-conscious laugh, I add, "Sorry to intrude so late."

"Nonsense!" she says, waving one well-manicured hand. "It's so rare that Jade brings *anyone* home. That is, anyone *female*." She chuckles to herself. "After all, Jade's hardly known for playing nice with others—especially other women. Indeed,

I haven't heard her mention a girlfriend since that tiff with Hana Benatar."

"Are we finished, Leonora?" Jade says, grabbing my hand and tugging me toward her room. "Because *some* of us have to *work* in the morning."

If Leonora Bishop's words were meant as some kind of warning, my impromptu sleepover at Jade's cleared up whatever wariness I might have otherwise felt. We wound up staying up late and talking, which wasn't such a great idea, since we did have early go-sees. But I think I might wind up being a good influence on Jade. Not only did I get her out of bed in time for her go-see, I even convinced her to have some yogurt and fruit with me in the morning, instead of her usual three cups of coffee. Maybe I feel so close to her because I miss the closeness I shared with Liza, who is just as immersed in her boyfriend this summer as I am in modeling. Or maybe it's because Jade feels like a lifeline to me. It's like I have someone to turn to in my time of need—and in this business, that's pretty rare. Some girls pair up, but only if they're different enough from each other that they won't compete for the same job—a weird basis for friendship. I hope there's more to it between Jade and me, but on the surface we do complement each other, so there's no competition. She's light, I'm dark; a client wouldn't pick one over the other.

Of course, that might work when it comes to modeling. But when it comes to men. . .

"Never date a model," Jade tells me as we sit over herbal teas between go-sees. Not that I've managed to convert Jade into a health nut, but getting her to Leaf is easy enough, as it's the teahouse to sip and be seen at—tea being the new coffee, and Leaf being a model haunt anyway, owned as it is by Joni Eldredge, another former "supe" made good. Massive in the '90s, Joni had a limited run—her choice, as I understand it. She quit to paint, but painting failed to prove lucrative, and Joni, already accustomed to a certain lifestyle, opened Leaf ahead of the curve of the tea craze, predating Moby's Teany even. It's been a goldmine. Jade likes it, since it's close to home; I approve, since everything on the menu has some sort of nutritional value. The vibe is very chill, Joni's tranquil, turquoise landscapes lining the walls, Joni herself a constant presence, traipsing ethereally about in her Theory tunics and toe rings.

"No exceptions," Jade says, her eye moving to the hunk standing in the entrance. "It's one of the axioms you need to live by, hon-bon."

I'm trying to pay attention, I really am. Except Duncan Shiloh has just stepped into the doorway, the yummy male model who is prompting this impromptu lecture from Jade.

Sometimes I think she takes this whole mentor role a little too far.

"Photographers are cool to date. Especially ones who work a lot—they end up booking you for all their jobs so you work constantly. It's a great trade-off," she continues. "Ditto designers, only that's pretty much a moot point, since most would rather *be* us than bed us. But a male model? *Verboten*. Taboo. The no-no of all no-nos. There are straight guys in the biz—prime examples of male ego run amok."

I flick my gaze to her for as long as I can manage to tear it away from Duncan, who looks just so sort of . . . innocent standing there. I wonder if he's here alone. Or if he's meeting someone. . .

"In their defense," Jade continues, "I think they're just not equipped to handle the attention. Girls who've always been too tall or geeky in high school are happy to be in a scene where they are considered beauties. They are like caterpillars who become butterflies in the modeling world. They thrive. But being attractive isn't supposed to matter to men, so incurring worship for chiseled cheekbones and piercing eyes and a killer bod is a strange trip—not very macho. Ergo, they're fucked-up over it."

I smile at her, nodding in agreement, though I'm not sure I've paid enough attention to know what I've just agreed to. Maybe he is alone, which would be wild, since Duncan Shiloh, is only *the hottest* guy in Delish's men's division. Got off the plane from Tennessee and walked directly onto a Times Square billboard. You can't miss him, rising high above the city, brandishing the new iPod. Dreamily lost in music, he looks like a cross between a dark-haired Jesus Christ and a green-eyed, *Excellent Adventure*–era Keanu Reeves, as rendered by Michelangelo. Even his knuckles are sexy. He's perfect. Almost too perfect.

And apparently alone. And shy! At least, he looks shy, standing there awkwardly, wondering if anyone is going to offer him a spot at their table. The joint is packed and everyone assembled has the same reaction, awed yet subdued acknowledgment of the masterpiece of manhood come into our midst.

And Duncan . . . he looks, well, oblivious. Is it possible he doesn't know how cute he is? He approaches the counter in black biker boots, stoops to study the goodies on display, stands erect again, and lets his endless, oceanic eyes meander from table to booth, ottoman to cushion.

Am I the only one noticing the way his well-worn plain

white T-shirt glides over his shoulders and chest? How his glossy dark hair is impeccably tousled and his facial stubble grown out just enough to delineate the structure of his sculpted face? Even Joni, whose name has been linked with some of the planet's most powerful men, seems indifferent.

But not me. I'm not going to let dear Duncan sip tea alone. Because that's what kind of girl I am.

I wait for his eyes to amble our way, and when they do I lock with them, give him a smile and a little wave. "Hi!"

A thrill moves through me when he ambles our way. I turn to Jade, trying not to bubble over with excitement, and am shocked to discover that she is staring daggers at me.

My eyes widen at her. I don't know what she's making such a fuss about. I'm just being friendly.

"Well, heyyyy . . ." Duncan's smile claims his face in a lazy, almost shy, way, so that when it's in place, in all its sparkling glory, you're almost prepared for it. Almost—but not quite. "Is it all right if I sit here?"

Jade and I have one of Leaf's round cocoon booths to ourselves—there's ample room. She doesn't move her bag or books from the spot beside her, so I scoot over and tell him, "Sure."

"Well, thanks." Long legs are an under-the-table conundrum; ultimately he has to extend them out. "I'm Duncan." Everything about him, including his voice, has this wonderfully unhurried quality, as if time were pennies in his pocket.

"Yeah, Duncan Shiloh, right?" Jade's quick, prickly manner is even quicker and pricklier in contrast to Duncan's warm molasses drawl.

He looks at her like she's psychic or something, his lips parting, his brow furrowing.

"We're with Delicious, too," she explains. "I'm Jade; this is Mac."

Duncan turns his gaze on me again. "I got to thank you for saying hi, letting me sit with y'all. I've never been in here before, but folks tell me it's a good place to come if you want to stay out of trouble." He turns slightly, as if abashed. "You know, barrooms and such. I promised my mama I'd stay away from all that."

Jade squelches her sarcasm, with difficulty—he really is kind of a hoot—as Joni glides over to ask what she can bring him; Duncan scans the menu and shrugs. "Frankly, ma'am, I don't know what from what on here. But if you have any sweet tea, I'd love the biggest glass you got."

Joni says she can handle that, and the three of us proceed to talk shop. Duncan says he's more surprised than anyone that he landed iPod on his very first go-see, and Jade tells him something very similar happened to me.

"Don't be silly, Jade." I brush it off. "It's just this editorial thing with three other girls in *Teen Vogue*. Nothing like a billboard on Times Square."

She mugs at me, then gets a call and dashes outside with her cell to take it, leaving me alone with Duncan. Somehow the subject of weird things we've seen on the subway comes up, and after he tells me the story of some "dueling crazies—a guy playing air guitar feuding with a woman in a rainbow wig"—he admits to feeling bad later for laughing. "It's not right to laugh at unfortunates, people who have mental problems and such," Duncan says with a rueful tenderness that makes me woozy.

Right about then, Jade storms back in. "Give me five, ten, fifteen, twenty!"

I stand, and we slap both hands in the air twice—Jade's version of patty-cake.

"I just got Spiked Tea!" she crows.

"Jade, that's awesome!" Damn, did she ever earn it—had like three callbacks for the campaign. "*You're* awesome!" I say, and I mean it sincerely, even though I'm a tad jealous. I didn't even have a go-see for Spiked Tea, but I was up for this Nokia phone thing, doing three callbacks with the casting agent before they wound up choosing someone else. Very disappointing. The rejection was on two levels. First it was personal, second, I would have made $25K!

"You know this can only lead to one thing." Jade's way too psyched up to sit down. "Parrrrr-tee! I can't very well shill for the alcoholic equivalent of Kool-Aid till I know for sure I like it. That wouldn't be very honorable, now would it?"

It flits through my brain that there's something perverse about her hyping liquor—she's technically a minor, after all—but the thought's soon pushed out by Jade's staccato patter as she plans a night of debauchery. I'm getting caught up in it, to the point that I forget Duncan is still in the booth. Jade, however, does not.

"So, you, Duncan!" She snaps her fingers. "Come on, let's have your digits. You want to be invited, don't you?" She flips her phone, ready to punch in his pertinences.

"Well, sure," he says. "You bet I do."

Jade taps in his number and smirks. "Naturally, you realize that if you come, you'll be breaking that promise to your mama every which way but loose."

Eight

Jade never ceases to amaze me. Turns out not only is it *not* an issue that she's peddling liquor at a tender and innocent nineteen, but she's actually encouraged to do so. Vyung Ltd., the company that manufactures Spiked Tea, Rhombus Inc., the importers, and Mercant and Silkes, the ad agency, are all too happy to join forces and turn her party idea into an A-list, E-ticket PR blowout. All she does is send a teensy e-mail to her contact at M&S, saying she thinks it would be fun, and he runs with it. Talk about cooking up a buzz.

Within days, a promoter is hired, a club booked, invites printed, and cases of Spiked Tea rolled through customs. I'm almost excited about it. If I can just get this niggling thought out of my head that Jade is trying to weasel in on my man. Okay, he's not my man. But she went from warning me away from him to inviting him to her party. What's up with that?

I'm trying to remain cool, though. I mean, she's being really, really nice. Even letting me stay over her place tonight for the party, sparing me once again the indignities of the Valencia.

I've even been invited for the pre-party prep, with access to Jade's considerable closet.

I should be happy. And I am. Really.

"The thing is, I don't even *like* parties," Jade says, standing before her closet in nothing but a black push-up bra and lacy thong. "Imagine if I bailed on my own bash. How enfant terrible would that be?"

"Very," I reply, a touch of huffiness entering my tone, despite my efforts.

"Hey!" She pokes me in the ribs as I'm about to try on her burgundy Rebecca Taylor. Annoyed, I rear back and swat her with the dress. Which only causes her to poke me again.

"Stop it, Jade!"

"What's with you?" she demands. "You mad at me?"

"What possible reason would I have to be mad?" I say, practically yelling now. *I'm not mad*, I tell myself, stepping into the dress. I'm just fried. I shot the Bloomingdale's catalogue this week and catalogue work, I'm discovering, is such a tiresome treadmill. I feel like I'm recovering from a killer workout—I ache all over!

"Don't be passive-aggressive with me, missy," she challenges. "I'll give you a reason: some very privileged contact information programmed into my phone."

I study myself in the mirror, assessing the degree of décolletage on display. "You mean Duncan Shiloh?" My tone is milder, though I find myself whipping off the dress as if it's infected. "Honestly, Jade, I couldn't care less. He's nice, I liked talking to him, but if you want him, be my guest." *As if he's mine to give away!*

"I *don't* want him. Not my brand of boy toy, hon-bun," Jade says. "It simply would've been impolite not to invite him, considering how we were discussing it right in front of him."

"Yes, and we all know what a paragon of politeness you are, Jade."

"Touché!" She smiles, slipping on a boldly graphic Dolce & Gabbana blouse, which happens to look great on her. But that's the thing: *everything* looks great on her. I don't want to be jealous. I like Jade. She's becoming my first real friend in this business. As much as I can call anyone a friend.

"You know, I only pulled this party together for your sake," she says, whipping the top over her head and dropping it to the floor, as if it didn't cost more than the pay I earned on my catalogue shoot this morning. "You're a Delicious model—time you partied like one. *And* I hooked you up with a sort-of date. Not that I recommend you mess with your own kind; indeed, as you know, I discourage it stridently." She flops on the bed and serves me with a wounded, sulky stare. "You try to do a nice thing for someone and they don't appreciate it and it really sucks."

Seeing her pout like that, I suddenly feel an urge to laugh. Instead, I try for a light, teasing touch, puckering my lips and filling the air with smooches. "Thank you, thank you, thank you, Lady Bishop, my benefactress—I'm forever in your debt!" Returning to the closet, my gaze falls upon a dress so pretty I feel a shiver up my spine. "How about this?"

"My vintage Dior? Girl, you've got to be kidding. That's practically a museum piece."

"Oh, but Jade, your generosity knows no limits!"

I hold the dress up against me, a sigh escaping my lips at the way the filmy material makes my skin tone positively shimmer. I catch Jade's gaze in the mirror and know she's going to give in. She invited me here, after all, on the claim that it's "essential" I borrow her clothes because mine are, in her words, "pathetic." "Judged as we are by the company we keep, I cannot very well be seen gallivanting around with the fashion-challenged," she said over doughnuts at the agency one morning—and I do mean doughnuts, as Jade polished off three of them to my none.

I step into the Dior, zip up, and evaluate the effect—which is devastating, the cinched waist and fluted folds of the skirt a foil for my newly svelte figure. Those extra two pounds I lost have really made a difference. I'm fitting into Jade's hottest dresses!

"What do you think?" I ask, turning to face her.

"What are you, trawling for compliments?" She rolls her eyes. "You just don't get it, do you?"

I blink at her.

"Your body is so sick it's cancer, especially now that you've pared off those fifteen pounds."

"Twelve!" I correct, gazing at my reflection once more. "I have three more to go."

She sighs. "Go for it—wear the Dior. But if you get a stain on it, I'll have to kill you."

I squeal, leaping into the air and clapping my hands. "Thank you!" Then, eyeing the closet that I know holds a veritable treasure trove of shoes, I say, "Do you mind?" Then, without waiting for an answer, I begin to scavenge for the perfect shoes, like a kid in a candy store.

"Don't touch the Marc Jacobs pumps!" she says, getting up from the bed. "If you're going old school, I'll be thoroughly modern, maybe pair the Daryl K with Heatherette. The Marc Jacobs pumps would be the icing on the cake."

I decide to leave my hair loose and Jade puts hers in pigtails. We agree to forgo makeup entirely. One cool thing about high cheekbones and high-end clothes is they do the work for you, no gussying up required. Of course, you must possess the body, the carriage, and above all, the hauteur to pull them off.

I glance at myself in the mirror, realizing that in this regard, I am, in fact, blessed.

Riding in the limo to Marquis, site of the Spiked Tea soiree, I flash on the conversation Jade and I had while getting dressed. How I'm required to party like a big-time New York model now. And how Duncan will be there—only the most amazing thing with a Y chromosome to hit this city in eons. Not that I consider him my date; chances are he won't even remember me. If he comes at all—Duncan really didn't strike me as a club person. It's just the prospect of rising to the occasion is a little intimidating. So I decide: from this moment on, Melody Ann Croft is officially retired, a relic of Morristown, New Jersey. I *am* Mac, even now, after hours. This realm I've entered demands an alter ego—with all the makeup, all the clothes, it's the last thing you put on, the finishing touch, before stepping out before the camera . . . or onto the red carpet, which I'm about to do. Private lives are for other people. In this business, the line between working and socializing is beyond blurry. If you're out—you're on.

The club is maybe a mile from the Bishop apartment. Ridiculous that we even have a limo. But tonight, someone else is paying for our transport—the liquor company or the importers or the ad agency—presumably for photo-op reasons.

"Now, remember, hon-bun, the correct way to air kiss is left cheek, right cheek, left cheek." Jade's voice ratchets up half an octave, almost shrill as we pull up in front of Marquis. "Otherwise you're likely to wind up with a broken nose." She gives me a look I can't decipher—her eyes jittery, teeth about to bite—then turns away. The velvet rope is unlatched.

Turns out Jade's expression is the first in a series of the evening's incomprehensibles. First of all, why are they taking pictures of everyone—including me—in front of a board that says Spiked Tea on it? Isn't Jade the only Spiked Tea girl? And why have they laid the red carpet on the dirty sidewalk? My mother doesn't even allow us to walk on the living room rug with shoes on! Once we are inside, what I really want to know is why the music is so loud, when there are all these people who want to talk to you? Or is it that they don't want to talk to you—they just want to be seen talking to you? And who are they, anyway? The crowd is very different from Lindo's. Top-model central, with the predictable assortment of designers, photographers, stylists in tow. A lot of random downtown scene-mongers, their clothes a Dumpster-meets-diva mix of thrift shop and chic boutique. Men? Rock-star types, athlete types, actor types—the kind of men that go with models like peanut butter goes with jelly. I spy Patrick Stump from Fall Out Boy and Jensen Ackles from *Supernatural* straight off. Older hangers-on and wranglers abound as well—PR and magazine and advertising people. Going from one end of Marquis to the other is like walking a gauntlet. So it only makes sense to grab something long, tall, and cool off a waiter's tray.

I don't do alcohol but it looks like finding a glass of water right now isn't going to be easy. And I suppose I should at least sample the product Jade is here to promote.

Mmm, refreshing. Only here's another thing I don't understand—the whole concept of Spiked Tea. Pretty colors—pink and orange and blueberry blue. Packed with herbal ingredients like ginseng and echinacea. But bottom line, the stuff is 20 proof. Are we supposed to be suckered by the easy-to-swill flavors and nutritionally trendy touches, to tell ourselves this isn't booze? So bogus! So yummy! I'd better be careful. I put the drink down on the first table I see.

"Come on, this way." Jade gives me a nudge. "We're being beckoned by the bottle host."

How she can tell in the multitude I have no clue—but what a bottle host is, I'm about to learn.

"Ladies, this way to your table," says a handsome hipster, slipping his arms through ours and escorting us to an elevated area. Here, the corporate powers-that-be who arranged this affair await us. As Jade introduces me, a waiter materializes with a tray. "Now I know this is a Spiked Tea joint, but you've got to indulge in Marquis's signature cocktails," says the bottle host, whose job, I surmise, is to slake the thirst of bigwigs willing to pay five hundred bucks for a few rounds. "They're called Vapors, and you will love them."

Much to my surprise, the label on the liquor bottle reads Roberto Cavalli. Who knew designers were doing vodka now? Ketel One and Grey Goose have been demoted to the level of Georgi, which I only know about because of boozy Uncle Frank—whenever we see him at holidays, he's got his trusty pint of rocket fuel in his pocket.

The drinks are mixed with a flourish and poured into elegant stemware. I take a sip to be polite. Jade knocks half of hers back in two sips, then leans into me. "No way am I sitting here with suits all night," she whispers, then pulls me up by my hand. "Gentleman, thanks a million." She finishes her drink in two more sips. "But now—we dance!"

As she leads the way to the floor, I try surrendering to the mindless beat of kitschy '90s house music, which was made famous in Europe and imported to the United States. The crowd comes with us, though, and in no time we're the epicenter of a mass of wriggling bodies and blank faces. Only Jade's face looks alive, wildly alive. Then again, she probably slept till noon while I worked a twelve-hour day, a slave to the Bloomingdale's catalogue. Clearly Jade got her work ethic from the grasshopper in Aesop's fable. With her wealth and lackadaisical upbringing, she never learned to apply herself, I suppose. Her party ethic, now that's a different story—Jade's idea of fun borders on hysteria. I notice that she isn't really dancing with me; she's dancing with everyone. And it's enviable. I wish I could be like that, able to turn off my brain and immerse myself in this sea of strangers. *Mac, Mac, paging Mac!* I think to myself. *Will Mac the model please report to the dance floor immediately!* It helps; I fake it till it turns into the genuine article.

That's when I spy him. Duncan! He's standing at the edge of the dance floor, and I think he's watching me. You know how when you go to a concert, and the singer delivers the ballad straight to you? Well, every other female from front-and-center orchestra to nosebleed balcony believes the same thing. It's kind of like that. I want to know for sure, so I close my eyes and really let the rhythm own me. When I open them again, Duncan's right there in front of me, moving in time with me. He doesn't move much, just enough, yet simply by entering the fray he causes the crowd to swell and surge. Guys and girls alike press in against us, vying for our attention. It feels good—even though it feels like drowning.

It's not my intention to touch him, only it's as if we're bouncing around in a refrigerator box—how could I not accidentally brush a part of him with a part of me? Once that happens—for scarcely a second—it's like a mutual decision to be out of there. Duncan searches above the crowd, scopes our escape, then grabs my hand and steers me away from the roiling mass.

"*Whoa!*" I say. "*Phew!*"

Duncan doesn't say anything, just gives me a small bemused smile.

"This place is insane!"

He casts his glance at one of the couches that line the club, leading me there and offering me the place beside him silently—again, conveying his thoughts with the depth of his eyes, the curve of his mouth. We sit beside each other touching slightly leg to leg, and shoulder to shoulder, my heart pounding as I feel him touch my hand. I wonder if it's accidental and then he touches me again. We look at the crowd. We look at each other as his hand explores my hand, caressing and moving over the curves of my fingers. As he brushes my palm with the tips of his fingers, I feel heat rising to my face, my heart pumping so hard I feel like I'm going to explode

"It's really hard to talk in here," I say.

He just continues to play with my hand and I sense from him that's why he's not talking.

Not talking—what a concept. To simply sit with each other, and be together, while humanity rages all around us. Experience, without making a sound. Just our hands touching, our eyes on each other, as if we are the only two people in the world.

Duncan takes my hand freely in his, his eyes on mine as he kisses my fingertips. His touch is so sensual, it's as if we're doing something more than we actually are. Like sharing a sexy secret.

Suddenly, out of nowhere I get this tingle. It starts in my stomach then jumps to the base of my spine and works its way up until it ignites my brain with a single thought: Jade!

I left her. But she's all right. Isn't she? Of course she is. She's a big girl. Well, tall, anyway. And so streetwise-sophisticated. Unless that's her facade. It's not that I have any real reason to stress over her—I just do, like she's my cosmic sister and we're linked on some level. Duncan senses my turmoil almost as soon as I do. When I stand, he does, too. "You know what, I need to . . . I need to find Jade. Excuse me . . ."

Urgency takes over as I move through the club. For a moment I wonder if I'm running from Duncan just as much as I'm running to Jade. I mean, it was pretty intense back there with him. I haven't felt that level of connection to anyone since . . . well, since Eric.

I slow down to negotiate my way. The place is a maze of little side lounges, up a few steps, down a few. Then it dawns on me: there must be a VIP room. Find that, I'll find Jade. I ask a waiter—shriek the question, actually. He points. I bee-line. There's a gaggle of people trying to get in; what makes me think I'll be granted entry? Must be the imperative of my mission, but I'm able to slip in on the tails of a cluster of wannabes. Then there's a doorman, complete with clipboard and attitude. *I'm a superhero*, I tell myself. *No nightclub nobody with a list can defy me.* But he does defy me, gives me a stony look, and asks my name.

"Melody Ann Croft."

He scans. Sniffs. "Sorry . . ." And his eyes slither away.

"Try Mac," I tell him.

He looks at me with scorn. "*Hmm?*"

"They probably put me down under Mac. Just Mac. Will you look again, please?"

He obeys, then *hmpfs*. "Go," he says, still unconvinced I'm not an imposter.

"MAC!!"

Jade perches on the bar amid several men who all seem to touch her at once. I head straight for her. "Ooh, Jade, I lost you . . ." It feels like a lie because it is a lie. I didn't lose her. I *left* her.

"Mac, bay-bee, hon-bun!" she cries—but she's not quite letting me off the hook. "Lost me, huh? Guess the aura of Duncan Shiloh got you all in a dither." She tosses back what's left in her champagne glass and grins. "*Awww*, Mackie-Mac, don't you worry your little head about that." She begins her dismount. "I'm goo-o-o-o-o . . ."

Not so good. She slides off the bar, bangs against an admirer, clutches at his shirt, misses, and veers backward. She desperately does not want to fall. Gravity has other ideas. Gravity wins. Jade's now flat on her ass, legs akimbo—and this time it's clear she is going commando. She's laughing, though; everyone's laughing, except for me. I crouch to cover her up and lend her a hand. She grasps, gets ahold of my knee instead, clambers up. I help her, support her, manage to get her reasonably upright.

"Mac, I want you to meet . . ." she waves a hand above her head. "Everyone. Everyone, meet Mac. She's my dear friend. And you know what? She's going to be the biggest thing ever. She is . . . on . . . her . . . *whoops!*" Jade sways, grabs my shoulder. When she breathes into my ear I realize exactly how loaded she is. Still, she tells me anyway. "Mac, I am fucked the fuck up. And I have to go pee-pee. Really badly. Will you come with me?"

Unfortunately, a different bodily function takes precedence. Before Jade can reach a ladies' room stall, she starts to wretch and heave, and as I'm trying to maneuver her toward the toilet she erupts—splattering me and the irreplaceable museum-piece Dior. Jade's eyes, bloodshot and watery, widen with the horror of what she's done. My impulse is to fling her convulsing form away from me and dive into the nearest sink, but as the second wave hits her my instinct to help kicks back in. When I'm a doctor I'll have to deal with much worse. I guide Jade into a stall, help her to her knees—paying no mind to the girls looking on in entranced disgust. Slamming the stall door in their faces, I put my back flush to the wall and squat. I lean over and gently tug Jade's pigtails out of the way. The back of her ribcage lurches against her shirt, vertebrae threatening to burst through her skin. I murmur susurrus syllables of comfort. I don't know how I know what to do; somehow I just do. I don't care that Dior and I have just been splattered. All I care about is Jade as the evening's every cocktail exacts its revenge.

It occurs to me, as I hold her frail, heaving body, that Jade needs me. Just as much as I need her. If not more. . . .

I'm forcing carrots and celery stalks into a juicer I found in the far reaches of the Bishop kitchen, worrying because I never did get to say good-bye to Duncan last night, when the yowl comes from the bedroom.

"Ma-a-a-a-c!"

I smile. Apparently the Spiked Tea mascot is awake.

"Mac Croft! Yo, bee-yotch, where you at?"

I turn on the juicer, wondering, not for the first time, where Mrs. Bishop is. I was glad she wasn't home last night to witness Jade's drunken return, but that she's still not here this morning makes me wonder if Jade really does live here alone most of the time.

The juicer stops and I look up to find Jade standing in the entranceway, looking almost innocent in girlish pink cotton panties and a Juicy Couture tank.

"There you are!" she says, beaming at me.

"You're surprisingly chipper," I say, pouring the contents of the juicer into two glasses. "Or are you somehow still drunk?"

"Sober as a nun." She presses her palms in a praying gesture, casts her eyes heavenward.

"You have the constitution of a Hummer." I say, handing her one of the glasses.

"Nice!" she comments after a swig.

"I figured you'd like it—carrots have so much sugar, they may as well be cotton candy." I point to a platter. "I made muffins, too. They're gluten-free."

She gives me an inscrutable stare.

"Thank you," she says finally. "For the muffins, the pulverized vegetables . . . you know, last night and . . . everything. I can't even remember coming home!"

I shrug, studying her as I take a sip of the juice.

"Let's go out on the terrace," she says, "We can recap."

"Fine, Jade, but don't you think you should put something on? Just a suggestion."

She makes a face and pads to her room.

When she joins me on the terrace, she's carrying the puke-splattered Dior.

"You ruined my dress, you polyp!"

I look at her. "*I* ruined it? I can't believe you don't remember that!"

"Well, you could have at least tried to stay out of the line of fire."

"You're kidding, right?"

"No, I'm *not* kidding. This dress is irreplaceable!"

"Yeah, but it's *your* puke on that dress. Not mine!"

We glare at each other, until her expression clears, as if she's made some sort of decision. Then she ducks her head in an uncharacteristically self-conscious gesture. "Well, I suppose maybe I could have drunk less. But you know how it is." She meets my gaze now, her eyes glittering with some emotion I don't quite understand. "You're in a bar, surrounded by strangers toasting you. Your only real friend dumping you for the first pretty face that comes along . . ."

If it's Jade's intention to turn the tables on me, it's working. "I'm sorry I left you, Jade . . ."

She shrugs. "Oh, c'mon, who could blame you, really? The man looks like a Greek god. So tell me, where did you and Duncan slip off to?" she asks, in a tone that sounds suspiciously nonchalant.

"Nowhere. I mean we just . . . hung out together for a while. It was nothing, really," I say, afraid to remark on the *something* I felt with Duncan. I'm sure now is not the time to emphasize the deep connection I felt with Duncan, especially when it feels like the connection I've forged with Jade is hanging by a thread.

"So where did you do him? In the bathroom or the limo? Please tell me it was the limo, hon-bon. I'd hate to think Mercant and Silkes wasted all that money on car service just to take us to and from a party."

Bristling, I respond. "I didn't *do* him, Jade. It wasn't like that. Duncan's not like that."

"Oh, come on, Mac. You need to get a clue. If there's one thing I know about male models is that the gay ones are off-limits and the straight ones are trying so hard to prove they're *not* gay, they sleep with whatever willing female is within their sights."

I shake my head. "I'm sorry. I know you'll think this is nuts, but as gorgeous as he is—and yes, I admit, Duncan Shiloh is hot—I can't really envision him in any kind of . . . doing anything . . . *uck*, Jade, it's like he has all this warmth, this incredible warmth of the soul and the heart, but he's just not guylike, or not like the guys I know. Where the horny hormones just pop off them like sweat. It's as if Duncan's above that."

Jade shakes her head. "I'm not buying the whole warmth-but-no-heat concept when it comes to a male model, especially a straight male model. Mark my words, if you don't put out for Duncan Shiloh, he's going to need to find someone who will. It's an ego game," then she glances away, gazing into the distance. "I just don't want you to get hurt."

I look at her, wondering at her words. And it occurs to me that maybe it's *Jade* who is afraid of getting hurt.

Nine

"Mac, darling, I have *fabulous* news," Francesca croons over my cell phone as I'm hoofing it past Henri Bendel on Fifth Avenue. "We have a shot at a layout—with *cover*—for *Ocean Drive*."

I stop in my tracks. My first cover! Then it occurs to me that I've never heard of the magazine she's talking about. "What's *Ocean Drive*?"

"Only the premiere fashion and lifestyle magazine of South Beach."

"South Beach? As in Florida?" Not only is this the first time I will be on a plane, but it will take me to a beach! South Beach to boot—I've never been to Florida. Ha! I may just get to the beach this summer, after all. Fun!

As if reading my mind, Francesca says, "You won't be spending much time down there. Two days. Three at most. As it is, I had to reschedule a shoot, which isn't *ideal*, especially for a job that isn't definite. But you did make the short list of models *Ocean Drive* wants to see, and if you get it, well, it could lead to other things. Bigger things."

As soon as Francesca finishes a mini-lecture on the proper

levels of SPF I'll need to take with me, I hang up and call Jade, too excited to keep this news to myself. Though I'm not sure what's more thrilling right now—the hope of having some much-needed beach time, my first plane trip, or my first cover.

Okay, the cover wins, followed by the plane ride!

Jade seems more impressed by the scene. "Oh, South Beach. I *love* SoBe. I'd give my right arm to do a shoot down there."

"So come!" I exclaim. "I'll already have a room you can crash in. And Francesca wants me to meet with our affiliate agency down there, and possibly do some go-sees." I roll my eyes. "God forbid I should have any time for R and R! Anyway, I'm sure you could meet with some people, too, if your booker lets you go. . . ."

Not only did Jade's booker, Vanessa, let Jade go, but she even lined up a few go-sees for her.

"Who knows, maybe she's hoping I'll work better in another market," Jade says once we are seated side by side on the plane and I remark on how easy it was to arrange for Jade to come.

I frown. "What are you talking about, Jade? You're *already* working in the New York market."

"Of course, I'm working, hon-bun," she says, graciously accepting a gin and tonic from the flight attendant, who was so interested in our being models that she didn't even bother to proof my nineteen-year-old seatmate. "But the fact is I haven't *hit* yet. You know, landed the big advertising contract—"

"You just got Spiked Tea!"

She sends me a look. "Yes, and don't think I'm not grateful for the exposure, not to mention the income. But a cosmetic endorsement it is *not*. I want the four-year-long contract, not the six-month hit or misses. *Maybe* my ad will last two cycles, but that's it. Certainly not enough earnings to retire from go-sees."

"What do you mean two cycles?"

She sighs. "Do I have to teach you everything? Ads run in cycles. If the ad hits or is successful, the client will buy it for more than one cycle and make a commercial from it. Sometimes if you are really lucky, like Justin Long who did the Mac commercial, you get big exposure. Justin did a role in *Live Free or Die Hard* with Bruce Willis after he got such great buzz from that campaign."

"Wow!" I reply, my mind still mulling over Jade's worry that she hasn't hit yet. It's the first time I've ever heard Jade talk like that. True, she hasn't gotten any big covers or contracts, but she seems to get a lot work. "I don't think you have anything to worry about, Jade."

She gives me a funny look, then she smiles, eyes gleaming as she raises her drink. "Oh, I'm not worried, hon-bun." Then, tapping her freshly mixed cocktail against my bottled water in a toast, she says, "You and I are going places. And I'm not just talking about South Beach."

This is the irony of my life right now: three days in South Beach, and I can't even lie out in the sun. Tanning is taboo. Being tan is fine as long as it's fake, but Francesca won't let me walk half a block without a thick coat of SPF.

"Mac, do you have any idea how devastating free radicals are?" she railed when I told her how I hoped to squeeze in a little time, poolside.

Actually, I do—and I don't want to invite premature aging

or melanoma. But I also know that sunshine is the greatest natural source of vitamin D.

Of course, with my schedule, I may just have to take a vitamin D supplement. Within an hour of landing, I'm off to the editorial offices of *Ocean Drive*, where I meet with Marguerite Moller, fashion editor, and Lucian Gilbert, a photographer I've never heard of but who Jade swears is the toast of South Beach, as far as fashion photography goes.

I'm not sure what my prospects are. In fact, I'm not sure I'm even visible at this meeting, since both Marguerite and Lucian speak about me—or rather, my breasts—in the third person.

"Look, Marguerite, real breasts!" Lucian exclaims when I enter the room. "They must be a C cup!"

"And they photograph well, too," Marguerite comments, glancing from my book, which is open on the desk before her, to my chest.

I wonder if this is a good thing, seeing as South Beach seems to be the silicone capital of the world. I think I spotted sixteen boob jobs alone in the cab from the hotel to the *Ocean Drive* offices. I try not to glance down at my own breasts, which were probably a C cup a month ago, but, of course, I lost so much weight I was bound to lose it in the good spots as well. Still, I don't correct her assumption about my size.

"Do you think she'll even work in the Thakoon?"

Marguerite shrugs. "She *is* much thinner in person."

I smile, knowing *this* is a good thing.

Lucian's gaze travels farther north. "She does have a very long neck."

I resist the urge to touch my neck. Long? Really? Is that a *bad* thing?

Then, handing me back my book and addressing me for the first time since I came in the door, Marguerite says simply, "Thanks for coming by."

"Is my neck too long?" I say to Jade when I find her dangling her long pale legs in the shallow end of the hotel pool.

"Too long? Hon-bon, has a fashion editor gotten her nasty little paws on your self-esteem? You're gorgeous."

I smile. "Thanks, Jade. It's just that I didn't get a good vibe during my go-see at *Ocean Drive*, and I hate to think Francesca sent me down here for nothing."

"Well, not for nothing. Just look at this place," she says, gesturing to the palm trees that tower over plush recliner chairs, the jewellike pool.

"Are you done for the day?"

"Hardly. Apparently Vanessa spoke with one of the reps from Spiked Tea and they want to do something down here, some kind of beach scene. I couldn't believe they were able to put together a shoot so quickly, but apparently they have an office down here. Of course, they'd never shoot at high noon—midday would put lines and shadows on the face of an infant. They'll call me when they need me. God, I just hope they shoot the thing quickly. All that cavorting in the sand is going to overdevelop my calves, and I can just hear Renee: 'Look at you! Legs like a linebacker!'"

The impersonation is spot-on. Sometimes I wonder why Jade doesn't go into acting—with her arsenal of accents, the easy way she can adopt attitudes, I bet she'd be great at it. It's got to be easier than modeling, so many breaks between takes, and there's the bonus of working with men. Straight men, that is. Jade's always bitching that she never gets laid.

"C'mon," she says, sliding her legs out of the water. "Let's go grab lunch or something."

Lunch, right. I still haven't lost my quota, those last three pounds like barnacles stuck to my hull. But I skipped dinner last night, and plan to hit the treadmill in the health club later—we're in a boutique hotel but it has a fully equipped gym, as well as a world-class spa, I'm told.

Jade knows her way around, and we get a cab to a Cuban-Asian fusion place on Ocean Drive (of course) that's all the rage (of course). If I didn't know better I'd think the main occupation in South Beach is to sit around cafés all day. It seems only a miracle will get us a table, but Jade just waggles her fingers in the right direction and—abracadabra—one appears for us.

"God, the SoBe scene is such a farce," Jade says. "I mean, look at these chicks—oh so generic, cookie-cutter cute, and they all basically dress alike, too." She adds loudly, "Can I get some diversity here, please?"

What she gets is a menu. Glancing around, I have to agree with her observation. It's not that everyone's the same color, just the same type—beautiful but bland girls fiddling with gadgets and talking in sighs and singsong. Jade orders *ropa vieja* with *maduros*, those sticky-sweet fried plantains. The waiter waits for me. God, even the salads have pork in them.

"*Ummm*, I'll take the stuffed artichoke, hold the stuffing." I've never actually eaten an artichoke, but how dangerous can a vegetable be? When it arrives, I'm not so sure—the thing looks like a hand grenade.

"The heart is the best part," Jade says, gesturing to my artichoke.

Taking her cue, I start to pull off all the leaves, then dice the soft center into as many pieces as possible, so at least it feels like a full meal.

"Mac, what in the world . . . ?" Jade says, looking up from her meal, which she has already started to devour. "Please tell me you know how to eat an artichoke!"

A sharp spine pokes the roof of my mouth as I stalwartly attempt to chew. "Of course . . . ," I start to say, removing the offending greenery with as much etiquette as I can muster and concealing it in my napkin. "Not," I finish.

Jade just laughs. "Allow me to demonstrate. You have the heart there already, you just have to clean off the spikes before you eat it." She laughs at me. "As for the leaves," she says, grabbing one, "you drench it in melted butter." She looks at my face. "But we can skip that part." Raising it to her lips, she continues, "You just scrape the leaf between your teeth."

It's actually kind of disgusting, leaving a litter of scraped leaves in the bowl, but eating an artichoke is strenuous enough a chore to burn calories. About halfway through the meal, a plump, busty girl sidles up to us. I'd take her for a college student if it weren't for the diamond and platinum chunks on her fingers and wrists, and the Bottega Veneta bag. "Hiyeee!" she says. "Are you models?"

"Aahhctually . . ." Jade puts on her oh-so-sophisticated voice. "I'm a Pulitzer Prize–winning playwright, and my friend here is going for her doctorate in nuclear physics. But thanks—I'm sure you meant that as a compliment."

"Huh-huh-huh-hee!" the girl giggles. "No, seriously, I know you get it all the time. But if I did not come talk to you, I would be remiss in my duties. My name's Charisse; mind if I sit?" She doesn't wait for permission. "I'm with La Donna, which I'm sure you know is Miami's number one agency. So are you new in town? Are you with an agency yet?" She juts her chin at Jade. "Girl, check you out, I didn't think anyone ate meat nowadays."

Charisse is a bulldog, but her bubbly personality is infectious, and she's so direct, we give up the charade. "We're down from New York," I tell her. "Doing some go-sees."

"We're with Delicious," Jade says. "You've heard of it, surely."

With a little snort, Charisse implies that she's well aware.

"Well, then, you know it's no use attempting to poach us," Jade says haughtily. "We're good. *Real* good. And we're already in the best market in the world—New York City."

"*Mm-hmm*, I feel that," says Charisse. "But Paul Anders better watch his back—our roster is mighty impressive. We have Jolie Nesbit, you know . . ."

"Ooh, Jolie Nesbit! Winner of the *Tyra Banks Comedy Hour*!"

Confusion must show on my face, since Jade turns to me. "That's what *real* models call *America's Next Top Model*. Reality TV—*pffft*, right. As if Jolie Nesbit is going anywhere."

Charisse lets the comment slide. "Stella Cheever, too. And we all know where Stella's going."

Meow! That's the worst possible thing Charisse could've said to Jade. Not that Jade's got a grudge against Stella Cheever, or has even met the girl personally, it's just that Stella's recently signed a very juicy exclusive with Victoria's Secret—it was all over the New York gossip columns last week, and the industry is all abuzz over it. Victoria's Secret is the Holy Grail for a model, the sign that you're a supe. So it's a real bone of contention for Jade, since she's . . . well . . . Jade's amazingly beautiful and she's got a great body, the kind of toothpick proportions most designers love to dress, but truth be told she *is* kind of flat-chested. Just mention Victoria's Secret and she'll take off on a rant about breasts—real breasts, fake breasts, what she refers to as the "pendulous udders that have hypnotized the populace."

At the moment, Jade simply seems to have trouble swallowing, a florid smolder of natural color rising under her makeup. Maybe she's flipping through her vicious vocabulary, gearing up for a good tirade. But if she comes up with anything juicy, we'll never know because suddenly her cell phone rings.

"Excuse me, it's my contact at Mercant and Silkes," she says, standing up. "I have to take this."

She disappears, leaving me to fend off Charisse alone.

"Mercant and Silkes?" Charisse asks. "Is she shooting something for them?"

I nod. "Yup. She's the new poster child for Spiked Tea."

"Oh." Charisse smiles in a way that says *I could do better*. "And what about you?"

"I just had a go-see with *Ocean Drive*. For a fashion layout."

"*Ahhhh*," Charisse replies, smile widening. "So you're the girl from New York Lucian was waiting on."

I blink at her. *Huh?*

"Jolie Nesbit is meeting with *Ocean Drive* as we speak," Charisse explains. "You're the competition."

"Oh." A frisson of nerves moves through me. As if running into my competition's booker is some kind of bad omen.

"According to Lucian, you're pretty hot in New York."

I try to swallow back my surprise at her words but she picks up on it.

"Lucian and I go way back," she explains. "In fact, I'm

shocked he was able to get you down here for a shoot for a regional magazine. If I were your booker, you'd be doing a cover for *Vogue* by now."

I digest this, trying to see it simply as boasting on Charisse's part, but then she says, "In fact, I got Stella a cover in her first month. Who's your booker?"

"Francesca DeLongue," I reply, my gaze moving to Jade, who is striding back toward our table.

"*Huh*. Never heard of her," Charisse says.

Suddenly I remember Jade's words, about how she should be doing fashion and cosmetic contracts at this point in her career. Stella Cheever's been working at this a lot less time than Jade has, and she's already landed Victoria's Secret! Had I been too hasty signing up with Delicious? Could I have had a big endorsement by now if I'd gone with a different agency?

As if reading my mind, Charisse says, "If I had a girl as hot as you, I'd strike while the iron is hot. Maybe you should look at other agencies." Then she slides a business card across the table at me.

To be nice, I take the card. Then in order to dissolve the clutch of nerves forming in my throat, I joke, "Maybe I should."

Charisse smiles, looking like the cat that swallowed the canary. Then she stands just as Jade returns. "It was *so* nice meeting you both." Smoothing her skirt, she smiles sweetly. "Hope I didn't come on too strong, but we do have a lot to offer down here. A *lot*. You wait till you get a taste of our South Beach hospitality."

I have no idea what Charisse means by that, but it doesn't take me too long to find out.

* * *

The sweet triumph of winning the *Ocean Drive* layout and cover is almost dampened by my conversation with Charisse. But not quite.

After all, I've never had my own layout before.

When I arrive at the shoot at 8:00 the next morning to find the stylist and makeup artist there waiting to serve me and me alone, it's an ego boost, I'll admit.

I do miss the energy of having other models on the set. And if Lucian is as "hot" for me as Charisse claimed, you'd never know it. As he takes me through the poses and the setups, I feel as if I might just be another prop in the whitewashed art deco mansion that is our setting, as easy to maneuver or manipulate as the soft pink settee I'm draped upon, or the cascades of silk drapery I pose against.

In fact, Lucian's only acknowledgment of me is served up at the end of ten hours of shooting. "You were wonderful," he declares, treating me to a two-cheeked air kiss. And then he disappears.

If this was a first date, I wouldn't be too sure I was getting a second.

Still, I'm happy to be done for the day. Happier still when I come back to the hotel to learn that a little pampering is in store for me and Jade.

"Hey!" I greet Jade when I discover her lounging on the bed, remote in hand. "Did you book us massages?"

"No, I didn't, and don't tease me."

"Are you sure? Because the front desk just asked me to confirm our spa appointments. We're supposed to be down there at eight."

"Really? Hoo-fucking-ray!" She leaps up, throwing her arms around my neck. "Carry me?"

Laughing, I gently shrug her off. "Come on! I haven't had a massage since physical therapy after I hurt my knee playing tennis, and I've never been to a real spa."

As we check in to the spa, I'm wondering if maybe Francesca set this up because I landed the *Ocean Drive* shoot. Then I grimace, realizing that if she did, I'll probably find it subtracted from my salary. But right now, I don't even care. A massage would be positively medicinal after the day I've had.

Jade and I are adjusting our terrycloth robes and slippers in the locker room when a white-coated attendant comes to fetch us. "You ladies are booked together," she says, which strikes me as strange. I have at least seen pictures of spas even if I haven't gone to one; I'm not completely in the dark. Besides, it seems to me that a massage should be a private matter. The room we're led to is a temple of understated sensuality; dimly lit, with scented candles flickering and ambient music floating in from hidden speakers, the padded massage tables arranged side by side. Perhaps our appointments were booked last minute, and this was the only space available.

"They must be twins," Jade whispers when the massage therapists enter the room. "And *muy caliente*."

She's not kidding. Both are studiously muscled, with bronze skin, fine features and matching fuzzy goatees. They introduce themselves as Diego and Felipe, and we shake hands.

"We will step out for a moment while you ladies remove your robes and lie facedown on the tables, a towel across you," Diego or Felipe instructs.

Jade tosses her terry and settles in, fitting her face into the table's little face cushion. "Go on, Mac—assume the position," she urges me, but the truth is, the whole situation feels kind of . . . weird.

But seeing Jade's ease with the circumstances soothes my nerves. Shrugging off my robe, I climb on the table, carefully arranging the towel to cover me.

Our therapists return and get down to business, oiling their hands and starting with our shoulders.

"How is that pressure?" I hear Felipe or Diego ask Jade in a soft Spanish accent.

"Just delicious," Jade replies, practically on a sigh.

"And how about you? This is okay?" Felipe or Diego asks me.

"It's *ummm*, fine," I answer, trying to relax and failing. Closing my eyes, I attempt to zone out as my therapist's fingers travel from my deltoids across the span of my back, rubbing and caressing, deeper and lower . . . and lower . . . until. . . .

"Oh, my God!" I shriek, scrambling to sit up without losing my towel. "What are you *doing*?!" I cry. "Stop! Stop that! Stop!"

"*Shh! Shh!* It is all right!" soothes Diego or Felipe.

"Don't you *shush* me! Don't you *dare* shush me!" I reply slapping at my therapist as I make my way off the table. I look at Jade, who is staring at me in surprise.

"Jade, are you . . . can we?" I sputter, suddenly very glad she's in the room with me as I grab my robe, throwing it around me swiftly and tugging the sash tight.

"Yes, yes, I hear you," she replies, her tone resigned. She gives Felipe and Diego an apologetic face and hops off the table. "Don't worry, hon-bun, it's cool—just a misunderstanding."

"Jade, we have to get out of here now!" My voice sounds thin in my ears.

"I know, okay, don't worry," she says, tying her robe a bit too leisurely for my liking. "I'm coming . . ."

Talk about random acts of crazy! What happened down there in the spa—what *almost* happened—I couldn't conceive of such a thing in a million years. Not Jade, however. She doesn't seem to think it's bizarre at all . . . which is even more bizarre.

"Mac, look, you need to lighten up a little," she says calmly as I pace our room, fuming and shaking. "Partake of the perks."

"Perks!" I practically spit the word. "Some guy I don't even know tries to . . . take liberties with me on a massage table and you call it a perk?"

Sitting cross-legged in the middle of the bed, Jade observes my tigress routine. "I understand you're upset and maybe an orgy isn't your cup of tea, but technically, yeah, it's a perk," she says. "That chick Charisse must have set it up to get us to jump ship. Hey, you're the one who told her where we were staying. She thought we'd like it, and, well, perhaps a fruit basket would have been more appropriate, but what can I say? Rival agencies can be incredibly cutthroat."

I stop in my tracks. Could it be? If she's right, then what in the world have I gotten myself into? Modeling is just . . . there's no logic to it—it's like falling down the rabbit hole. "I mean, really," Jade continues, "it's not like we were expected to *do* anything. Just lie back and enjoy."

I have to laugh. It's too ridiculous. I'm in some whacko wonderland, and who's trying to explain it all? Jade, the female Mad Hatter! I sit on the edge of the bed, shake my head. "Well, it was humiliating," I say. "A violation." This would be a prime opportunity to let Jade in on a secret I've been harboring, but I decide against it. Not that I'm ashamed—or, at least, Melody Ann isn't—but this is one fact that probably isn't right for Mac's image.

Jade unfolds herself to poke me in the ribs. "Think what a funny story it will make to tell your grandkids one day," she says. Then we both crack up. "Maybe not."

A long hot bath later and I'm able to get it together and go out with Jade, who has learned from her contact at Spiked Tea that there is some kind of record launch party going on tonight at midnight for a band I've never heard of, but Jade claims we were "lucky" enough to get on the guest list for. I don't even want to go out, but the truth is, I don't want Jade to think I'm a total party pooper. Still, I dread running into Charisse, who must be a big shot on the South Beach social scene. Well, we see Paris Hilton, we see Sacha Baron Cohen (though someone has to ID him for me—he's actually kind of nice-looking when he's not in character), we see Beyonce (who's apparently recording in the basement studio at the Raleigh), but we do not, thank goodness, see that major psycho from La Donna Models at the restaurant or any of the three clubs we hit.

I don't know where Jade gets all her energy. Must be all that food she eats. She seems like she could party all night—and she would, if I didn't plead a headache at 2:00 a.m. and beg her to go home. Of course, she could stay on by herself but loyal girlfriend that she is, she simply rolls her eyes then, blowing air kisses at everyone within range, heads out with me to hunt down a cab.

"Why haven't you called me back yet?" Francesca demands, after I roll out of bed the next morning, bleary-eyed, to find my ringing cell phone in my clutch.

I blink, look at the clock, which reads 7:00 a.m., then glance at Jade, who rolls over with a groan, covering her head with a pillow.

"*Ummm* . . . I haven't had a chance yet?" I whisper, slipping out on to the small balcony off our room and sliding the door shut behind me. "What's going on?"

"What's going on is I got a call from La Donna Models last night telling me you're signing with them."

"What?"

"Apparently you've given this Charisse some sort of verbal okay to put together a contract!"

"I did? Francesca, that's—"

"I wouldn't have believed it except that I must have called you three times last night and when you didn't answer, I didn't know what to think."

I take the phone away from my ear, see the little message blinking icon in the corner of the screen. "I'm sorry, Francesca, I was out. I must not have heard the phone—"

"Then this morning I get a fax with a picture of your new calling card for La Donna, complete with pictures I have never seen before."

How the hell had she gotten ahold of pictures? She did say she was friends with Lucian; did he give her digitals from yesterday's shoot? Panic fills me and my mind races, trying to fill in the blanks. Had I said something to mislead Charisse?

"Look, Melody," Francesca continues, barely able to keep the anger out of her voice, "if you're moving on, I would have appreciated the call to come from you. Now I need to know where we stand. Because I'm here arranging your whole next week, but if you've got other plans I need to know about them. I haven't got time to waste on a girl if we're not going to work together—"

Surprise fills me, followed by a rush of tears, which is even more astonishing. "Francesca, I had no idea—"

"Well, something's going on, because this woman seems to think you're on board with La Donna."

"She's lying!" Then I remember Charisse's confident smile when I took her card, joking that maybe I should look at other agencies. "If I did say anything it was only as . . . a joke."

"Well, I don't have time for funny business, Melody Ann. If you want out, then that's fine—"

And suddenly I *am* crying. Maybe it's exhaustion, or maybe it's the thought that Francesca would shrug me off so fast, leaving me to that conniving . . . vulture of an agent. "No, Francesca. I don't want out."

Hearing my tears, her tone immediately softens. "All right, sweetheart, *all right*. I'm sorry to yell. It's just I get this call and then I can't get in touch with you, what am I supposed to think?"

I swipe at the tears on my face and take a deep breath. "I would think you might know me better than that."

She's silent for a moment. "I guess I *should* have known you better than that, Melody, but modeling is a cutthroat business sometimes. You never can be too sure who's on your side."

I sniffle, getting a grip on myself once more. "Well, maybe I was just wondering the same thing."

"Melody Ann Croft, if I'm not on your side, nobody is. I'm your *booker*. There's no one who wants you to succeed *more* than I do!"

"Well, *am* I succeeding?" I ask, remembering Charisse's words about where I should be in my career.

"What the hell is that supposed to mean?"

"Charisse said I should be getting bigger bookings. She thinks . . . she thinks I'm really . . . *hot* right now."

She pauses. "Oh, for goodness sake! Is that what you need to hear? That you're *hot*? Of course, you're hot! In fact, you're so hot, Renee wants to take you to meet Albert Lazar the moment you get back to New York City."

"Really?"

"Of course, darling! This cover will be good for your book, but Albert will be great for your career! Oh, we've got plans for you . . ."

By the time we hang up, any doubts I may have had about Delicious are soothed, though the conversation took a toll on my emotions. I've never felt so vulnerable in my life!

"What's up?" Jade asks, when I step back into the room.

I look at her for a long moment. "I'm meeting Albert Lazar next week," I say finally, just moments before I burst in to tears.

Ten

My meeting with Albert Lazar is a carefully cultivated sham. While Renee has filled me in on Albert and purred in his ear about me, we will act, when introduced, as though we've never heard of each other. The encounter itself has been orchestrated to look impromptu. A pretty funny notion, since Albert Lazar is one of the few designers who even my own parents would recognize, his name as synonymous with American fashion as Calvin Klein's. In fact, Renee told me that Albert and Calvin were contemporaries at FIT and even grew up in the same New York City neighborhood. Which is wild, since there couldn't be two designers more different than Calvin Klein and Albert Lazar. While Calvin is known for his clean lines and monochromatic color schemes, Albert is known for exotic fabrics and girlish silhouettes.

"Remember, banish recognition from your face. Be charming, be delightful, but above all, be clueless," Renee lectures on the way to Tilda, a restaurant near Albert's atelier where he can predictably be found over a late lunch (see? I even know the man's eating habits). "Do you understand me, Moch?" Renee has finally taken to calling me Mac, but pronounces it as though she hails from a country you couldn't find on any map. She's rumored to have grown up in Paris but some—like Jade—believe she was born in Iowa.

"Yes, Renee, I've got it." In other words, play dumb.

Tilda is an airy yet cozy place with tantalizing aromas wafting from the kitchen. The nondescript man at a corner table is basically the only other customer, yet Renee pretends not to see him, focusing instead on the apple-cheeked, pear-shaped woman who bustles out from behind the bar with a welcoming *"Ah!"*

"You are so naughty, Renee. You have not been here in ages." Kiss, kiss, kiss!

"I know, Tilda. Your cassoulet has been calling my name, but I am so busy!"

They laugh merrily—at what, I have no clue. Standing behind Renee, I flit my gaze at the plants and knickknacks scattered around, trying not to let my eyes rest on the corner table, but it's like trying not to look at a pink elephant. Chirping like hungry sparrows, Renee and Tilda catch up as we get seated, but Albert still doesn't glance up, which is weird—not to sound conceited, but I usually turn heads when I enter a room.

"So you will be having the cassoulet?"

"Ooh, no, I couldn't," Renee says sadly. "I am just coming off a juice fast—my system would go into shock."

Tilda clucks, then recites the menu for us. I'm tempted by the aromas to order a big plate of steak frites, but since I just miraculously shed those final three pounds—*yes!*—I follow Renee's lead and order the goat-cheese salad, light on the cheese, heavy on the frisée. We sit, making small talk, which is nerve-wracking enough, since this is the first time

I've been out alone with the president of the agency. I would have been more comfortable doing this with Francesca, but since Renee and Albert go way back, she has taken charge of this little venture. I do my best to make chat, though it's no easy feat; Renee's an icon and she makes sure you know it—I feel as though she's judging my every breath. Then, as if some internal mechanism goes off, she emits a squeal.

"*Alllllll*bert!"

Slowly, he responds to the sound of his name and invests a few seconds letting Renee register. Then he cries out: "Ren*eeeee*!"

Like two stags with locked horns, Albert and Renee battle to see who will approach whose table. It's Renee who rises, and soon they are chatting in hushed tones, their heads bent together. My challenge is to remain perfectly still and expressionless— no fidgeting with the saltshaker, no water sipping, certainly no smiling, just stare off dreamily, waiting for Renee's summons. No wonder models have a rep for being stupid—it's all a show.

"Moch!" She raises her voice to get my attention.

Playing my part in this charade, I wait a beat, then put on a fraction of a smile.

"Moch, my love, come here," Renee summons. "I want you to meet someone."

I glide over and increase the smile by two millimeters. When I'm asked to sit, I crank it a touch more. But it's not until Albert speaks to me directly that I give him the full effect of my smile, and he basks in it like illegal sunshine. Renee recedes into the virtual background—it's all about Albert and me. And he's really nice. Regular-person nice. Pale blue shirt with the sleeves rolled up, Brillo hair, and nose like a blob of clay, there's nothing about him that screams "fashion!" Albert talks easily yet eagerly about commonplace topics—baseball, gas prices, the latest celebrity to put his foot in his mouth. The only giveaway that there's something going on beyond a casual gabfest is Albert's eyes—small and black and bright, they make him resemble an alert, intelligent mouse.

"Mac, can you move?" he asks, completely out of nowhere.

At first I think he means literally—like he needs to go to the bathroom and I'm in his way. This throws me off until I realize that Renee has pricked up her ears.

"Albert asked you a question, Moch," says Renee, rattling me further.

"Look, Mac, you're lovely, and you're bursting with life." Albert rubs his chin with his napkin and tosses it next to his plate. "But I need girls who can propel my clothes—who can put them on and fly, and make everyone want to take off after them."

Whoa! We were just sitting here shooting the breeze, and now Albert has cut to the chase before anyone said ready-set-go. Am I expected to answer him verbally? Get up and show him? The restaurant wouldn't make much of a runway for a Barbie doll. In fact, it's starting to feel claustrophobic. Maybe I should grab Albert's hand, run down West Broadway with him. Or . . . or what? I've got to do something. As Renee found necessary to remind me, the man asked me a question.

Okay, I know. It may not work but I don't have a whole lot of options. Not to mention I haven't done this since I was sixteen— an exercise my trainer taught me to develop balance, agility, and killer quadriceps. Probably never before attempted in a pair of sling backs. But I smile, my playful smile, the one that hides my teeth but ignites my eyes. I slide out of my chair—it's a sturdy, stocky wooden chair, and that's in my favor. I stand beside it and . . . here goes nothing: tense, find a focal point on the wall, engage every muscle, concentrate . . . and . . . spring! Two feet up! Then land squarely on the seat, solidly yet gracefully. Yes!

Lowering my glance I see Albert and Renee staring up at me in astonishment. Tilda and the waitress are riveted, too, as a rush courses up from the soles of my feet, racing through my heart and out to my fingers, tingling my scalp. I've pulled off a physically remarkable feat, but more than that, an act of nerve—what's known in New York as chutzpah. Only trouble is, I don't know if it's the kind of thing that will snag me a spot in Albert Lazar's fashion show or a gig with Ringling Bros. Circus.

Two nights later, I strut into the kitchen, where my mother is hard at work on what looks like a troughful of fettuccine Alfredo I surely won't be able to eat.

For the first time in two months, I can honestly say that I'm not even *hungry.* I'm *way* too excited to eat!

"Guess who's walking in Albert Lazar's show at New York Fashion Week?" I say, doing an amateur catwalk over to my mother, who looks up in surprise.

"You're home!" she says, grabbing up a dish towel to wipe her hands as she leans in to give me a kiss. "I've been wondering what train you were taking . . ."

"Did you hear what I said?" I ask, blinking at her beaming face and wondering if my news even registered.

"Oh, yes, that's *wonderful,* Melody! Albert Lazar—fancy!"

I smile, happy to see her reaction, though it confuses me a little. Up until now, any enthusiasm Mom has shown for my career has been cautious, at best. But today she's positively glowing with what looks like genuine happiness for me. Which is good, because there's another possible side to my participation in Fashion Week that she's *not* going to like so much. Since it takes place the same week I'm supposed to start at Penn, I may miss my first few classes, not to mention orientation. . . .

"Guess what came in the mail today, sweetheart?" she says, rushing into the living room, where she grabs an envelope off the secretary she keeps there. "A letter from Penn about your scholarship!" Then she looks abashed. "I know I should have waited for you to get home to open it, but I couldn't bear not knowing any longer . . ."

A mix of excitement and—surprisingly—dread winds through me. There's only one thing that could make my mother *this* happy.

"You got the scholarship, Melody! Your tuition at the University of Pennsylvania will be paid in full!"

"I just heard the news about Albert," Jade says when she opens her apartment door to me the following day, dressed in nothing more than a knee-length red silk robe. "You are on your way, hon-bun!" She holds up a hand in the air.

"Thanks, Jade. I'm really excited." Raising my hand to hers, I give her a halfhearted high five.

She lifts an eyebrow at me "You sure? Because you sound about as enthused as the 'before' chick in the Paxil commercial."

"It's kind of complicated . . ."

"I like complicated," she replies, leading me to the terrace of her building. Below us, the streets of TriBeCa swell with after-work party-mongers.

Once we're seated, she turns to me with an expectant look.

"You'll think I'm a dork . . . ," I begin.

She reaches out and touches my hand. "Mac, hon-bun, darling, I already think you're a dork. There's nothing you can say to make me think you're any dorkier."

I stick out my tongue at her, then give her a flat-lipped grin, one you won't find itemized in the model's smile file. "Well, it's like this. Up till now modeling was this goof, this crazy way to make money for school." I stare off at the city and beyond, toward the Hudson and what everyone outside New York and the industry refers to as the real world. "But ever since Albert asked me to walk for him, modeling has gotten very . . . I don't know, substantial, viable. Before it was as though college was meat and potatoes, and modeling was cotton candy . . . only not anymore. Like, I can really do this. This is an option. I hadn't realized I was thinking that way until I came home last night and learned I'd gotten awarded a nice fat scholarship to Penn."

"Well, la-di-da. Not just rocking the modeling world, but academia as well."

"That's just it, Jade. I don't think I can do both. I mean, in the back of my mind I *knew* getting into a show during fashion week would mean that I'd have to miss my first few days of classes at Penn. Which wouldn't have been a big deal. Yeah, I would have liked the freshman bonding experience of orientation and whatever, but I figured I could sacrifice that in the name of making more money for tuition. Francesca already told me that I'll make five thousand a show and she seems to think that now that Albert wants me, everyone will want me to walk for them."

"And not just in New York, Mac, darling. Chances are the Europeans will want you to walk, too. Of course, we won't know that until Fashion week unfolds in New York City."

I bite my lip so hard it almost bleeds, which won't do at all, since I have a go-see for a L'Oréal lip shine ad tomorrow morning. "Two months ago, I never would have thought I'd be saying this, but . . . I want to go to Europe, Jade. I feel like I have half a shot at this, and I want to take it. But I can't. My plans are already set. I'm maybe starting late, but I *am* starting at Penn this fall. My parents have so much wrapped up in me going to college, really making something of myself. But of course it's not just them—this is my life I'm talking about—I know that. I mean, I have a plan: go into medicine, help people, make money, have respect. *Be* somebody. It was a sure thing. Modeling may be lucrative, it *may* be—it's so iffy. And it's not exactly the kind of career that allows you to contribute to society—there's no modeling equivalent of the Nobel Prize."

"Well, except maybe the CFDA model of the year award," Jade chimes in.

I must have looked at her weird, because she added, "Just kidding."

Closing my eyes momentarily, I realize how exhausted I am by my own thoughts, which have been rolling through my mind ever since my mother's jubilant news yesterday. Yeah, jubilant for her. But I realize now that I was almost hoping that I *didn't* get the scholarship, as it would have made this decision that much easier. Having the scholarship compels me to go to school. How can I give up a free education?

In fact, my mom was even making that fettuccine in my

honor because she knows it's my favorite dish—*was* my favorite dish. These days I don't even like to be in the same room with anything as remotely caloric as Alfredo sauce, which didn't make my mom too happy to hear. Sometimes I wonder if she's trying to mutilate my modeling career through any means possible. Death by Parmesan.

I'd laugh, if I had any energy left. Instead, I look at Jade. "I have to make a decision about this scholarship and it's been keeping me up all night."

She stares at me for a long moment, her expression pensive. "Not that I can possibly relate to what your grappling with," she says finally, "but the way it seems to me is, you make a decision, and if you don't like it, you change your mind."

"Sounds good in theory. But if I chose modeling, I lose my scholarship. And my father has already made clear that if I don't go to college this year, I won't get help from him next year. And who knows what kind of money I'll be making by next year. I mean, modeling is a gamble. What if I lose?"

Jade gives me an inscrutable smile. "Forgive me for getting all New Agey on you, Mac, but things do happen for a reason," she says. "You're here, in New York and on this terrace, with Albert Lazar and the fulcrum of fashion at your feet for a reason. So what the fuck, give it a whirl. You don't like it, say buh-bye, modeling, hello, Penn—here, take this big fat check, I don't need your scrubby little scholarship."

I smile at her. She makes it sound so simple. Except it doesn't *feel* simple. Why is it so scary to trust?

Easing back in my chair, I take her hand in mine. Together we watch the last of the sunset made violently colorful by New Jersey pollution.

"Hey, maybe Albert will want you, too," I say after a while.

"I don't think he's chosen everyone yet. Maybe I could even talk to him about you."

Dropping my hand, Jade lets out a humorless laugh. "Thanks, hon-bun, but that makes me feel about as desirable as dirty socks."

"I didn't mean it that way—"

She turns the force of her gaze on me. "Look, Mac, from what I know of Albert's aesthetic, I don't have the look he likes—that energetic, amazon, cheerleader thing. Which is fine. So I'm not Albert Lazar material. I'm not about to be pounding steroids and stuffing my bra."

"Well, you'll walk," I say, trying to make up for the pothole I inadvertently put in her confidence. "Designers will be jumping over each other to book you. I was just . . . I was just hoping we could do a show together . . ." Grabbing her hand once more, I continue, "But one thing's for sure, Jade. We'll be doing Fashion Week together. I just know it." Then I squeeze her hand, as if I had the power to control both of our futures, even as my own feels like it's spinning out of control.

When I go into the agency two days later, the place is abuzz with news of designer picks. Word is that Jade and I are the hot girls of the season: Darryl K, Fillipa K, Thakoon, Nili Lotan, and Heatherette all request Jade for New York Fashion Week. When I pop into her office, Francesca practically explodes with the news that I've landed Alice Roi, Derek Lam, Zac Posen, Cynthia Steffe, Joanna Mastroianni—and this is amazing!—Marc Jacobs.

It's all because of Albert; not only do other designers want me now, all the top magazine editors will see me walk, so they'll want me, too. There's a cash register in my head going *cha-ching!* every time someone asks for me. Five thousand dollars just to walk down a catwalk! Okay, it's not really 5K for twenty minutes' work; there are fittings and rehearsals, hours in hair and makeup, even a class Francesca wants me to take to learn how to rule the runway, silly as it sounds. Still, it's all so incredible.

"And it's only the beginning, darling," Francesca chirps. "You just wait until the Europeans get a look at you on the runaway. I'd say Milan, Paris, and London are a lock for you!"

My stomach twists into a knot. "There's something we need to talk about, Francesca . . ."

She raises an eyebrow at me. "What's that, Mac, darling? You don't know what to pack for Europe in September?"

"That's just it, Francesca. I can't *go* to Europe in September."

Her eyebrows draw down, her expression thunderstruck. "What do you mean, *can't go?*"

I shake my head. "I told you before. I'm starting Penn in the fall." Injecting a cheerfulness I don't feel into my voice, I add, "I've even been awarded a scholarship."

But Francesca is not impressed by my academic achievement. "Mac, you can't tell me you'd honestly throw away a *career* all so you can don some god-awful argyles and do the whole college girl thing?"

"It's not that I don't want to model—I do. It's just that I can't throw away my scholarship. I can't not go to school!"

She stands up then, her face flushed. And just when I think she's going to toss me out on my ear, she grabs me by the arm and drags me down the hall to Renee's office.

"Renee, could you *please* talk some sense into this girl, because I've given up!"

And with that, she storms off, leaving me to Renee's mercy.

"Moch, darling, what's going on?"

And so I explain, in the best way I know how, the confusion living at the core of me these days. How much I want a chance at Europe and a career; how the thought of giving up Penn and my dream of becoming a doctor is impossible, not only for me, but for my parents.

Renee is surprisingly compassionate. "Did you know I had a chance at a big position at a French soap manufacturer that I gave up to become a model?"

"Oh," I reply, trying to see this choice to give up a career making soap as compelling as a giving up a career saving lives.

Then she launches into a nostalgic trip down memory lane, in which she details her startlingly quick rise to Supermodeldom in the eighties. Not that I don't know this whole story already. Jade filled me in on all the details. Of course, she didn't have to, as it doesn't take Renee much to start talking about the days when everyone from Helmut Newton to Irving Penn wanted her in front of their camera lenses.

Still, I get caught up in it, so much so that there are tears in my eyes when I say that as much as I want to follow in her illustrious stilettos, there is no way I can give up my scholarship.

Her eyes widen. "Moch, no one is asking you to give up your scholarship. Why not simply defer it for a year?"

I blink. "Defer? Is that even possible?"

"I don't see why not. Other girls have done it. It's called . . . what is that word? Ah, yes! A hardship waiver. You need to say that you cannot take the scholarship right now due to some sort of a problem."

"Is that really possible?" Can this decision I have been

aching over really be so easy to fix? And if so, why didn't I know about this? Why didn't my parents know about this?

A weight starts to lift off my chest. If Penn allows it, a waiver would be the perfect solution! This way I could try out modeling for a year, see where it goes, and if it doesn't go anywhere, I have Penn to fall back on.

"Renee, you're a genius!" I say, leaping up and throwing my arms around her, which completely startles her. Tears of relief fill my eyes.

Uncomfortable with my sudden well of emotion, Renee gives me a quick pat on the back before disentangling herself. "Of course I am, darling."

My heart is visibly lighter when I learn, via a phone call to the financial aid office at Penn that I make just moments after I leave Renee's office, that I *can* defer for one year due to family obligations. In fact, I'm so happy to have this option, I practically skip to my first fittings for the New York shows.

I have more than one reason to feel so much joy. I also learned through the Delicious grapevine that Duncan Shiloh is also on the hot list for the fall shows, which means we'll be crossing paths more often. . . .

"Well, heyyyy . . ."

Whoa, the power of positive thinking! I'm sitting in Leaf, catching my breath after my first fitting for Marc Jacobs, which was easy and fun, since all the clothes he's having me wear are *fantastic*, when once again I feel Duncan's presence before I hear his soft drawl. Drinking him in, I realize all at once why Duncan's so unlike the guys I know—he's not a *guy*, not a *boy*, there's a *manliness* to him, but not in a dad or doctor or teacher way, either—after all, he's only twenty. It's not exactly maturity that oozes out of him, and he's definitely not jaded, but he's got this quality of being aware and centered, what I think people mean when they call someone an old soul. Being near him makes me feel fully as one with the world. The antithesis of nervous, totally at ease. "Duncan! Hey yourself."

"Is it all right if I pull up a chair?" he says.

I tell him sure, and we grin at each other in silence for a few moments, then start comparing itineraries. "Yeah, Duncan, I'm doing Marc Jacobs, too."

"That's real cool. Maybe we'll get to see each other some."

I flash on how nice that would be.

"You know, Mac, I'm here about six months now, but I can't say I've made a true friend yet." Duncan's eyes are earnest embers. He makes my soul glow. "I met a lot of people, sure. Cool people. Fun people." He laughs, a husky, unhurried chuckle. "Some downright crazy people . . ."

As if on cue, Jade hurtles into the tea shop, pigtails flying behind her like streamers on the handlebars of a little kid's bike. "Mac!" She throws herself into a chair. "Get this!" For half a second her demeanor changes—a quick lick of her lip as she says, "Duncan." Then she slaps both palms flat on the table. "Willie Santana wants me now!"

The sentence hangs like an ominous cloud in the space between us. Of course it's wonderful that another big designer wants my best friend to appear in his show. I want to, need to, have to congratulate her. Yet I seem to be struck mute. And Jade doesn't seem the least bit surprised. Neither, really, does Duncan. After all, we're fashion insiders. We know full well that Willie Santana, in addition to being a huge talent and a notorious downtown party boy and a heterosexual (if you believe those recent photos of him and Ashley Olsen), is the archrival of my biggest supporter in the realm of the runway, Albert Lazar. They've been feuding since they were freshmen at FIT.

I have a feeling Jade and I are mere pawns in their ongoing mission to mess with each other. "You can always say no, Jade."

"Surely you jest!"

"No, I don't jest. You're doing a bunch of cool shows, and as you've told me about three dozen times, you've got London on lock."

"So? I have expenses—like a mother who confuses Cristal with Perrier. Forgive me if that's not as noble as saving for a college education."

I roll my eyes. "Jade, please. Money has nothing to do with it." I stab at my nonfat iced vanilla chai with my straw. "At least Albert wants me for legitimate reasons."

She narrows her eyes at me. "What are you trying to say?"

"It's obvious: Willie knows I'm Albert's discovery, and he found out you and I are friends . . . Jade, no offense, but he's only after you to bug Albert. I've heard how petty and vicious Willie Santana can be. He's probably counting on some sleazy publicity out of pitting us against each other."

"Sleazy publicity?" She gives me a smile that looks feral. "You're just jealous."

"Ex*cuse* me?"

"No—excuse *me*!"

"No . . . *um*, excuse me . . ."

Oh, dear. Duncan. Forgot about him. I shut my mouth with an audible clap, my fingers flying to my lips lest any other hateful sound escape. Urgent eyelash action ensues as Jade and I both blink back tears. What mean, nasty, despicable girls we are. Worse, we were mean, nasty, and despicable in front of a guy.

Yet somehow, that's okay. If anything, Duncan looks sympathetic . . . and—could it be?—a bit amused. "It's almost funny," he says. "Right before you came in, Jade, I was telling Mac about how much I could use a friend. Now, I may not know either one of you too well, but I do know there's something true between you. The way you step up for each other and reach out to each other . . ."

"*Mm-hmm?*" I say, my gaze taking a quivery detour toward Jade. "What about the way we just ripped into each other?"

"*Aw*, that's nothing!" Duncan says, tipping back his chair.

He cannot be serious. Jade and I are mongoose and cobra. "Duncan, you can't disregard how awful I was to Jade just now." I look at Jade ruefully. "I don't know where it came from, Jade—I'm sorry."

"No, I'm the one who ought to be tarred and feathered, or drawn and quartered, or whatever corporal punishment befits being a monster in the first degree."

Duncan shakes his head at us. "Best friends are going to tussle now and again," he insists. "It's human nature."

I see Jade on the verge of spilling into laughter, probably over Duncan's using the word *tussle*. Ignoring her, I ask, "What do you mean, it's human nature?"

"I couldn't tell you, but I could prove that it's so," Duncan says. "If you had a picture of yourself and a mirror, that is."

"A picture?" Jade says, heaving her leather-bound book onto the table. "Duncan, I'm a model—I've got a whole portfolio."

"Well, wait, hold on now—it can't be just any picture." Duncan opens Jade's book and begins flipping through. I have a momentary thought that I'd like to be showing him *my* book—after all, what girl wouldn't want to show the guy she likes some studio shots of herself in artful poses with perfect hair and makeup? But I find myself caught up in looking at Jade's book, which it occurs to me I've never seen. There she is in vivid color and artsy black and white—some test shots, some bona fide tear sheets. On a boat in Bermuda. Coming out of the Métro in Paris. Natural curls, silken blowout, jet-black wig with bangs. I'm momentarily envious, not only at the variety of pictures but the sheer numbers. My book is just halfway full. But that will all change after Fashion Week. . . .

"Won't work with a profile or a three-quarters shot," Duncan says, flipping through. "Oh, all right—this ought to do."

He finds one way in the back of Jade staring dead-on at the camera and wearing blue eye shadow, which makes me wonder if this was taken last season, when blue eye shadow was all the rage.

"Oh, don't use that—I hate that," Jade says, placing her palm over the shot, smudging the protective sleeve.

"Well, Jade, it's got to be a full face," Duncan explains. "Anyway, the photo's only one element. I need a mirror, and I can't use any old mirror, either."

Curious about what he's up to, I rummage through my bag. "Here," I say, pulling out a large round compact. "Use this."

"Nope, won't work. It's got to be a flat mirror; at least the size of the picture, too." Duncan shrugs. "Maybe one day I can show you."

"Wait . . ." Jade pulls a frameless, rectangular mirror out of her vintage patent-leather clutch. "How's this?" She hands it to Duncan.

"That'll do fine." He lays the portfolio open on the table

as Jade and I hover around. "Now you'll see why one picture's worth a thousand words." Using the mirror like a knife, he proceeds to slice Jade's face directly down the center, then tilts it slightly to show one side joined to its reflection. What we see is beyond bizarre. The image is Jade, all right . . . but different. Wider, rounder eyes; fuller lips; her brows highly arched, and her face broader, a pure and absolute angel.

"Wow, Jade," I say. "You look so sweet and innocent."

"*Mmmm* . . . ," she says, examining the image. "It looks like me, but . . ."

"It *is* you." Duncan sounds almost ominous. "One side of you . . ." Then he swivels the mirror to reveal the other half of Jade's face joined seamlessly to its twin.

Jade and I gasp in unison.

"Unholy shit," Jade says quietly.

We stare at the image of Jade. We can't stop staring at it. *This* Jade. Chin practically pointed, nose sharper, something sly and twisted in her smile. And the eyes! Narrower and slanted up, with a glint that says they've seen it all. There's mischief there, and worse—it scary to see. This girl—this Jade—is the sort of vixen who'd spit in your drink and steal your wallet and beguile your boyfriend simply because she could. All she needs is horns.

Eleven

I'm alone in my room, which is starting to feel like a foreign country, with its tennis trophies and sunflower curtains. Even more so now that my future plans have taken on a more solid shape. Last night I told my parents my decision to defer my scholarship for one year.

They were not as disappointed as I expected. Well, my mother seemed to have reservations. But my father came around to my way of thinking more easily. In fact, I think he might even be genuinely proud of me. Mostly because that very afternoon, he'd accidentally-on-purpose opened an envelope that had come in the mail from the agency, which happened to contain a check for thirteen thousand dollars.

"It's not a terrible plan, Margaret," he said to my mother, arguing on my behalf. "In the last two months, she's already made almost as much as a rookie fireman earns in a year. She can do this for a bit, then go back to school."

My mother looked at me uncertainly. "*Will* you go back to school, Melody?"

I knew she was thinking about how she had given up college after two years to become a homemaker. She wanted more for me. Always had.

"Oh, she'll go back," my father declared. "Chances are this whole modeling thing will be over by the time she's twenty-one!"

Even my mother looked offended by that. But what he said is not too far from the truth.

"That's why you have to save all you can, while you can, Melody," he warned, his tone becoming ominous. "You can only wear one pair of shoes at a time—so don't buy a lot of shoes. I'm sure it won't be long before you can probably afford anything you want, but maintaining this 'model lifestyle' might do you in financially. The upkeep has got to be expensive and I don't want to see you waste your money."

"I won't," I said, mentally putting the Marc Jacobs bag I've had my eye on back on the pristine shelf in the boutique where I spotted it two weeks ago. "I promise."

Though it's a promise that might be a tad hard to keep, I realize now. Home for the weekend and restless, I start going through my closet to see if there is anything passable I could pack for the shows. I'll be staying with Jade for the week and I'm still grateful to her for her offer. I'm hoping she might offer up her closet, too. I just put on a pair of trousers I bought three months ago and they are swimming on me! As are *all* my skirts *and* my favorite pair of jeans!

I'll confess the sight of my clothes sagging off me makes me giddy at first. It's one thing to weigh in at fifteen pounds lighter on the scale. It's another to actually see the tangible results. At five eleven and 126 pounds, my body does look different, I realize, as I study myself in the mirror. Not just slimmer, though you can see my ribs; I guess the word is willowy. My limbs seem to float when I walk, my neck is like a pedestal for my head. Plus, there are contours and hollows I never had before, and my breasts actually look bigger, despite that I've gone down a bit in size. But being thinner all over makes them stand out more.

Do I look better? Hard to say. I sort of miss the muscles of my tennis body, which made me feel impenetrable, like nothing could knock me down, physically or mentally. My model body seems to have a power of its own, to do what? I'm not sure.

Grabbing a box of trash bags from the pantry in the hall, I head back to my room to begin a mass purge of my possessions. It's something I need to do and there's no better time than the present. Besides, I'm still waiting on Liza, who's coming by tonight. It's probably the last time I'll see her before she leaves for college in the next couple of weeks. She invited me to a party last night but I begged off. My ex was guaranteed to be there and I just didn't want to deal.

Sighing, I open a drawer and begin going through stuff. Did I actually wear these clothes my mother made? I love the woman but she's no Albert Lazar. Everything, everything goes into Hefty bags; everything, everything off to Goodwill. On the floor, I come across some books from my childhood—*Clifford the Big Red Dog* and *The Magic School Bus*. I hit the wall with a shoebox of old photos. It's as though they have power over me, forcing me to go through them, recollect each occasion or goofy nonevent. Such awkward poses and insecure smiles—no one would ever imagine the girl in those pictures poses for a living now. All of a sudden I remember that thing Duncan did with Jade's photo. You think a face is symmetrical, that your eyes are a matched set, but it's freaky—at least it was in Jade's case.

What about me?

I ransack the shoe box for a full-face shot. The argument Jade and I had at Leaf totally unnerved me. Some of the things I said—was I just being honest, or defensive, or really, truly rotten? In tennis, competition is simple—you play your heart out and your ass off, and if you're better, you win. Modeling, another story. So much goes on under the surface, behind the smile. That's why I attack a mirror I got for my birthday a few years ago, hacking away with a sewing scissors to pry it out of it's seashell frame. If I can pull it out intact without severing a vein I can see both sides of me for myself. . . .

But footsteps race along the hall, and my door bursts open. "Melody!"

"Liza!" I throw down the mirror and the scissors and the whole mess of photos and jump up and we're hugging, and suddenly I feel normal and carefree for the first time in ages.

"Or should I call you Mac, Ms. Model?" Liza's sarcasm is as counterfeit as a street-corner Fendi.

"Shut up," I tell her, and we hug again. With her uneven tan lines and sun-streaked hair, she looks happy and healthy. She kicks off her flip-flops and we sit on my bed. Liza doesn't mention the garbage bags that lie around the room like silent walruses stuffed with my past. Intuition tells us not to talk much about our summers—she's probably afraid hers will bore me and mine could sound like I'm showing off. What, then, do we have to talk about? Could the summer have really made us strangers?

"God, let me tell you what you missed last night." Liza gets inspired, and I'm relieved. "*Uck*, Devon and Dave are like this old married couple," she starts off, speaking about our high school friend Devon, whom we lost to her boyfriend, Dave, six months ago. "They're way beyond the gratuitous PDA phase and have moved on to grooming each other in plain sight, like a pair of chimpanzees. And Marianne Shefflin got drunk—"

"Marianne Shefflin?"

"Crazy, right? She was always so timid. Oh, and—hey!" Liza punches my thigh. "Look, the new Victoria's Secret commercial."

I'd forgotten the TV was even on in my room, the sound muted. I don't bother to turn it up. Sure, there'd be music, an announcer gurgling about the lingerie conglomerate's latest line, but the voice-over might as well be in Portuguese. These sixty-second spots are all about the visual. A parade of usual suspects—Raquel, Adriana, Esther, Karolina—stalk individually in assorted bra-and-panty combos, and then the new girl, Stella Cheever, runs down the catwalk, barefoot on the balls of her feet, crimson scraps barely covering her most intimate areas.

"I swear, if only the right underwear could make you look like that!" Liza says.

"It has nothing to do with underwear and everything to do with lighting." I say this because it is often the truth. Not only do models have lighting on their side but full body makeup. Not that these tricks would help Liza, who has sort of a boxy shape—not much waist, a big but flat butt, thick legs—but I don't want her to get down on herself.

"Yeah, *uh-huh*, tell me another," she says good-naturedly.

That's Liza—solid on the inside, too. Billows of smoke swirl as supermodels evaporate to pixel mist pixie dust on-screen. Wouldn't you know it—a commercial for a new brand of frosting follows. Too cruel!

"Next year at this time, that's going to be you," Liza says.

"What? Someone's going to stick a spatula in me and spread me on a cupcake?"

"You know what I'm talking about. Don't be modest, Melody, or I'll have to smack you."

"Liza, really, next year at this time I'll be packing for Penn." The response is automatic, but I wonder: could I get Victoria's Secret? All that money—it's enough to make me dizzy. And the power, the prestige. The commercial replays in my mind, and with a tiny smile I decide that Stella Cheever's got "cankles." Oh, even if I got it—could I *do* it? Prance around in my skivvies, basically sell sex? Am I that kind of girl? I just don't know—it seems so easy for the other girls to make these decisions, why is everything so much harder for me?

"Girl, you're nuts!" Liza breaks the spell. "You know you've got the bod for it."

"Maybe," I say. "I just don't know if I've got the stomach for it."

I get the answer to that question sooner rather than later. Specifically, five days later, in Albert Lazar's atelier, where I've come to do my preshow fitting.

So far it's been a mutual-admiration fest between me and Albert, with me gushing over every new creation he gives me to try on, and Albert waxing poetic about how I was positively born to wear his designs. I'm so excited I can barely stand still as his tailors flutter around me, adding a pin or holding up a hem for Albert's consideration.

That is, until his stylist, a sullen Russian woman I only know as Alessandra, holds up a blouse so gauzy it might have been fashioned from an angel's wing. "Oh, this is *lovely*," I say, reaching out to touch the soft, sheer fabric. "*Umm . . .*," I begin, as Alessandra holds it out so that I might slip my arms into it. "Isn't there, like, a camisole or something?"

She shakes her head, then proceeds to sheath me in the blouse which I discover, once I'm gazing down at my nipples, is completely transparent.

"*Ohhhhhhh!*" The sound, which startles me at first, shudders out of Albert, who enters the studio once more, a freshly poured Perrier in hand.

Reflexively, I raise my hands to cover my nearly bare breasts.

As if anticipating my move, Alessandra touches my arm.

"Magnificent!" shouts Albert, oblivious to my unease. "This could be my testimonial piece!" Then glancing about the room, he shouts, "Pierre!" and his tailor hurries over and, eye level to my left nipple, begins pinning per Albert's instructions.

And I suddenly feel an urge to throw up. All over Albert's testimonial.

"It just can't be *done*, Mac," Francesca insists as I pace in front of her desk. "Calling Albert Lazar to tell him you don't feel comfortable wearing one of his designs would be career *suicide*."

"Well, if I don't commit suicide then you're going to have my murder on your hands," I reply. "My *parents* are coming to that show, Francesca! My father can't see me parading topless in Bryant Park!"

"You won't be topless, Mac darling, you'll be swathed in Albert's *fabulous* creation. You'll be making history! No one— and I mean *no other model*—will be wearing this design on the catwalk but you! Think about that!"

All I could think about was that in two weeks' time, my nipples were going to making their own bit of history. Half the guys in my high school wanted to see my breasts and I managed to hold out. *Now* I'm going to give it up for a gay man just because everyone else is too afraid to tell him no?

The whole thing just doesn't feel right to me. It's not who I am. It's definitely not who Melody Ann Croft is. And, I decide, it's not who I want Mac to be, either.

Unfortunately, Francesca won't budge. "This is *very* unprofessional, Mac. What's gotten into you?"

A sense of modesty? Does this woman even know me, I wonder, not for the first time.

"What about Renee?" I plead. "She knows Albert. Maybe if she just talked to him, told him it has nothing to do with his design and everything to do with my . . . my comfort level."

Shaking her head, Francesca marches me over to Renee's office and explains my "little dilemma."

Renee actually has the gall to laugh. I think it might be the first genuine emotion I've ever seen out of her. "Oh, *Moch*, don't be ridiculous. Albert will never understand. *I* don't understand. This is fashion, after all! And in fashion, anything goes. At least," she says, her expression becoming stern once more. "Anything *Albert* wants."

Twelve

Run, go, hurry, come on, sit down, stand up, shut your mouth, hold your breath, now, go, move it move it go! I've just arrived at Bryant Park for my first show and already I feel like I'm hanging onto a hurricane, the insanity swirling around me spurring my adrenaline. The madness starts in the farthest concentric circle around Bryant Park—cabs and Town Cars bleating for blocks, traffic inching in agony toward the summit of style. At the main entrance a security phalanx demands tickets and IDs and bag checks; pass through, and you've got a gauntlet of photographers to contend with, when what you really want to do is grab some swag from the sponsor booths—sunglasses, DVDs, chocolates, magazines, perfume. Fortunately—or unfortunately, depending on how you look at it—I go through the model's entrance, which means no swag, though we do have a bevy of photographers to contend with. Right up the street, behind the park, sits the main branch of the New York Public Library, that massive structure with stone lions guarding the tomes. I do wonder, just for a nano, how many of the fashion people stomping and snorting like rodeo broncos have read an actual book in the last decade.

Yes, indeed I do. I even wonder, briefly, how many books I'll be reading in the next year now that I've swapped college for career.

There are three tents—two big ones and a smaller arena called "The Atelier"—where the shows take place, and once inside there's this ongoing roar, the anticipatory clamor for glamour. Snippets of conversation come at me like dragon-flies:

"The nerve, asking for my ticket! I told him my face is my ticket!"

"He's a Peek-a-Boo—part Pekingese, part Bouvier. Have you ever seen anything so adorable?"

"Yes, it *is* divine—but you should have seen the first thing he sent! I was like, 'Give me the dress I want, or I'll be wearing Dolce to *your* show!'"

"It's the new leather alternative—costs twice as much as leather but I wouldn't be caught dead wearing cow now!"

"Such a shame she couldn't get first row. The day I'm seated anywhere else is the day I retire!"

Once I make it backstage, I spot Gwyneth Paltrow talking to Marc Jacobs. And who is she with? . . . *Ooooh!* Sarah Jessica Parker!

I tear my eyes away and break into a light run. I don't have time to stargaze.

Besides, I'll know where to find them later.

Jade already filled me in on the protocol. There are only two places to be during Fashion Week: in the front row or along the back wall. First row is for celebrities, influential magazine mavens, and big-shot buyers for the best stores. The back wall is the domain of models. We're pretty much all-access and can hop from tent to tent, but there's this unwritten rule that we all stand in back—that is, if we're not at the backstage W lounge.

It's ridiculous, of course. I'm just glad I managed to get passes for my parents, who'd be happy enough in the bleachers.

My parents . . . Just the thought of them sitting out there while I parade down the runaway in what my Catholic-school-weaned mother will classify as a pornographic outfit makes me ill. And my father! Forget about it. My stomach roils again. It figures that Albert Lazar's show is the only one they're coming to, mostly because his show is nearer to the end of Fashion Week. The biggest designers appear at the beginning and the end of the shows. When I first got my parents on board to come see me walk, I talked them out of coming to one of the earlier shows, figuring I'd be too nervous.

Me and my big mouth.

Which is exactly why I need to find a moment alone with Albert before I walk for him. I've decided to take matters into my own hands and talk to him myself about possibly putting a camisole under that way-too-saucy number he designed. Surely he'll understand. That is, if I can *find* a moment to talk to him. . .

Right now I'm hustling over to the promenade where I'll dress for Joanna Mastroianni.

My Fashion Week debut is less than a half hour away!

That thought alone makes me want to vomit.

"Hello, hello, who are you? Oh, Mac, yes! This way!" says a harried assistant when I reach the dressing area. She quickly shuffles me off to hair and makeup. Immediately, the hair team starts teasing, twirling, and looping. Last season, Joanna Mastroianni did minimalist hair, so now she's going all out . . . at the models' excruciating expense.

"*Ow!*"

Nothing, not even a sigh of sorry from the desensitized stylist yanking my strands into obeisance. No pain, no mane! True, I feel like there's a chandelier atop my head when they're done, but the style goes surprisingly well with the simple yet elegant gowns Joanna Mastroianni designs for . . . well, I don't know who, but I bet they have a Park Avenue or Hollywood address.

Next stop in the manic assembly line is makeup, the artist so gentle as she swabs my face and brushes color over my eyes, my lips, I feel almost soothed by the time she's done.

Almost. But not quite.

Now it's time to get dressed. The typical photo shoot is as calm as a yoga class compared to backstage at a fashion show. Here it's incredibly hectic, with lots of people running around, so my natural inclination is to stand behind my rack rather than go bare butt and full frontal. Trouble is, if I do that, I'll feel like an amateur, so I remind myself of all the times I stripped down in the locker room at tennis matches to force myself over my modesty. I peel like a banana and of course I don't touch a single thread of Joanna Mastroianni—heaven forbid I muss anything. It still kind of freaks me out, feeling a stranger's brusque hands get me in and out of clothes, like I'm some kind of life-sized doll. This dresser is a real pro, though—she puts me into the gown as quickly and professionally as a marine assembling his AK-47. Once she's done, I stuff tissues under my arms. I don't want to sweat all over the silk before the show, and I'm definitely sweating!

The final touch is accessories. I've known for a week I'll be wearing Jacob the Jeweler, yet I can't quite get over it when the real thing—an oval diamond centerpiece surrounded by twenty-five smaller stones and set in platinum—is clasped around my neck. The jewels lay coolly against my throat and dip into my cleavage, heavier than I expected—not that I had any clue how much 42.57 carats would actually weigh—and when the dresser fastens the matching bracelet it hits me that I'm about to strut off with $560,000 in blinding bling.

So I chuckle. It feels good to laugh about *something* today. Though my nerves are so frayed, the sound that erupts out of me is borderline maniacal.

"What's so funny?" The accessories stylist can't imagine anything amusing about all that ice.

"Oh, . . . nothing." I'm not about to let slip my fleeting fantasy of making a run for the border.

Breathe, I tell myself as I line up to take my first walk. No easy task, since this bodice I'm wearing is so tight it's cutting off my air supply. Oh, God, what if I suffocate in front of all those people? My stomach heaves for the sixth time this morning. Worse, what if I puke?

I try to relax by watching the small monitor near the entrance to the runway, where I can view the girls walking. So far, no one has tripped. So far, no one has puked.

Of course not. They're saving that number for me.

As the first models start to come back, I hear a squeal out of Lacey Alvin. "Tom *Cruise* is out there!"

"Where?" says the model behind me.

"Right next to Demi and Ashton!"

"Oh, Ashton is here. I *love* him!" another practically shouts in my ear.

All this excitement is doing nothing for my nerves. If anything, knowing I'm about to face not only the Fashion World but half of Hollywood really makes me want to run and hide.

I lurch forward as the strap of my Christian Louboutin stiletto digs deeper into my flesh. Do I even know how to walk in these shoes? Why, oh, why, did I bail on that stupid class Francesca wanted me to go to on how to rule the runway? So what if it seemed like Francesca was only trying to help out the poor girl teaching it by letting her make some money off newbie models! I *am* a newbie! I *need* help! Who the hell was I kidding?

I step out of line to take a brief practice walk—and nearly collide with Joanna Mastroianni herself!

"Ah, Mac, let me have a last look at you," she says, and I stop breathing again as she gives me the once-over. I want her to be pleased with how I'm presenting her dress but I can't tell from her expression if she is. . . .

She gives me a quick smile, then moves on, quelling my worries. But only for a moment. Because suddenly the producer of the show taps me on the shoulder, signaling me that it's time for me to step forward, before the gaze of everyone who is anyone, and all their dearest cronies.

I move out onto the runway, my stomach twisting as I watch the swish of the dress on the model before me as she makes her way up the walk. The knot in my gut grows tighter, knowing the other models are now watching me on the monitor backstage. Once the model in front of me hits the mid-runway mark, that's my signal to go.

Breathe! my inner voice chides, even as I'm struck blind by the lights.

I can't see a thing! *Nothing! Help! Heellllp!*

And suddenly something in me relaxes. Suddenly my legs begin to move in slow, easy strides, hips gliding forward. It's as if I'm floating above the stage, the world around me one big blur of brilliant light. Soon enough, the end of the runway is in sight. Soon enough, I'm pivoting, pausing as I'm bathed in a sea of flashing cameras, before I saunter back, everything coming to me as if by instinct, or at least by memory of watching the other girls.

Before I know it I'm back in the clutches of my dresser.

I did it! I want to shriek at her, but she is already hustling me into a new dress, new shoes . . . a new life.

After the finale, during which models in thirty beautiful gowns circle the runway, Joanna herself comes out to take her well-deserved bow and I run backstage to get dressed. Better to get there before all the cameras and fans! Even if I've learned to undress in front of my colleagues, I certainly cannot go full frontal before cameras and strangers! And I do mean full frontal as I have no panties on under my skimpy silky Joanna Mastroianni gown—the lines would have ruined the flow of the dress.

I manage to put on my street clothes just as the hordes from the audience come streaming in backstage, the security guards unable to keep them out any longer. I marvel at the party happening backstage. I know it must be a great relief for the designer, this moment when the show is finally over. But, whether or not a designer has a success on her hands is something she will only find out in the next few months as the orders pour in.

I hope I'm still around as a model to witness the success of the shows I'm in.

By day four of the show, I'm a pro. Okay, not really. But I did a knockout job for Zac Posen today. So much so that I don't think anyone noticed that I tripped about two steps before my exit. Fortunately, Duncan came onto the runway just as I was leaving it, which I'm sure distracted the audience enough that no one even noticed my little stumble.

Duncan . . . At least I got to see him backstage. We're going to try and meet up at the W Lounge later if the shows don't run too late.

Since I know Jade wedged her way in to watch me in Marc Jacobs, I head over to Willie Santana to see her walk, traitorous as it is to Albert. *Fashion Week Daily*, the newspaper that covers the minutiae of the collections, picked up on the story and ran an item: "Dueling Designers to Wield Best Friend Girls." I have to admit it was a kick to see my name in print, even in that context.

I keep a low profile once I get to the back row of the Santana show, to ensure no photographers see me. At least I know Albert isn't around to see me paying homage to his rival. I went looking for him again this morning to make my case for a cami beneath his see-through design, but he was nowhere to be found. If I don't find him soon, I'm really going to freak out.

When Jade hits the runway as the last girl, I'm thrilled for her, as this is the testimonial spot. The most important girl in the show walks last! As she struts out in Willie's skimpy short suit, I momentarily forget my worries as I watch her kooky walk, long filly legs swerving and veering, arms swinging, attitude cranked so high it's almost mockery.

I break into a grin. What is the world is she up to? Could be she's poking fun at how seriously people take fashion, maybe she's just having fun—either way, I can relate. I was scolded by Francesca for smiling on the runway, but how can you keep a straight face when you're having such a blast? Watching Jade, I know she's feeling the same thing. . . .

At least I think she's feeling the same thing, until I see her start to tug at the jacket. Not just tug, but tear it from her body! I can practically hear the sound of the fabric shredding, my ears filling with the stunned *"Whhaaa!"* of the audience as she rips the jacket into a rag and twirls it over her head.

Clapping a hand to my mouth, I stare in stunned silence. And then I realize her brilliance. Leave it to her and Willie—aka Boy Flamboyant—to concoct such a move. What's her next trick—purposely splitting her pants? Whatever that may be, I can't stay to see the finale. If I don't hustle, I'll never make it to my next show, which begins—I glance at the clock on my cell phone—*yikes!*—in twenty minutes.

Every second counts. Be the tiniest bit late and you set the whole schedule careening. Just one girl spending half a minute extra in the bathroom in the morning means the last show of the evening won't start till 10:00 p.m. By mid-afternoon, everything's running an hour behind—yet nobody's too cranky, since apparently this is business as usual.

When I'm done for the day I could go home and crash, but this is my first Fashion Week and I want to catch as many shows as I can. Plus, I need to find Jade, congratulate her for wilding out in Willie's show, so I head for the W Lounge, where we said we'd meet up one way or the other.

Entering the bar, I do a quick scan for Jade and, while I'm at it, Duncan. He did say he might try to get here, too. But I don't see either of them.

"How's your friend?"

It's Lindsey Burton, who would sound condescending

saying "I love you." But I met this girl on my very first shoot; I'm used to her by now. "Jade?" I say. "I'm looking for her, in fact."

"*Hmpf*," Lindsey sniffs. "I was about to call Bellevue on her myself and then I remembered I really couldn't care less."

"What are you talking about, Lindsey? Is Jade all right?"

Lindsey cocks her head, an evil twinkle in her eyes. "That child is the definition of all wrong," she replies. "Last I saw, she was having herself a nice little nervous breakdown."

When I find Jade in the bathroom, she's attempting to tear out her own hair.

"Jade!"

I grab her hands, just as she's about to give her own face a wicked slap. "Jade, please! Stop!"

She doesn't seem to be listening. In fact, I'm not sure she is even seeing me through the glassy-eyed haze of confusion and anger I glimpse in her eyes. But then she collapses against me with a sob. "I hate myself, I hate myself, I want to die!"

Taking her weight, I half drag, half carry her to a bench, sit her down, and wrap my arms around her "It's all right, it's all right, whatever, Jade, whatever, I'm here, I'm with you, it's all right. . . ."

"No, Mac, it's not. It's not all right. It will never be all right."

I smooth a hand over her hair, surprisingly soft considering the amount of product it must have in it by now. "Why don't you tell me what happened."

Suddenly she spills out everything in a rush. How she couldn't get the buttons undone on the jacket. Those impossible buttons! Her off-the-cuff brainstorm to tear the jacket off. How her moment of rebel "genius" lost her spots in both the Thakoon and Nili Lotan show. How callous Vanessa was when she called her and gave her the news.

"I don't believe it," I say when she's finished. "I thought . . . well, I thought it was part of the show. I mean, it looked like fashion-as-theater."

Shaking her head miserably, she says, "I suppose it might have been, except the samples we wear are one-offs created just for the show." She lets out another sob. "Oh, Mac, don't you see? It's over for me. I'm ruined—a has-been who never was!"

Since I have no reassuring response for this, I simply continue to hold her, stroking her back, realizing once again how fragile she is, how childlike, despite her world-weariness. Was it possible that she hadn't known the consequences of her actions?

Slowly her hysteria ebbs. "I don't want to hurt myself anymore. I don't want to cry anymore," she says, meeting my gaze with mascara-smudged glassy eyes. "I just want to go home."

And so I help Jade to her feet and whisk her out of there before anyone else can witness her defeat.

I'm beginning to think my friend Jade is like her cat, Tom Jones, because the girl has nine lives. Remarkably, by the very next day, everything *is* all right. Sort of. Yes, Renee Kitaen rips her a new one the way she ripped Willie's jacket. And yes, she's out a bunch of money. But by that evening, she's all revved up and ready to join the scene at the after-show parties. Apparently, the word on the street is that Jade's little stunt had more than a few admirers. It seems a bad-girl reputation isn't the worst thing in this business. In fact, it might even prove to be an asset for Jade.

Though I did tell her I'd join her at the party *Elle* magazine is throwing tonight, I'm not sure I'm going to actually make it there, as I'm a model on a mission.

Today I learned from one of his assistants that Albert Lazar has dinner reservations at Jean-Georges, and I'm determined to bare my soul to him before I have to bare a lot more than that to the fashion world.

Of course, the maître d' has other ideas. "I'm sorry; I can't confirm whether Mr. Lazar is here. It's against our policy."

Clearly he thinks I'm some kind of obsessed fan. Do designers even have obsessed fans?

I decide to wait it out in a nearby coffee shop. Overdosing on herbal tea and rag-trade magazines, I read the gossip on the shows, everything from how Sarah Jessica Parker thought Narciso Rodriguez's designs were "to die for" to how Lindsay Burton stumbled on her way down the runway during Donna Karan. Jade got a full paragraph—complete with photo—on her stunt during Willie Santana, which the editors of *Fashion Week Daily* loved. Oh my heavens! There's even a photo of me and Duncan talking backstage at Zac Posen! I wonder, briefly, how someone managed to get that, then I settle into the thrill of seeing myself in print with Duncan, the two of us dubbed "Fashion Week's hottest stars." I study the picture dreamily . . . we make a pretty hot couple. Perhaps that's what the newspapers will be writing about us next. . . .

I'm so immersed in my reading that by the time I get back to Jean-Georges, I learn, from a busboy who can be bribed, that Albert Lazar's party left twenty minutes ago.

I get on the cell phone to Jade, who I know is probably already at the *Elle* party. "Are you coming?" she asks against a background of throbbing music.

"Maybe . . . is Albert Lazar there?"

"Albert Lazar? He *never* goes to these things. Especially not before his show. The rumor is he spends the night before in his atelier, probably sacrificing whatever assistants he can spare to the fashion gods."

"Okay, thanks," I say, hanging up before she can ask why I'm looking for him. I haven't filled Jade in on my dilemma with Albert's design. I have a feeling the girl who flaunts everything from T to A every opportunity she can just won't relate.

Instead, I hop in a cab and head to SoHo.

Feel a flicker of hope when I'm buzzed into the building where his workshop is. As I ride the elevator up, I say a little prayer to the fashion gods myself that Albert doesn't take offense at my even showing up here so late, never mind asking him to change his plans for one of his designs.

The elevator slides open at his studio, which is dark. Maybe he's *not* here. But if that's the case, who let me in? A shiver moves through me and I'm almost ready to jump back on the elevator again when I see Albert, sitting in a small circle of light at his desk.

I swallow hard, suddenly unwilling to disturb the intense concentration he appears to be in.

But then I muster up all my courage. "Albert?" His name slips softly, shakily, between my lips.

He doesn't stir. "Albert?" I say louder.

He looks up, eyebrows moving down in confusion. "Who is it?"

"It's Mac," I answer, stepping out of the shadows. "Mac Croft. I'm so sorry to bother you so late, but I needed to talk to you about . . . about the show tomorrow."

His expression is so stern, I feel like fleeing. But he's looking at me so intently that instead I spill everything out in a rush. How thrilled I am to be in his show. How in love I am with every one of his designs. Then, finally, how uncomfortable I am wearing one of those designs. . .

"It's not that I don't love it . . . It's just that, well, I wasn't raised to . . . to be so, *um* . . . *open* with my body. And my mother and father are going to be there because, of course, I wanted them to attend the best show . . ."

There is a long silence, during which I'm convinced that I have just done what Francesca predicted: I've committed career suicide.

He stands up, his hand on his chin as he looks at me.

How do I tell Renee I went against her orders and spoke to Albert without her okay? How do I make this right?

My knees begin to buckle as I see my career crashing before my eyes. I look around for something to hold on to so I don't hit the floor.

"Mac, Mac, Mac!" Albert finally shouts at me.

"I am so sorry, Albert. I should not have come here. Renee will kill me . . ."

"Yes, she would if she ever found out, but she won't because I won't tell her." His small, intelligent eyes narrow over his bulbous nose. "Could it be you are a witch?" Then, incredibly, he smiles. "Perhaps you are a fairy then. Because it's unbelievable that you have come here tonight, just as I was pondering whether that piece fits in with the landscape I'm trying to create." He picks up his list of show outfits for tomorrow's extravaganza and looks it over again.

"And does it?" I ask.

"I'm not sure. One is never too sure of anything in the fashion business! But you have made up my mind. I am taking this piece out of the show!"

Then, to my complete astonishment, he kisses me on the forehead, much as my own father would. "You are a very sweet girl. A one of kind—much like one of my designs, no? Don't ever change!" he orders. "Now go home and rest! We have a show to do tomorrow!"

As I turn to leave, Albert gently calls to me. "And Mac," he says. "Always stand up for what you believe in. Always defend yourself and your beliefs."

Wow! Was I just given great advice from the world's best designer? "Thank you, Albert. For everything." With a smile, I make my exit, leaving him to his work.

By dawn's early light, Jade bursts into the bedroom, brandishing the tabloids. "Don't believe a word of it." Still in her party gear and resembling a crumpled receipt, she plops onto the bed.

"A word of what?"

She points to the *Post*. "This." A picture of her and Duncan cuddling. "They're hinting we're an item but please—you know that's not true."

A weird prickly feeling breaks out all over me. For no logical reason—Duncan and I have nothing but a casual friendship at this point, and my bond with Jade runs deep. Besides, the idea of anything romantic between them? Jade and Duncan might as well be of different species. Yet the idea of those two touching consumes me like a flesh-eating disease.

"You know that, Mac, don't you?" Jade asks with a tense edge. "God, if those idiots at the *Post* had a nose for news they'd have sussed out what was going on in the limo between me and Everett Frye last night."

Whoever that is. I can only assume Jade made a conquest—the man behind her rumpled attire and smudgy mascara. She is *so* vulnerable lately. It really scared me the other night, the way she was battering herself, but she recovered in a snap, as if it had all been magically erased from her memory. Only I know Jade: she may pretend it never happened, but she was clearly angling for some positive press. Being seen with Duncan would do it—he's emerging as the male sensation of the collections. And he was just being nice, obliging her in a photo op—that's Duncan to a tee.

"Of course, Jade," I say with a yawn, trying to be nonchalant about the whole situation. "So . . . you had fun?"

Sighing, she begins to offer tidbits of her rendezvous with Everett, but I refuse to discuss penis size before sunrise. "I don't mean to cut you off, Jade, but I've got Albert today and he wants us there early to do a rehearsal. Can we catch up later?" Then, giving her a quick hug, I'm off and running again.

I'm happy enough to be busy so that any anxious thoughts about Duncan and Jade are pushed from my mind. They had to have a picture, right? Well, I have shows to do. I just hope that once the tents are taken down and the fashionistas go back to whatever office they hide in for most of the year, I have a chance to make something real happen with Duncan. Not just a stupid photo. . .

The show goes great. So great, in fact, as I do my final turn at the top of the runway, Albert whooshes out, slips his arm through mine, and we parade to the end, all the other girls pouring behind us. The crowd cheers, and Albert gets on tiptoe to spin me around one more time, his peach silk swirling around my thighs. It's his achievement, yet it's my moment, too. Waves of envy and admiration wash over me, and I can almost feel the editors in the audience taking mental notes: Get Mac! Get Mac! Get Mac!

The import of all this, of course, is lost on my parents, who meet me afterward for a celebratory dinner at Houston's. I guess I was in the mood for something more splashy than a chain restaurant just as easily found in Ohio as in New York City. I try to drag Jade with me, but there's no way she's going to miss the *Moda* party in favor of ribs at my dad's favorite restaurant.

But Francesca joins us, again and again via cell phone. "Darling, I'm sorry to interrupt again but I just have wonderful news! Anna Wintour, via her assistant, just requested that I send your book over!" she says during one phone call, which makes me so excited I can barely eat the broiled salmon platter the waitress places before me. Over cups of Lipton (they don't even have herbal!) she calls again to tell me that I'm going to walk for Anna Molinari for Blumarine, and Moschino in Milan.

"So I guess you *are* going to Europe then," my mother says, her face already lined with worry.

I nod, glancing at my father. "Five thousand a show. Can't beat that." Though it's not even money I'm dreaming of anymore. It's success. Power.

As though sensing this, my father smiles at me, but something in his expression, perhaps a wistfulness for the teenager I once was, gives me a pang. Suddenly going to Europe makes me feel like a five-year-old contemplating her first day of kindergarten. Only I can't let my parents see a glimpse of any vulnerability I feel—they're worried enough. So when I go with them to Penn Station to see them off, I kiss them good-bye and hug them, and hug and kiss them again.

Now it's as though my mother and I have reached a truce at last. Exposing her to the reality of fashion, proving that I'm a viable, significant part of a multi-billion-dollar industry that shapes the consciousness of the culture, has had its effect. Modeling may never fully appeal to her staunch sense of righteousness, but she's off my neck for the moment. I've earned her praise, if not her pride.

So why is it so hard for me to let them board the train for home? I head for the number 1 train to Jade's place, trudging—literally dragging my feet. It's hard to feel grounded in this business. You enter this world and it's as though you're a helium balloon held by a spoiled, fickle child. At any moment his attention could be diverted, he could let go, and you'd go floating off to nowhere. I know that's my mother's greatest fear—and it comes from love and is based in truth. It's my great fear as well. But the only thing I can think to do is face it.

Thirteen

Entering JFK airport, the members of Delicious Models must seem to the casual observer like a squadron of elite fashion enforcers. There are fourteen of us going on the same flight to the Milan shows—up-and-comers and established girls requested by various designers—all of us five ten and over and all marching together in long-legged, hip-hugging formation. Sunglasses inside the terminal, luggage trailing behind us like logo-embossed toddlers, multi-liter water bottles stuffed into low-slung satchels.

Our fearless leader, Renee Kitaen, ushers us to the gate in a state of constant kvetch. "Oh, for the days of the Concorde!" she decries the injustice. "New York to Paris in three hours. Four grand a ticket and worth every penny. I could shuttle you girls to Milan and have you working the same day."

I smile, glad to have Renee along, despite the drama she displays wherever she goes. According to Jade, it's not usual for the president of the agency to travel to the European shows, but Renee, never one to miss a party so close to her homeland, has decided that there is a new model in Paris she simply *must* see and woo to New York. Though Jade claims she's just coming to cluck over us like a mother hen, and keep us from getting in trouble.

I've got no complaints. I just can't wait to touch down in Milan. I'm in nine shows, Jade's in eight, and we're in three together: Moschino, Iceberg, and Anna Molinari for Blumarine. Most of the biggest names didn't pick either of us, but I don't feel snubbed. To me it's so amazing to be going to Milan Moda—that's Italian for Fashion Week. Then there's Paris and London . . . Despite the nightmare of packing for the various weather conditions of each country, I'm thrilled.

If Jade is equally as excited, you'd never know it. The moment we take our seats, she's out like a light due to the arsenal of pharmaceuticals she filched from her mother's medicine cabinet and popped into her mouth at the gate.

Good thing I've got an armload of magazines. Got to keep up with what's going on with the competition, after all. . .

From the moment we touch down at Milan, I truly feel transported to another world. Another time, even. It'll be hard to see much of the city itself—its art, its monuments; I'm no goggle-eyed tourist with a map and a fanny pack. For the most part it's the shows, the nonstop nightlife in Corso Como (you *have* to be spotted in the VIP area of Hollywood, Milan's eternally famous club) and our hotel, the Clotilde, which Jade proclaims a dump but basically all the girls stay here, except for the tippy-top models. Supes are ensconced at the Four Seasons, where we all head post-show, the lobby and bar a model mecca where there's always a good chance of meeting a photographer or a designer or an editor and making a contact. The point is this is not a vacation. Fashion is a huge worldwide business; millions are at stake, and so the frantic vibe is serious—everyone is tense and hyper and in a hurry, and in Italian that passion cranks to an even higher level, like some kind of crazy opera. With crazy costumes to match.

Compared to New York, the Italians are far more fantastical—even the priciest luxury designer in NYC has some clue about real life, whereas here they seem to be creating for the denizens of an opulent, outrageous Disneyland. I probably wouldn't want a closet full of these clothes, but they sure are a trip to wear and watch on the catwalk. The shows are addictive; like being inside a kaleidoscope—Jade and I want to see them all.

Above and beyond the color and the chaos, though, are the Italian people. The designers I've met are so incredible—as talents, sure, but as human beings, too, just so sweet and down-to-earth, treating you like family, even though, frankly, I don't understand a word anyone says to me. Even Italian models are incredible, like Carla Balti, the Italian supermodel. She's like a homecoming queen—everyone wants her, it's a national pride thing. Her schedule is unbelievably demanding, but she's not stuck up at all. Like today, as we troupe to the Four Seasons, we see her surrounded by all these boxes and bags. Gifts of one-offs from the designers are a major perk when you're a supe, and we lesser-known girls cannot help but gaze at them longingly.

"Hi, Carla," I say.

"*Allo, allo, Moch!*" She pronounces my name like Renee does, and gets halfway off the sofa to offer a flutter of kisses. "*Allo,* Jade. Look at me, I am drowning, no."

We hover around, and I hope I'm not turning noticeably green as my fingers absently toy with one of the bows. Carla extracts a cute purple T-shirt with fluted sleeves from a Moschino bag.

"What was Rosella thinking, she is so silly—I cannot wear *porpora*. It's bad luck to Italians! She should know that, no?" She flings the item back at the bag just as Jade snatches it midair.

"It's not bad luck in America," Jade says, her smile ingratiating.

"But of course! You must take it then, Jade. It will look so lovely with your pale skin."

"*Grazie*," Jade replies. "That's very generous of you, Carla."

"Oh, you silly, it is nothing," Carla says, gaily dismissive. "Moch, you stay around, I find something for you."

She does, too—a Gucci hat and scarf combination! I take it without feeling greedy, or in any way bad about basically accepting Carla's rejects, since the entire exchange is sincere and genuine. That's Italians for you.

Which is really great. Except when it isn't—except when it's really, truly way too creepy and weird.

Starving is an even harder feat to accomplish in Italy, since all Italians want to do is feed you. I may need to have my jaw wired shut for the duration of this trip. Thank God, the salads are so delicious—arugula and dandelion. Who knew you could eat weeds? Blessed as Jade is, metabolically speaking, her only real dilemma is choosing between farfalle and fusilli. We don't have any time to sightsee, but when Jade and I venture out for a quick walk down Via Montenapoleone with Colleen Deverhardt and Joie Howe, two other newbie Delicious models who tag along with us, we nearly cause a riot. Somehow word reaches the street that we're Americans from a particular New

York agency, and next thing we know there's a clot of men, stamping their feet and chanting *"Delizioso! Delizioso!"* It's insane. Italian men are merciless, they flirt like it's war, and during Milan Moda, when the town is awash with beautiful women, they lose all control.

Of course, there's only one man I'm interested in. But unfortunately, he's the model *everyone* is interested in. If I thought seeing Duncan at the New York shows was hard, seeing him in Europe is nearly impossible.

I've all but given up. In fact, instead of going to the Four Seasons yet again in the hopes that he'll turn up there, tonight I head back to my hotel with the thought of catching a few winks before tomorrow's round of shows. Between the challenges of the language barrier, the manic mania of the shows, and fending off the men, I'm exhausted.

Of course, the Italians, or rather, one Italian in particular, has other plans for me.

"AAAAAAAHHHH!" The sound comes out of me involuntarily as I swing open the door to my hotel room to discover a man in my room.

"Ah, bella!" he begins, then lets out a string of Italian words that I suspect, judging from the way he's practically salivating at the sight of me, are designed to seduce.

I would laugh, if he hadn't just scared me out of my wits. How the hell did he get *in* here?

"You need to leave," I say, as nicely as possible. It occurs to me that I might be able to take him, if need be. He's maybe as tall as my elbow. In his mid-thirties and impeccably groomed in a hand-tailored dove gray suit, he's the antithesis of the younger Milanese males we'd seen around, who are all into American style hip-hop clothing. He has large brown eyes and an aquiline nose, and his expression is bewildered when I gesture frantically for him to leave, miming the action of him walking through the door.

It's only then that I notice the transformation my room has undergone.

Candles flicker on a table that has been set up near the window, supper for two laid out with linen napkins and several bottles of wine. In the middle of the bed lies a pretty box, done up in distinctive wrapping and ribbon: La Perla, the exclusive Italian lingerie line.

And that's not all. Because suddenly my Italian paramour is holding out a long, thin box, which he opens to reveal a diamond and sapphire bracelet.

Oh my.

My hand goes involuntarily to it. So pretty . . . I glance at my pursuer. How far do I have to actually go to get the bracelet? Dinner? Maybe a kiss . . . ?

Suddenly I come to my senses. What am I, *mad*? Clearly all that glitter is making me lose my mind.

"*Um*, would you, *um* . . . *scusi!*"

And with that, I dart out the door and down the hall.

"Jade!" I yell, banging on her door. I don't know why I'm expecting her to be here. Knowing her, she's probably at that party at Club Plastic that's going on tonight.

I nearly fall through the door when she opens it. "You're here!"

"Just leaving actually. Aren't you going to the party?"

"No, I . . . Jade you have to help me. There's a . . . a *man* in my room!"

"*Brava*, hon-bun. Though I have to say, that's not *such* a hard task in this town."

I shake my head. "No, no! I don't . . . He's just . . . Listen . . . I came home and found him *in* there. Uninvited. And I can't seem to get him to leave!" I give her a weary look. "I'm having a total communication breakdown. Could you just come explain to him that I'm not interested in his company?"

She shrugs. "If that's what you want."

A few moments later, we're both standing in my doorway. My little Italian friend grins expansively at the sight of Jade by my side, perhaps under the mistaken belief that that bracelet bought him the luckiest night of his life. This is offensive, even to an open-minded person like me—does he think all American girls can be bought off with a meal, some pricey underpants, and jewelry?

Okay, the jewelry was tempting. . .

"*Signore* . . ." Jade says, beginning to converse with him, translating the pertinent parts for me.

"His name is Luciano; he's heir to a textile fortune . . ."

"He saw you in Miu Miu today and has fallen madly in love with you. . . ."

"He has 'an arrangement' with the concierge—in other words, he bribed his way into your room."

"Oh Jesus—you remind him of his mother! This is too disturbing."

"*Ick!* Jade, please! Just get him out of here! Tell him we'll call the police."

"Now, Mac, chillax. He probably has the cops in his pocket, too. I'm guessing he's used this routine with other American models he's fallen madly in love with over the years. He keeps saying he can't understand why you won't dine with him. But I know for sure that if you give in and dine with him, he'll want to know why you won't drink with him, and if you drink with him he'll wonder why you won't kiss him, after all he's done for you . . ." She smirks. "Italian men can be super stubborn, you can't say you don't like him, or that he's too old; he won't relate."

"Won't relate? I don't care! I just want to crash."

Luciano looks from me to Jade, clearly uncomprehending. "Just let me think a minute," Jade says, wandering farther into the room and perusing the table, where the pasta is already starting to congeal. I watch in disbelief as she picks up a slab of melon dressed in pink marbleized prosciutto, and pops it into her mouth.

Of all the times to eat!

"Luciano, Luciano, Luciano," she says, once she has licked her fingers clean. Her tone is one of wistful sadness and her tale must be something else because before I know it, he is blushing and exiting the room in a storm of *"scusis."*

I stare at her, pooped but impressed. "Jade, how did you do it?"

She continues to pick at the foiled romantic spread. "Elementary, my dear Mac," she says. "I told the poor fellow that for moral reasons you're a devout vegetarian, that by bringing dead animal products into your room he upset you profoundly to the very core and essence of your being, and it is because of that, and for no other reason, that you couldn't possibly have anything to do with him whatsoever. He should have done his homework and he was embarrassed that he didn't."

I summon whatever strength I have left to applaud. *"Brava,* Jade. Thank you. Really, I appreciate it. Now take whatever else you want and let me hit that bed!"

She raises an eyebrow at me as she picks up another slice of melon. "A very generous offer—and I intend to take you up on it!" Then, hooking her finger in the bow of the La Perla box, she scampers out.

Once she's gone, I look around the room, but I see he didn't leave the bracelet. I'm disappointed about that, in spite of myself. . .

Next stop, Paris, and I've got to pack. This country-to-country travel is dizzying. I've never gone to more than one destination on a vacation, much less three! And this is far from a vacation. Renee's cracking the whip to keep us on schedule, but between the few souvenirs I was able to buy at the pharmacy across the street—I couldn't believe I found beautiful scarves for my mom and Liza in a drugstore!—and the endless freebies, I've accumulated all this stuff. I'm still cramming my bag when Jade arrives at my door.

"Good, you're here—help me zip this. Hey—what's that?"

She tosses the box at me. "It's yours," she says.

Right, of course, I recognize La Perla's packaging. "What's the deal? I thought you wanted it."

"No no no," Jade shakes her head firmly. "That was selfish of me. *Scusi*."

I eye the box. "This is one souvenir of Italy I can leave behind."

"Don't be stupid, Mac. You haven't even seen it. It's gorgeous. And probably costs about fifteen hundred U.S. dollars retail."

"I don't care." But, well, it wouldn't hurt to take a peek. The bow had been undone, the tissue mussed—Jade made a vain attempt to put it back the way it was.

"Go on, girl. Check it out," she says.

I grin. "Okay!" I lift the top, part the crinkly paper. It's a bodysuit, but not the sort of thing you'd do gymnastics in. A teddy, that's what it's called, and it's exquisite. I've never seen, or felt, such fabric—as though it were spun from thin air, like it might dissolve if you breathed on it. Black, sheer, and trimmed in a delicate edging of lace like icing on a cake. I've always been a Jockey girl, never owned anything this whisper soft, this impractical, this sexy. Could I possibly push away the thought of the oily modelizer who picked it out? *Uck*, I don't think so! "Wow," I say. "But Jade, it's much more your style than mine."

Abruptly, her face goes cross. "Yeah, well, you're wrong about that," she says. "In fact, you couldn't be more wrong!"

She turns from me angrily, starts for the door. "Jade, what—what did I say? Hey, stop! Why are you mad?"

"I'm not mad; I have to finish packing."

"Jade, come on—don't be like that. You helped me out of a sicko situation; you should have this. It's not being selfish, really. This is your reward."

Finally she turns around. "Mac, you don't get it, and I really don't feel like breaking it down for you."

But I can tell she does. "Look, I can't apologize if you don't tell me what I did."

Jade stares at a corner of the ceiling, then sighs. "It's not what you did, it's what you are. Mac, I can't wear that thing because it won't fit me. It's your size. Old Pukey Playboy must have gotten your measurements from some mole at Miu Miu, or he took a wild guess. Shall we say 34C? Or are you a D?"

"Is that what this is about? My boobs?"

She gives me a sneer. "Want to trade?"

I am speechless. Jade doesn't know how good she has it being a natural born beanpole. She needn't calculate the calories of every single grape and cornflake, worry that Renee will grab hold of her waist and yell something nasty about how donating my body to science will be like a two-for-one deal. My figure is something I fought for, and continue to fight for, on a daily basis. So if my boobs seem to stand out more now that I'm thinner, well, I earned that. That's the one place on my body I don't have to stress about.

"Yeah, didn't think so," Jade says bitterly.

This is weird. The way Jade likes to prance around in the buff, I assumed she thought she was hot stuff. "So you don't have big breasts, so what?" I say. "You've got those endless legs, and killer abs, and you can eat anything you want without gaining an ounce—"

"You know what, Mac? Just shut up. I don't want to hear you itemize my attributes, as you see them." She begins to pace the room. "You've got to have a rack in this business. Name me one supe who doesn't. So how can I compete? Clearly, there's no Victoria's Secret contract in *my* future." She picks up the teddy, hurls it to the bed again. "Oh, it'd be bad enough if I was only a genetic loser careerwise," Jade rants on. "Breasts also happen to be what define you as a woman—ergo, no man will ever really love me."

Could she actually believe that? As if breasts, or any other physical characteristic, have anything to do with love. In some ways Jade is so deep, so wise. Can her concept of love be so woefully deformed? "Jade, that's . . . ridiculous."

She sneers. "Oh, really? My mother's flat as a board and see how long she held on to my father!"

Evidently this is a huge issue for Jade. What a dolt I am not to have picked up on it. Dare I suggest the obvious? Half the girls in the industry must have bought their boobs. But if she's so breast-obsessed, she's no doubt already grappled with that. Only I don't know. Other girls get the surgery, no problem, but Jade isn't other girls. She's a lot of things, a lot of crazy, conflicting, tempestuous things, but fake isn't one of them. Jade has to be Jade, 100 percent.

Bang, bang, bang! on my door. I stare at Jade, her eyes brim. *Bang, bang, bang!* I race to answer; it's Renee, bags stacked, bad hair day camouflaged in a Hermès scarf. "Moch, come, we must go now!" Jade charges out, toward her room. "Jade Bishop, are you making trouble again?" Renee accuses. "If you are not downstairs in sixty seconds, we'll leave you here!"

"Please, Renee, don't worry, we'll be there." I quickly stuff the La Perla into my bag—surely there is *someone* I can give it to—then summon superhuman strength to close my suitcase and go after Jade.

It's been raining for four days straight in Paris, and yet . . . I'm in love. I've caught the French fever, drippy weather and all.

The sentiment seems to be mutual, too. Designers who hadn't requested me at first are scrambling to fit me in. Renee's behind it; she's been launching a Mac Attack on everyone of influence. So wherever we go—restaurants, clubs, the shows themselves—I can feel a palpable buzz in the air preceding my entrance. And the paparazzi! They were out of control in Italy and Paris is no better.

But it's lonely. I haven't seen Duncan at all beyond a brief, giddy conversation we shared outside just before one of the shows, about how he might have landed a *GQ* cover. Unfortunately, the men and women's shows rarely ever mix. And Jade, well, I feel like I haven't had a chance to have a real conversation with her since we left New York. At least we are doing the

Costume National show together today. When I get there and see her waving at me from the makeup chair, I'm so happy to see her I feel like leaping into her arms.

"Guess what?" I tell her, after gracing both cheeks with kisses—not air, but genuine kisses, albeit in the European paired fashion. "I'm getting the new Dior bag, the one I carried in the show! They won't even be manufactured for months, and the waiting list will probably be a year. But they're sending the one-off to the hotel. I wonder if I should have it insured."

"Awesome, hon-bun," she tells me, sotto voce, "but you might consider lowering the volume. It's bad form to squeal about one design house while dressing for another."

I giggle, mostly because I've really missed Jade's smoky-voiced advice, then slip into the makeup chair beside her. Jade sends me a look and I turn to see Lilly Benedict enter the dressing area. Spotting us, she starts walking over. That's *the* Lilly Benedict, number one in the Delish roster, the face of Estée Lauder, the girl who doesn't get out of bed for less than ten thousand dollars a day.

"Mac, you were fa-a-a-a-a-bulous," Lilly drawls.

"Oh, thanks so much, Lilly. So were you," I say, thrilled that she even noticed me.

"You're going tonight, right?"

At my nod, she says, "If you're smart you'll go back to the hotel for a power nap. It's bound to be a late night." She swats me playfully, platinum bangles pealing. How very strange—if Lilly Benedict acknowledged me a week ago, I'd have fainted with shock. Jade even went as far as to suggest a few weeks back that I was a threat to her, since we're both the same dark-hair-blue-eyes-big-boobs type. I'm happy to learn that was merely Jade's cynicism talking.

"Good idea," I say now. "But I'm so excited—me, at a Gold Fire!" I still can't believe I was invited to this party. The legendary annual soirees are the most exclusive events on earth. Nobody knows in advance where it will take place, the one hundred guests whisked off to an undisclosed location, much to the pique of paparazzi.

"Shush up! You know you're not allowed to breathe a word."

I mime locking my lips, and once we exchange *"à bientôts!"* I shut my eyes to let the makeup artist swab my face.

"So you're going to the Gold Fire."

I open my eyes again and glance her way. "Yes! And here I thought I was going to have to get the recap from you tomorrow! I'm so excited!"

Jade, clearly, is not as excited.

"You are going, aren't you?"

Her eyes narrow into hard slits but not before I glimpse the hurt in them. "Not me. I've got better things to do than hang around with a bunch of egos in taffeta."

How was I supposed to know that Jade wasn't invited? I thought all the models were. Jade's exclusion from the party almost puts a damper on the evening for me. But once I'm dressed in tiers of Chanel chiffon and making my way through the streets of Paris in a Mercedes limo, I can't help but feel a glimmer of anticipation.

Like any female with a romantic bone in her body, I considered Paris the ultimate someday honeymoon spot. And like any young tennis player, I had the French Open on the brain. But never in a million years did I envision executing a coup d'etat on the City of Light, stunning the glitterati in fashion shows by day, hopping from bistro to VIP room to a genuine

Baroque castle by night. Two days ago, I had no clue what a Gold Fire was, and now I'm one of the privileged invitees.

As I arrive at the party, I wonder at the pile of paparazzi outside. If this is such an exclusive event, how did they find it?

Then I smile. What would be the purpose of all this Chanel chiffon and the hair and makeup if there were no press around? I suppose that every party has its "invited" paparazzi. Otherwise, why bother?

As I step out of the limo, I gasp at the sight I see: candles line the walk way up to a beautifully kept castle.

Guards block the front entrance. Before I can even open my mouth to give my name, I'm waved in. My face is my credential!

Inside, everyone is dressed as if they are at the Prince's ball in *Cinderella*. Gowns and furs swish by me. Men in tuxedos, or "smoking" jackets, as they call them here, hold out their arms to gallantly help the women up the stairs to the main ballroom.

The lighting is romantic—nothing brighter than a flickering candle—and the music is divine, some classical piece coming from an orchestra playing on the balcony. I feel like I have been transported back in time to another era, one of gallantry and finesse.

However, it isn't long after my arrival that I realize a party in a castle isn't all it's cracked up to be. In fact, it's a little stuffy, like partying in a museum. I wish Jade were here. But even when I told her I'd give her the address in case she wanted to keep up her bad girl rep and crash, she merely shrugged and gave me one of her inscrutable smiles.

Jade isn't the only model missing from this stiff-necked affair. Duncan isn't here, either, though I learned from Lilly, whom I've already air-kissed hello, that he was invited. That he's not here yet makes me wonder if he's coming. Does Duncan care so little for the scene that he would blow off a Gold Fire? Maybe he got a better offer, though anyone who is anyone in the industry is here tonight.

Unless he got an offer from another woman. The last time I saw him he was surrounded by a bevy of them; magazine editors, models, photographers. A couple of them looked like they were quite chummy with him, and if I didn't know Duncan better, I'd think he was enjoying the attention.

Actually, I don't know Duncan very well. He *could* this very moment be enjoying *someone's* attentions.

Stop obsessing, I remind myself. And just when I'm wondering how to keep my mind off Duncan, I notice someone riveted on me, his hair so black it makes his tuxedo look faded, his teasing smile setting me off-kilter. Once he's sure I'm aware of him, he begins to pursue me all over the palace—as if flirtation were an Olympic sport—until, finally, he maneuvers me onto the dance floor, taking me in his arms.

He's broad and tall, taller than I, which is nice, and now that I see him up close I can tell he's about my age. That's nice, too. He won't look at me while we spin and sway—I figure this is part of his game—but I feel the excitement in his breath as it tickles my neck. Waltzing is like walking to him, second nature, and I'm just glad I can follow his lead. Me, Ms. Independent, surrendering to the leonine strength of his embrace and the smooth, fleet moves of his tasseled Lanvins. By the third song, an older gentleman cuts in, and next thing I know I'm dancing with the entire European elite. Finally, I excuse myself, begging off to get a beverage. I'm parched, but the waiters tote only flutes of champagne.

"Evian, *s'il vous plaît?*" I request, leaning against a cool marble column while my eyes circle the vast ballroom, searching absently for Duncan and failing that, the distraction of my first partner, who was pretty dashing himself. But oh! Here he is, right beside me, two other men in tow.

"*Pardonez-moi, mademoiselle. Parlez-vous français?*" one of them asks formally, his accent not exactly French.

"*Un peu,*" I say—which means "a little" and is basically a lie; I know less than that. The men consult in a different tongue, and I surmise from their tone they find it amusing but not incomprehensible that I don't "*parlez.*" Then one of them asks, "You are the model American by the name of Mac Croft?"

The stilted English sounds funny, but I don't laugh. "That's me," I say.

"Here I am most honored to make you acquainted with His Extreme Highness Baron Alexander Igor Krossier of Romania."

Well, an evening with a baron! That's almost as good as my prince.

My raven-haired admirer takes my hand, murmuring "Lexi" into my ear. I smile my breezy smile, as though I'm introduced to royalty on a weekly basis, and let Lexi steer me to the dance floor again. Everything converges at once—the vaulted ceilings and gilt-framed portraits, the swirling violins, and the hottie with a title who pilots me expertly across polished marble. Without my even realizing, he pilots me into uncharted territory—an unlit alcove beneath a sweeping staircase—but we're dancing, still dancing, and Lexi braces the small of my back and bends me into a dip.

He holds me there a moment, my spine arched, the strands of hair I'd left out of my updo falling away from my face, his gaze penetrating mine. Then he smiles, shifting me back up again and I don't know whether it's the look in his eyes or the momentum of going from horizontal to vertical in seconds flat, but suddenly I'm breathless.

"*Pardonez-moi*," I say, exercising the few words of French I do know. When he doesn't let go of me, I wonder if I pronounced them wrong. "Excuse me . . . I . . . I need to go to the, um . . . *toilette*." Not so much because I have to pee, but because I need a moment to get my bearings. This dancing with a baron stuff is pretty heady, and I need to keep my cool with him. If I can. . .

Whether he understands me or not, he releases me. With a smile, and an awkward curtsy I realize is totally unnecessary, I make a dash for the bathroom, only to discover I have an entourage. Not only is Baron Alexander Igor Krossier my personal escort to the ladies' room, but his two cronies as well.

Reaching the door, I turn to smile again just as I'm about to slip inside, and suddenly I *am* inside—with Lexi.

I giggle nervously and attempt to explain to him that the female silhouette on the door he just went through is an international symbol meaning "no boys allowed." But then I realize Lexi has another international language on his mind.

Suddenly I'm up against the tile wall, the length of his hard body up against mine.

It occurs to me that it's been way too long since I've had a hard body up against mine.

And then his mouth is on my mouth, tongue tangling with mine in a way that makes me ache with longing.

"*Mmmmm . . . ,*" I murmur against his lips, wrapping my arms around his neck and pulling him closer.

In response, his hand moves up my rib cage, making me realize that despite how often I have hands on me—hands of dressers and designers—*no one* has touched me with any sort of intimacy in months. . . .

It feels good. Too good.

Especially when his fingers move to my breast in a caress that feels . . . *too* intimate.

"Lexi," I whisper, trying to catch my breath. "I need . . ."

"Yes," he answers. "I give it to you . . ."

"No," I say, smiling against his mouth, gently moving his hand away from my breast. "I need to go a little slower . . ."

He ignores me and I wish I knew more French than kissing, especially when he plants his erection between my legs. I can feel him throbbing against me, even through all those layers of Chanel. "Lexi—"

"I could take you right here. Very hard, very quick. You will like. You will pop your booty and then I keep your wet underpanties for my souvenir."

His English returns to him—clearly he learned it from a winning combination of romance novels and rap lyrics. "Lexi, *no!*"

He laughs and why wouldn't he? There's no one around. He's got his bodyguards posted outside the door. He could do whatever the hell he wants with me.

And he appears ready to, yanking up my dress and pulling my panties off in one quick maneuver.

"No!" I yell again, struggling against him to no avail, worried for my borrowed Chanel—as well as my morals. What was I, crazy, to let things get this far? I feel his flesh against my skin and then, spurred by a mix of fear and adrenaline, I react, taking the very sharp, very pointy, heel of my pump and plant it, very hard, very quick, somewhere in the vicinity of his big toe. The thin leather of his Lanvins hardly provides much protection. Lexi emits a regal yelp, releasing me long enough for me to scoot into the adjoining water closet.

Thank God the Europeans had the good sense to keep the toilet in a separate room. Otherwise, where else would I have escaped to, with his thugs posted outside?

But then it occurs to me that I'm trapped. At least until this royal dick gives up and goes away.

Fortunately, the baron doesn't have the stamina to wait me out. "I did not know that *no* means *no*—it never has before!" he shouts to me behind the door. "I am a baron! You should be lucky that I even look at you!" Within moments, I hear him exit, muttering a string of words I can only assume are curses. In this moment, I'm very glad I don't understand French!

I open the door a peek, and seeing the coast is clear, I slip out, taking the hall around back instead of the shorter route through the ballroom.

As I hit the cool outside air, I breathe deeply, looking at the melted candles that just a couple of hours before held such beauty.

I spot the valet and again, my name is not required. When my car pulls up in front of me, I pile in, pantyless, but a little smarter.

Alone in the Mercedes speeding me back to the center of Paris, I feel lonelier than I've ever felt. I cannot help but think about Duncan. The blue-jean boy from Tennessee has more inherent honor and refinement than that boorish baron in a monkey suit could hope for.

When the car pulls up to the hotel, I'm exhausted and eager to find Jade. I could use a little girlfriend comfort right now.

I head straight for her room, only to find the door ajar and, aside from an empty champagne bottle and a torn thigh-high stocking abandoned on the carpet, the whole suite has been cleared out.

Fourteen

As it turns out, Jade was not abducted, though that was my first
suspicion when I saw her room, abandoned as it was. Unless you
equate running off with a rock star with being kidnapped. Or
I should say, running *after* a rock star. Rather than sit around
the hotel room and brood over missing the Gold Fire, my best
friend boarded an earlier flight for London, with some idea
of attending the Roman a Clef show at the Brixton Academy.
Of course, Jade wouldn't condescend to simply *go* to a rock
concert and worship Roman Price and his battalion of leather-
clad bandmates from afar. Not the Jade I know and love. The
Jade who lived in London in her teens and befriended anyone
within spitting distance of the band she worshiped since pu-
berty. *That* Jade not only sat in press seats, she even got invited
to the backstage party.

That Jade, I learned when I trailed into London three days
behind her, is not only having a hot affair with none other than
Roman Price himself, she's falling in love. Or so she claimed
during the brief welcome I got when I arrived.

I would be happy for her. Really I would. Except I've never
felt so lonely and miserable in my life. Marooned in my hotel

room, all by myself—while my best friend does who knows what, who knows where. Who with? That I do know. Ever since I got to London, it's been "Roman, Roman, Roman!" Jade all aglow like the filament in a lightbulb.

I meet the Boy Wonder briefly backstage at Gareth Pugh, and while he certainly stands apart from the fashion pack, he's not at all what I expect. This lanky, almost gangly, guy with pale skin, close-cropped hair, and shabby clothes doesn't remotely resemble a rock star. Only his magnetic eyes command attention—when they're on you, pinning and dissecting you, it's impossible to look away. Fortunately, after a cursory examination and a sullen "hullo," Roman narrows his gaze back on Jade, grasping both her wrists in one of his large hands, he pulls her close and kisses her, devouring her mouth with his. "I'll see you later," he tells her. "I'll send a car. Round midnight, yeah. Wear the red thing. I like that."

The thuggish way he talks to her, giving orders in succinct sentences, melts Jade like a stick of butter. "Yeah," she says, her voice soft despite adopting the brusque cadence of his speech. "All right. I will."

The words are few, but the air between their bodies crackles with voltage. Then Roman kisses her again, taking her mouth like robbery, leaving Jade dazed. Do I wonder what she sees in him? Nope, not at all. A willful girl like Jade would have to fall for a guy even more selfishly insistent than she is; she'd trample anyone less adamant.

Once he's gone, Jade snaps out of her hypnotic state, and for the rest of the day brims with fierce, edgy energy. She seems to be on the phone every free second, taking and placing calls, making plans for later. That evening, when Adelaide from Models 1, an English affiliate agency, has the Delicious contingent dine with some execs from the OPT Group, Ltd., a prominent British advertising firm, Jade exhibits no sign of slowing down. Flitting around the table from suit to suit, she laughs at their jokes and sits on their laps. She's like one of those desserts that get splashed with brandy and set aflame. Later, Adelaide wants us all to move on to Farouche, a new private club in Knightsbridge, but Jade pleads a sudden headache, and I pick up the cue and say I'm tired, too. I may not ever bond with Roman Price, but I'll give him the benefit of the doubt, for Jade's sake. Besides, there is something intriguing about his anything-can-happen aura.

"So, where are we going?" I ask in the cab.

"What do you mean?" Jade wonders innocently, then tells the driver. "The Conrad Hotel, please."

I nudge her thigh. "Come on, Jade. I've heard you on your cell all day, and I know you're hooking up with people . . . with Roman."

"No, no—he canceled . . . everything fell through. I'm disappointed but it's all right. I really do have a pounder."

So why is she telling me this with her gaze glued to the window? Does she think I'm too uncool to party with rock-and-roll society? Is she just getting back at me for Gold Fire?

"Really," she insists.

But just after midnight I ring her room. And surprise, surprise—she's not in it. I try a few minutes later, in case she's in the bathroom, and a few minutes after that. It's obvious: Jade dumped me. Me! Now that she's met some guy and connected with his whole London crew, she leaves me flat. How could she be so thoughtless? Not that I wanted to hang out with the band—I don't even *like* Roman a Clef, and I'm not too crazy about Roman Price, either. Did he tell her to lose me, since clearly she does everything he says? I can't help but feel hurt. You don't just abandon your best friend, the person who's there to resuscitate you every time you crash and burn—which, if you're Jade, is a pretty regular occurrence. Ha! Talk about crash and burn, when Roman Price gets sick of her, Jade is bound to go off like a nuclear bomb!

I'm just leaving my hotel room the next morning when I get the news about Veronica Gesso. I didn't know her well, but we were living parallel lives, as she was also in the first six months of her career and doing her first European shows.

Which is why her death shakes me to the core.

The first person I seek out is Jade. And I find her, looking a bit like death warmed over herself, sitting in a makeup chair backstage at the Clare Tough show.

She appears to be sleeping. At least I hope she's sleeping.

"Jade?"

She cracks open one bloodshot eye.

"I'm so glad I found you. Have you heard what's happened?"

Her eye closes again. "Whatever it is, I'm sure it can wait."

"No, it can't," I say, shaking her.

"Please, Mac," she implores me. "If I don't get in a little nap before this show, I'm going to die."

"Jade, don't say that—don't *ever* say that," I say. "Veronica Gesso really is dead." The tears that rush into my eyes surprise me. I had only met Veronica once at the agency and I didn't know her very well. As a newer model, I guess I felt an empathy and sisterhood with her. I feel close to her in this moment. Like we were sharing the same struggle.

"Veronica . . . ?" Jade says with a frown.

I grab her hand. "It's so sad, so crazy. Everyone's talking about it. She collapsed on the catwalk at Thelbay and Royce yesterday, and they tried to cover it up . . . but she died on the way to the hospital."

"Died? As in death?" She sits up in the chair. "What . . . how . . . what of?"

"All they're saying officially is the cause of death was an infection, some mystery infection. But Jade . . ." I grip her wrist in my hand. "Jade, she weighed ninety-two pounds. And they found . . . between her toes . . . needle marks . . ."

Jade's expression becomes shuttered, her body stiffening.

"I just—it's so horrifying and scary. What does this business do to us?"

I look at her, waiting for something—compassion? Anger at the injustice of it? But what I get is a complete surprise.

"Oh, don't be such a baby," she snaps. "Only the strong survive, hon-bun. I thought you figured that out."

"How can you be like that?" I say, noticing for the first time the dark shadows under her eyes and the pale cast to her skin. "What is wrong with you? Do you know you were passed out just a minute ago and practically drooling?"

"Spare me the playback, Mac."

"No, Jade, you don't understand—I was mad, I was hurt and embarrassed that you left me, but not anymore. Now I'm just so worried about you, what could happen to you. I know you lied to me last night, I know you went out with Roman, left me behind because I'm too bourgeois for your hipster rock-star scene. . . ."

"What are you, spying on me?"

"No, I—listen to me. Forget what you did last night. Today—"

"Today I'm about to steal the show at Clare Tough. That's all I know. That's all that matters," she says, color rising to her cheeks as an energy fills her, surprising me, considering the state she was in five minutes ago. "I'm gonna shine today. And I'm going to do it my way, with balls-to-the-wall Jade Bishop punk rock panache. I'll show London who's boss, and I'm going to ride that wave all the way back to New York."

Then she narrows her eyes at me. "You needn't concern yourself with me; I'm not about to succumb to drug-induced anorexia like that B-list Brazilian wannabe. So instead of wringing your hands over me, worry about yourself—you're the one who doesn't eat. I, for one, have a bacon, egg, and cheese on its way down to me, and I only hope I can squeeze in a nap before it gets here!"

I stare at her. "Jade, please, don't be like that. I thought we were friends. And friends look out for each other and . . . I just really need to talk right now."

Then she smiles, a smile I recognize from her model smile-file, the innocent-angelic, which I'm discovering usually precedes something her listener doesn't want to here. "I hear you, Mac, I do. And your concern is very . . . sweet. But I assure you it's unwarranted. And right now *I* need to nap."

Then she shuts her eyes, waving her hand at me to go away, shutting me out. Again.

If Jade Bishop is haute couture's latest casualty, I haven't heard the news. I haven't seen her in more than a week. Not at the parties for the end of London Fashion Week. Not on the plane going home—I have no idea if we were even on the same flight.

My parents pick me up at Kennedy, and that is a trip in

itself. When I didn't see my mom after I cleared customs, I sat on the stairs leading to baggage pickup to wait, mindlessly watching the passersby. When I finally see her, I smile—and she looks right past me, as if I don't exist! With disbelief, I watch her look from face to face. I know I'm exhausted, but seriously, how could my own mother not recognize me? Involuntarily, tears begin to leak out of the corners of my eyes.

"Mom!" I call out and she looks at me startled, her eyes filled with surprise—and then worry. What must I look like to her? Skinny, pale, tired. Nothing like her sports fanatic, nutrition-crazy daughter.

"Melody," she says, sweeping me up into her arms, and I surrender to a sadness that has been stalking me all the way from Europe, my eyes burning, blinded by my tears.

My father is waiting for us in the car and together they whisk me back to Morristown, where I give them the few gifts I managed to pick up during my frantic trip through Europe, mostly from pharmacies near the hotel and airport gift shops. The house is so quiet—my brothers have already gone back to college, and I didn't even get to say good-bye.

Being home is a brief respite—a chance to sleep, watch DVDs. I try to answer questions about this country or that, but the ghost of Veronica Gesso lurks wherever I look. Fortunately, the tragic story hasn't reached suburban New Jersey. Then I'd be fielding things like: "Did you know her?" "Did you know she was on drugs?" "Did she look sick?" Or, "Maybe you should eat something. You don't want to wind up like that Veronica Gesso." My mother doesn't need any anti-model ammunition.

Chilling with family ought to make me feel serene, normal, grounded, and it does—except for the moment I want to scream. Could I possibly come from this provincial place of strip malls, softball fields, and culs-de-sacs? Am I really related to these people, with their TiVo and tube socks? And why oh why is there so much goddamn food in this house? Are we harboring a platoon in the backyard? Seventeen different types of cereal! Cookies in boxes, cookies in bags, cylinders of raw cookie dough begging to be baked, or eaten raw.

"Honey, I'm going to the market—you want to come?" my mom asks.

What, is there some variety of cheese she inadvertently left behind during her last foraging excursion? "No thanks," I say as nicely as humanly possible. If our kitchen cupboards are agony for me, how could I endure the aisles of a middle-class supermarket?

"Oh, . . . okay. Is there anything you want me to pick up for you?"

Is she insane? Deliberately trying to sabotage me?

I sigh, realizing I have to ask for something or she'll worry I'm not eating. "Maybe just some fruit, Mom. You've got great salad fixings—I'm going to make myself a big one for lunch."

It's not just to throw her off the scent. I *do* make a salad. But first I pour what's left of a bottle of ranch dressing down the drain, so I won't be tempted. This is a crucial time—I can't afford to blimp. The major magazines are gearing up for their big shoots. Now that the shows are over, the magazines will shoot those same collections. Francesca and Renee are confident I can get *Vogue*—real *Vogue*, not just *Teen Vogue*—*Elle* and *T, The New York Times Fashion Magazine*. Plus maybe some designers will book me for their ad campaigns. Those are my next hurdles and I aim to soar above them without breaking a sweat.

Something happened to me in Europe, something kicked in. The death of Veronica Gesso, and Jade's callous reaction, made me realize that no one is truly your friend; this is a cold, callous business I am in. But the accolades I received overseas, particularly in Paris, showed me how far I can go with modeling if I want it bad enough, and I've decided: I do. How else would a girl like me get to see the world? Or make this kind of money. I'm eighteen; if I'm smart I can do this for five years and retire a millionaire, still go to college if I want and pay for it out of pocket, no student loans—just like everyone says. Maybe get my family a house by the shore so we can all vacation together. Set up financial independence for the future, for my own family someday—all that stuff. And just on a personal level, achievementwise, I want to see if I can really make it. Yes, I know I'm good, but how good? Can I land Lancôme or Revlon, be a "face" like Lilly Benedict? Maybe segue into acting—I think Uma Thurman was a model once.

But I have to do it right. Veronica Gesso wanted it bad, and it killed her—a mixed bag of substances in her blood and a body mass index (BMI) of 14.3. Of course, in the aftermath, the industry is all in an uproar, talking about drug tests for models and making it so that a girl must have a minimum BMI of 18 to work the collections. Talk about the fashion police. Maybe that will help, maybe it won't—bottom line you have to take care of yourself. Deliberately, I tear up some low-sodium turkey breast and add it to my salad. Rather than measure a specific ration of sunflower seeds, I just sprinkle them on. What about this nonfat Swiss? I sample it—it has the consistency of plastic and tastes like it, too, but the package says it's got calcium so I throw some of that on top. Now, doesn't that look healthy and satisfying? Yeah, sure, whatever. Taking care of myself—that's what I've got to do.

What about Jade—who'll take care of her? At times I feel as though I shouldn't even associate with that girl. People judge you by the company you keep, and Jade's company is . . . I guess "erratic" would be the kindest way to put it. Maybe I should look into finding a place in New York so I won't be forced to stay with her—or worse, at the Valencia, on those late nights. I can get a roommate—someone stable, someone sane. I'm sure the agency must know other girls looking for an apartment and I can certainly afford to share a place. But who am I kidding—sane and stable aren't words you hear a lot in fashion. In fact, they're unfashionable. And to me, modeling and Jade Bishop are inexorably linked—I just can't see doing this without having her to bounce things off and commiserate with and laugh about.

It'll be difficult going it alone. This is already a lonely business—traveling alone, working alone, eating on location alone, going to go-sees alone. But I have to make a decision—Jade or my career. I have to let Jade take care of Jade. I'm going to be too busy to moonlight as her nursemaid, and besides, she thinks she knows what's best. She doesn't want my help. She thinks she's got it under control. Whatever "it" is.

On the pretext of needing to pick up things I'd left at her place during Fashion Week, I text Jade and ask her if I can stop by her apartment.

When the text comes back, "anytime, hon-bun. I'm home right now," it feels as though nothing has changed between us.

I want to believe it's true, but I know it's not. I have changed. And I can't go back to the way things were.

"Hey," she says, opening the apartment door, a pint of ice cream in hand. She leads me back into the kitchen, perching herself on a stool before the island at the center.

"What're you doing?" I ask.

"Not much. Drowning my sorrows." She holds out the pint to me and I take it from her, which causes her to look at me, really look at me for the first time since I arrived. I dig in, sans my usual harangue about empty calories or cholesterol or how I'm going to be America's fattest model.

She raises an eyebrow.

I smile. "I've missed you."

She smiles back. "I've missed you, too."

"But—"

That eyebrow shoots up again. "Oh? So there's a *but*?" She takes back the pint.

"Fine, make it an *and*," I reply. "As in . . . *and* I intend to concentrate very seriously on my career. I think I can really make it, but I'll need to focus. I can't always be watching out for you, Jade, cleaning up your messes."

She cuts her eyes at me. "Oh, like I never helped you out of a jam?"

"Okay, point taken. You have been there for me." She holds my gaze. "But that's different. When I need you it's because the situation is screwed up, not because of some poor judgment call I made. With you, Jade, I just never know *what* you're going to do—but I do know you can be very inconsiderate at times."

She shrugs, her gaze on her spoon as she mines for pecans. "You're right—I can be a first-class selfish twat. Maybe it's an only-child-of-a-broken-home thing. Or a you-only-hurt-the-one-you-love thing. What can you do?"

I sigh. "Nothing, I guess. You're you, Jade, and I'm me."

She passes back the pint. "Finish it." I take two bites, sliding into the chair across from hers. We look at each other.

"I *do* love you, you know," she says.

"I know that, Jade. And I love you, too."

Then I smile, realizing that somehow in all this madness, we have managed to forge something real. Something that might carry us through whatever obstacles come our way.

Jade and I resume our friendship, fall back into our pattern of cell phone calls and texts between go-sees and shoots, the odd cup of tea shared at Leaf, and though it doesn't feel the same as before, I'm grateful to have *some* sort of camaraderie again in a business where friends are few and far between. Not that I have time for friends; any leisure time I have is more limited than ever, now that Francesca and I have our hearts set on a big cover and a big ad campaign.

When we do talk, it's usually about the sad state or our lack of a love life. Although Jade enjoyed several idyllic AWOL days with Roman in the English countryside (his manager owns a cottage there), she left not knowing when (if!) she'll see him again. As for me, I haven't even seen Duncan since the few glimpses I got of him in Europe. Rumor has it the shows were a big success for him, too. There's talk that he's up for the Calvin Klein campaign. I'm happy for his success. The grand irony is that we're both the same—ambitious, hardworking. And it's that very commonality that keeps us apart.

Maybe we can retire together in a few years. The thought makes me smile.

The cool thing is Jade doesn't come off as though her

relationship is more valid than mine, even though hers has been consummated and all I've got so far is an unrequited crush. She acts as if Duncan and I are an "us," and that helps validate . . . us.

Really I have nothing to complain about. Late October is a glorious time in New York City. The weather is getting cooler, and there's a general rush of excitement in the air. I window shop from appointment to appointment, even allowing myself to plunk down a silly amount of cash on an Hermes scarf, a little gift to myself for my success at the collections. I'm wearing it today because I've got another potentially big meeting—one of those accidental-on-purpose run-ins, à la the one I had with Albert Lazar.

Renee and I head to the flower district—a full city block devoted to blooms, blossoms, and plants. This is where florists come to select their wares, but it's open to the general public, too—any member of the general public nuts enough to require fresh-cut flowers before sunrise. Apparently, that includes the fabled photographer known only as the Corsican.

"Whatever you do, don't go near any carnations. The Corsican abhors carnations," Renee warns as we wander from stall to stall. The aroma makes me light-headed, and I feel a bit clumsy amid the hustle and bustle—this is a place of business, after all. Then all at once a hush falls over the immediate vicinity as an older gentleman with a deep tan and a sweep of silver hair browses our way, his arms laden with lilies, larkspur, and amaryllis. Everyone seems to know him, clearing him a path with subdued smiles.

Renee waits until he makes a selection from a nearby stall, then springs into action. "Ah, what a delight it is to see the Corsican!" she says with reverence.

"And you, my dear? Ah, . . . it is you, the skinny kitten!"

"Oh, the Corsican remembers me! I'm so pleased. That work we did together for YSL in the eighties is perhaps the pinnacle of my career."

"Perhaps?" the Corsican raises a snowy eyebrow as if offended, but lets it go. "And what brings the skinny kitten out before the dewdrops?"

Renee nudges me forward. "Moch Croft, my latest discovery, simply adores flowers, and as a reward for her extraordinary work in the collections, I told her I would bring her here."

The Corsican tilts his head as if deliberating adding me to his bouquet.

"Hello," I say with my three-quarter smile—the one that's excited yet a trifle shy.

"*Ah*, the chestnut orchid," the Corsican says. "You are pleased to meet me."

Huh? "Oh, yes, I am so very pleased to meet . . . the Corsican."

"And you, the skinny kitten, you are as sly as ever. You have brought the chestnut orchid here for me to pluck. Surely you're aware I'm in the throes of a new book for Taschen—a labor of love."

"But of course! I follow the Corsican's endeavors avidly. I also know you will photograph Dior's spring palette and do a pictorial for *Bazaar*."

The Corsican purses his lips. "*Ah*, not even the Corsican can live on beauty alone." He dips his nose into his bouquet and inhales deeply as if to purge this injustice. "So. The skinny kitten will bring the chestnut orchid to the Corsican's studio this week. Contact the porcelain frog—you are acquainted with the porcelain frog, who assists me?"

"But of course! The porcelain frog and I go way back! Oh, I am so glad for our serendipitous rendezvous!"

The Corsican looks down his nose. "Indeed . . ."

Okay, these people are so weird! Good thing for me I can keep a poker face.

When I relate this surreal encounter to Jade later, she cracks up—but she's impressed. "The Corsican's a celebrated eccentric—makes Karl Lagerfeld look like a frat boy," she says. "But shooting with him is huge, hon-bun. And if you think meeting him in the flower mart was whack, wait till you enter his personal domain."

She isn't kidding. The Corsican hires me for a book he's doing on fruit. That's right—fruit. He's got all sorts of actors and athletes and models, and regular people, too, posing with pineapples, mangoes, cherries, et cetera. Cool with me—I love fruit.

The vibe in the studio is one of purposeful tranquillity. Several fountains lend a gentle burble to the air, and nobody speaks above a whisper. Everything's white like a hospital—only cleaner. It's strange, but a refreshing change from the loud thumping hip-hop and screeching personnel of a typical photo shoot. Besides, I've been told to expect oddity, so I'm determined to go with the flow. First, I'm asked to disrobe completely and then I'm given a robe. Next, the hairstylist shrouds me with his sheet and proceeds to give me a simple, stick-straight blowout. My makeup is very basic, too, and takes forever, since it's supposed to look natural. Then, instead of being led to the dressing area, a sharp-featured man I assume is responsible for my attire stands me under a bright light.

"All right, Mac, remove your robe!" he whispers . . . authoritatively.

Knowing the drill, I shrug off my robe.

The dresser begins to scrutinize my body.

"Excuse me, what are you doing?"

"Checking for irregularities. Blotches, splotches . . . Aha! Carole! Come! I see a trace of tan line!"

As Carole daubs concealer on my shoulder, then proceeds to apply foundation to the entire rest of my body, it dawns on me that my costume for the shoot is to be my birthday suit! "Wait a second, I can't . . . can I? . . . I need to speak to someone. I need to speak to the Corsican!" It's extremely difficult to keep your decibel level down when you're as upset as I am right now.

"Calm yourself!" hisses the dresser. "The Corsican is waiting for you on set. He does not like noise!"

I glare at him, grab the styling sheet, and drape it toga-style, then march off, trying not to shiver at the clammy dull feel of my skin covered in foundation. How am I going to get this stuff off, anyway? I'm wearing my brand-new leather pants from Italy, and I don't want to get makeup on them.

The Corsican has replicated the Garden of Eden in his studio, and as I approach he is holding my prop—a perfect red apple. Okay, I get it—but I can't do it.

"Sir, I'm so terribly sorry, I had no idea—" I stammer softly, while the dresser, and the assistant called the porcelain frog, who's been alerted to my indignation, gesture and murmur to convey what's up.

"*Shh! Shh!* The chestnut orchid is dismayed, this I see, but not to worry," the Corsican soothes. "The Corsican is shooting the portrait only. The body will not be seen."

Phew! I think. "Oh, thank you so much—I'll just run and put my pants back on."

"Oh, no no no. You cannot do that!" the Corsican says, quiet yet absolute. "You are to *be* Eve! And you cannot *be* Eve in clothes! It is impossible!"

Moment of truth. Either bolt right now, or *be* Eve. Walk out on one of the most brilliant photographers of the century, or *be* Eve. Let my fear and modesty rule me, or *be* Eve.

I choose to *be* Eve.

A thousand shades of green surround me. A perfect red apple rests in my palm, plucked from a bag of one hundred apples bought just for this occasion. I am naked to the world—through the lens. I am the first woman on earth, uncorrupted and un-afraid and free of shame. I am beautiful and I am innocent and I am about to alter the fate of all humankind. I am Eve.

And then the Corsican calls a stylist and adds the one thing missing from this scenario: the serpent. I try not to scream—the Corsican does not like noise!—though I must have gone pale because suddenly the stylist is assuring me that the crea-ture he's wrapping around my naked body is harmless. I try to blank out what's actually happening, no easy task once I'm holding the full weight of the reptile artfully draped around my shoulders.

The snake is cool on my skin and sliding ever so slowly tighter around my waist. Funny, I always thought snakes were slimy, but this one is dry to the touch, his tongue slithering in and out in rhythm. I try to imagine that he is as scared as I am. Then I think of the slithery beguiler who offered Eve the apple; also known as the devil himself. At least he's nowhere to be seen on set, as far I know. Only later, at Jade's, where I'm spending the night tonight, I'm forced to come face-to-face with him.

Fifteen

It's been a very long, very trying, very naked, very slithering day, and I'm looking forward to some tea and sympathy—not to mention pajamas. Instead, chez Bishop is a loony bin, the chimpanzee cages at feeding time. Roman a Clef have descended on NYC, and Jade's place has been transformed into what looks like a welcome bash. Just what I don't need right now. Only what can I do? Order everyone out? It's not my apartment, and besides, I'd look like a fuddy-duddy. *Slap on a happy face, girl*, I tell myself as I force myself into the spirit.

"Ma-a-a-a-c!" Jade comes barreling toward me, lit up like a wrestling match between Times Square and Tokyo. "Guess who's here!"

"*Um*, the entire U.S. Navy?"

"No, silly!" She gives me a squeeze. "Roman! And the band. And . . . well . . . just everyone. Oh God, I was gobsmacked. He just . . . appeared! And he'll be here a week at least—they're doing a video. It's so amazing." She links her arm through mine and herds me into the melee, lowering her voice to say, "Oh, hon-bun, if only Duncan were here it would all be so perfect. . . ." then booms to the room at-large, doing her mock hip-hop MC, "Yo, everyone! Mac Croft is in da house! *Whooooo!*"

This is very weird. I'm accustomed to seeing celebrities nowadays—the circles I travel in, the clubs I hit—but bumping into them in the place where I'll be resting my head tonight is a different story. There's an Olsen twin on our terrace, a Madden brother pulling a beer from our fridge.

"Hey, hi, you know what kind of cheese this is?" asks Mischa Barton, tentatively sniffing a hunk of yellow substance.

How would I know? I feel like I haven't eaten cheese in years. "No, sorry, I don't," I say, filling the kettle at the sink. Mischa Barton, fresh from the cover she just did for *Elle*, is leaning against the same kitchen counter I do every day. And she's smelling cheese. See what I mean about weird?

Taking my mug of chamomile into the living room, I decide to do a once-around mingle before escaping for the bedroom. Only this proves to be harder than I thought. Every square inch of me has begun to ache, payback for sitting perfectly still all those hours in the Corsican's studio. About halfway through my circuit it occurs to me that I haven't seen the guest of honor yet. I hope I will. My first impression of Roman Price wasn't the best, and I've got a mental block against him because of that night Jade left me in London. This is something I need to get over, if he's going to be my best friend's boy. Half an hour later when I still haven't run into him, I have to give up—I feel as though if I don't lie down, I'll fall down.

I'm glad Jade's bedroom is down a hall and a ways away from the central living areas. With the roar of the party behind me, I'm so ready to crash I pull off my top without bothering to turn on the light. Actually, I don't need to, I realize, seeing the glow from the desk lamp. . . .

"Hullo, Mac."

At the sound of my name, I just about jump out of my skin. "Who's that?" I tug my top back on in a hurry.

He's sitting at the desk, the bulk of his black-clad form a shadow made of mass. He swivels the elastic neck of the lamp toward his face. "Surprise!"

The hollows of his eyes are caves. "Roman . . ."

"Scare you?"

"Yes—a little." Actually, a lot, but I feel my pulse return to normal.

"Sorry." Scraping the chair along the parquet floor, he opens himself to me, his long legs extending. "Just had to get away from the madding crowd a bit. You know how it is."

"I guess," I say. "I know I couldn't deal with it."

"Bad day?"

Roman doesn't ramble, yet his economy of words urges me to speak. "No, not bad. Just . . . difficult. I had to work with a snake—you know, the animal kind—and it was a tense situation." I lean my neck to one side, kinks and cramps attacking muscles and tendons I didn't know I had, but Roman's steady study—intent and impersonal as a cat—makes me uncomfortable in another way. I catch my hands in front of me, as if reciting, and go on. "The photographer is a living legend, so shooting with him is a feather in my cap. But, well, if you'd have told me a year ago I'd be sitting still as a statue in a bogus garden without a stitch of clothing on for ten hours straight, I'd've said no way."

I know Roman's looking at me, and I wish I could see his eyes, but he'd swiveled the lamp again, putting me in the spotlight, himself in darkness. "Got to respect the unexpected," he says.

What's that supposed to mean? I wonder.

"I'll be off, then—give you your room back."

Though it's not exactly my room, I happily take him up on his offer. "I'd appreciate that. I'm not usually this antisocial, and it *is* nice to see you again, Roman, but I'm really out of it."

"S'cool," he says. Yet he doesn't move. "Mac?"

"*Hmm?* Yes?"

"Want to do a spot?"

"A what?"

Roman maneuvers the light onto the surface of the desk, and I see what he's really been up to in here. "A spot—oh, right, a line in American. A bump."

I can barely speak. What is it? Cocaine? How—he—I can't believe this! Yet of course I do believe it, absolutely and completely. Here I am, talking to him, trusting him, while he's been using Jade's bedroom as a drug den. "No . . ." is all that squeaks out.

"You sure? It's the finest . . ." He stops, chuckles. "Oh, right. You're a healthy person. Jade'd told me. All apologies." Then he bends his head over the desk and snorts up everything in front of him in one fell swoop. And still he sits there. "Mac, confidentiality agreement, yeah? I'd prefer if Jade didn't know about this. Quite a little Hoover, that one, and the truth is I'd rather she didn't . . . partake. Wish she were more like you actually. Body is a temple and all that."

Finally, he stands, twirls the wrists of his big bony hands. "Funny, innit? Only in the country six hours and already hooked up. One of the perks of what I do. Everybody wants to turn on the rock star." Roman rubs his nose, inspects his fingers, licks them quickly. "Thing is, I can handle it. Jade, though. If she got bad . . ." He shakes his head once. "Be a pity."

* * *

Guess I glazed over during those just-say-no sermons in middle school. It was always a no-brainer for me—an athlete, a scholar, I had no interest in polluting myself. I also kinda like the way my brain works when sober; I never wanted to mess with the formula. So now I'm scouring the net for a refresher course on the effects of various drugs, as well as indications someone you know might be abusing. Jade's my closest friend in the business, and I'm finally seeing her capacity for self-destruction—I can't pretend it's okay by me if she kills herself with drugs. So although I pledged I wouldn't be her nanny anymore, here I am, her narc.

Only I don't know. Maybe I'm overreacting. Some people take drugs without becoming addicted. Jade could have a history of dabbling with pills, pot, powders—the whole smorgasbord of mortality testers—dating back to third grade. Yet she manages to function . . . in her trademark dysfunctional way. Trouble is something's different now—something tall, pale, and British.

Not that I'm blaming Roman; in fact, I believe what he said about wishing Jade wouldn't "partake." And I doubt she's doing it for his sake, to look cool for him or whatever—Jade answers to no one but herself. Still, Roman's presence is ominous. As he himself admitted, he basically has people throwing drugs at him left and right. Hang out with him and you're bound to get hit in the crossfire. Which is why I'm going to Roman a Clef at the Bowery Ballroom tonight—to be a sort of deflective shield.

"So hon-bun, where do you want to watch?" Jade asks when I meet her in front of the club. "From backstage you're closer, and you can hobnob, but in the audience you're part of the *experience.*" In her skinny pants and sky-high heels, T-shirt torn up and reconstructed, silky ropes of hair in an undone bun, she's glowing with life, on top of the world. A full 180 from the wraith who could barely drag herself around the apartment two days ago. Jade swore it was the flu, but I'm skeptical of everything she says now. Seeing her tonight, it hurts to think a girl this incandescent would risk it all . . . for what? some numbed-up, dumbed-down sensation that wears off in a few hours?

"You decide," I tell her.

She arranges a laminate badge around my neck. "This is for later," she says, and leads me into the crowd for the *"experience."*

It's pretty packed inside, but Jade's annoyed. "When is America going to get with the program?" she scoffs. "God, the guys are massive in Europe. Their Brixton show, there was like three times as many people."

I reserve judgment till about three minutes into the concert; then, for lack of a better term, I'm hooked. Basically I'm into pop, radio tunes you can sing along to, and Roman a Clef are definitely dark. But they play with a contagious urgency, as though it means so much to them, and at the same time there's this pervasive sense of pleasure—they're having a terrific time up there. It's like a tennis match, except all four guys are on the same team, and there's no competition. They're all in it together—the band, the fans and of course their raucous ringleader. While his offstage persona is deliberately aloof, Roman goes for the jugular in performance, stalking back and forth in a simple, single-breasted Prada, his lanky extremities seemingly made of galvanized rubber, his voice a large animal off its leash. Guys and girls, straight and gay, succumb to his charisma. I feel the crush and movement of the crowd around me lulled by his voice into a single big mass, moving and twisting as if one. During one song he's pelted with roses as if on cue. By the end of the number he's practically knee-deep, and once the applause dies down Roman selects one from the pile, throws back his head, opens his mouth and does a sword-swallowing routine with it, thorns and all.

Jade hoots and hollers from start to finish, and when Roman dedicates an encore to her—well, what he says is, "This one is for me moppet with a heart the size of China"—I think she's going to swoon at my feet. Backstage, however, the whole vibe changes. Roman has to "receive" people, a lot of them girls, and Jade can't very well force herself between her man and his fans. So she flits from the bar to the catering table, imposing fun.

"You all right?" I ask her at one point.

"Why do you ask?" she whinnies. "Because I've eaten about twelve cupcakes in rapid succession? You've got to try them, Mac, they're from Magnolia."

At least she's not on anything other than sugar and champagne—one of the things I learned in my AP pharmacology class is that drugs tend to ruin the appetite. Although Jade's appetite being what it is, maybe she's immune.

"Come on, Mac, live a little. Splurge!" She hands me one and we "clink" cupcakes, but after one bite she lopes off to greet a latecomer and I immediately dump the cupcake. There are people I know, too, so I wander—a shallow conversation here, a photo op there. All I'm really doing is biding my time, looking for an opening, clocking Roman's every move. And when I finally see him duck out to take a call on his cell, I hover till he's finished, then. . .

"Hey, Roman," I walk his way, attuned to the echo of my stilettos. "I really enjoyed the show."

"Oh, hullo Mac. Thanks so much for coming."

"So, I wanted to talk to you—if you have a second."

He sighs as though he knew this was coming. "Sure. What's on your mind?"

I make my voice flippant. "Well, I was wondering what your plans are. I mean, are you off on an American tour now? Or do you need to go back to London?"

"Or do we have a pressing engagement on Mars? That suit you, Mac?"

Heat floods my cheeks. "Am I that transparent?"

"A veritable Baggie, I'm afraid," he says, but his smile is actually friendly. "Look, Mac, you care about Jade. I understand. But if you *know* her, you know she's bound to do as she pleases. Hook or crook. That's Jade."

He's right. "I know—and I'm not saying you're leading her astray, Roman."

"Nor am I the only bloke in New York with a smack connection."

Smack? Oh my God! This is way worse than I ever imagined. A light-headedness overcomes me, and I actually start to stumble. Roman reaches for my arm, propels me toward a more secluded recess of the backstage area. I lean against the wall, glad that we're farther from potentially prying eyes. "Heroin!" I hiss.

Roman merely shrugs. "Or what have you. Bit of a human rubbish bin, your girl. She has no drug of choice—prefers to mix and match." He lets this sink in. Behind me the wall is a cliff of ice; I hug myself to quell the shivers.

"So to answer your questions," Roman goes on, "no, I

needn't return to London just yet, and an American tour is not on the itinerary, either—this New York date was just a lark, since we just shot a video here. Truth is I could hang about indefinitely. Maybe even experience a typical American Thanksgiving, yeah." He watches for my reaction, but the horror I feel fails to register on my face—it's like I've morphed into marble. "But I won't," he finally continues. "Look, Mac, I care about Jade, too; I think she's a brilliant, marvelous, magical girl. I may even be in love with her. So even though I can't protect her from herself, I *can* protect her from me."

Wait—what does that mean? "Are you . . . going to break up with her?"

"Been thinking about it. For her own good, of course." For the first time, I see a wet warmth in Roman's onyx eyes, and before he casts them away I can tell it's nothing less than tears. "Hard thing to do, you know? Breaking up with her is going to mess me up and drive me mad, but I think we might be better apart. She might be better."

My fingers fly to his arm, a gesture of comfort and support. "Roman, I . . . I'm so sorry! But I think it's the right thing."

"You'll be around to pick up the pieces. I mean, should her heart happen to crumble."

"Yes, I'll be around."

He bites his lip so hard I expect to see it bleed, but it seems to steel him, replace his facade of detachment. "Well, we've got a deal then."

"We've got a deal. And I've got to say, Roman, you really are a good person."

"*Shhh*, now. Don't be spreading that around. Wreck my reputation."

That's how we are, standing in the semi-dark, our smiles

small, my hand still on his arm, and our eyes full of secret, when Jade discovers us.

Something is very wrong. Jade's acting like everything is normal, so that's how I know. She never made a peep about discovering Roman and me in what could have been seen as a compromising position. Nor has she said a word about their relationship, which should no longer exist—and I can't imagine Jade taking the breakup in stride. Unless Roman lied to me, and had no intention of ending it. Or—uh-oh—what if his way of dumping a girl is the dreaded, ungentlemanly just-stop-calling routine? That would be the worst. Here's Jade, blithely going around like all is cool, assuming he's just busy with rock-star affairs, when he could be in Knightsbridge by now.

One way or the other I'll find out tonight. Heidi Klum is hosting the Models Masquerade, probably the most glamorous Halloween event in history. Designers will dress the Delish contingent in costumes and amazing masks that will be auctioned for AIDS research at midnight. Alice + Olivia is doing me as a sylphlike swan—an all-white matte jersey and ostrich feather gown plus a headpiece of Swarovski crystals. The party is a very big deal, celebrities and socialites and captains of industry uniting at the witching hour for a media-worthy charitable cause. If Jade and Roman are still a couple, he'll certainly be her plus-one.

What will I say if I see him? What will I say if I don't? Why did I get myself so involved in matters of Jade's heart? Maybe because my own heart is still stuck in limbo. I'm musing on this, alone in Jade's apartment, where I'm camping out in anticipation of the party, when our outfits arrive.

"Where do you want these, miss?" One of the building's porters slouches in the doorjamb with a rolling rack.

"Bring them to Jade's room, please," I direct him without hesitation. Usually for these events, we primp and preen together; it's our bonding ritual. So why should tonight be different? No reason—except for this nagging feeling the earth is about to go off its axis.

The costumes are sheathed in garment bags, and the first one I unzip happens to be Jade's. It's Rock & Republic, silver and black, gauzy, and, frankly, a little trashy. The designers and models were matched up by lottery, we had no input, but it wound up that my outfit suits my style, while this one is pure Jade. I couldn't possibly wear such a thing . . . could I? On impulse, I take it off the rack and go to the triptych mirror, holding it to my torso. The flared skirt is minuscule, with chains at the waist crisscrossing the belly to form the lines of a halter top.

"What are you *doing*?"

I spin around. "Oh, hey, Jade. Our costumes came."

"I can see that." She snatches the hanger. "This one's mine, I believe."

"I know," I say. "Hey, what do you think the masks will do to our makeup? I know it's Halloween and all, but I really don't want to look like a freak after midnight."

Jade shrugs distractedly, throws the outfit on her bed.

"You'd better shower," I remind her. "We need to be there at ten."

"Yeah," she says, but instead of the bathroom she heads for her dressing table and litters the surface with every compact, crayon, and tube in her possession. "Look at all this crap, what a mess," she mutters to herself as she starts rearranging the cosmetic mayhem.

I stand behind her. "Jade, is everything okay?"

Fixed on her task, she doesn't answer me. I lay a hand on her shoulder and she twists and jerks, sending lip gloss flying. "What!?" she shrieks.

Her eyes are wide and wild, with two tiny pinpricks in the center. Thanks to my online crash course in Druggie 101, I know that indicates some kind of speed.

"Mac, what?" Jade repeats, carefully, feigning sobriety.

Ripped up with anger, I want to slap her. I want to shake some sense into her and whatever she's high on out of her. But I can't—I love her too much. Standing there uselessly I summon a smile, annoyed with myself for inability to confront her. "Nothing, never mind. Just get moving, girl. We've got an entrance to make."

I'm forced to put my apprehension aside once we step into the Models Masquerade. The setting is dazzling, a former church that functioned as the Limelight nightclub in the eighties and was more recently rechristened as Avalon. Inside, they've rigged a mechanism to illuminate the stained glass as if the sun were streaming in. Our costumes probably contribute as well; the designers have outdone themselves to present the most magically turned out crowd New York City has ever seen. Even the music suits the mood—mysterious, entrancing New Age. Whatever the reason, I feel transported—lifted, secure, and serene.

The atmosphere seems to have a calming effect on Jade, too. As we glide through the room, pausing to chat or pose, her laughter is breezy, not brittle, and her comments flattering and sincere to everyone we meet. When she pats my arm—her palm reassuringly cool and dry—and tells me she is going off to talk to a photographer she knows, I promise to catch her later without the slightest trepidation. Tomorrow will likely turn topsy-turvy again, but tonight I know everything will be all right.

Circulating solo amid all the beautiful strangers is a funny kind of thrill. Chances are I'm acquainted with plenty of these people, but tonight I have no idea who's who. Except for one beautiful stranger who, despite the tawny suede suit and rosewood antlers depicting him as a stag of the forest, is not a stranger at all. Not to me. I know him instantly—by his stance, the set of his head and the breadth of his shoulders. I know him by his essence and his aura, and I know that as much as I've missed and mused about him, this reunion is so perfect it makes all the missing and musing worthwhile.

We don't speak—there's no reason to. We dance, but it's not really dancing; it's simply, sublimely, *being*. We play the game of ambiguity when all is pure clarity. And when midnight strikes and the masks come off, the whole assembly seems to be cheering for us, though we hardly hear them.

"Hi, Duncan," I finally say.

"Hey, Mac. I knew it was you."

"I did, too."

"I know."

A few heartbeats pass as we revel in the knowing, and then Duncan says, almost shyly. "Still, it sure is wonderful to *see* you."

"You, too."

He came back. He came back to *me*. How do I know this? Because of the way my chin tilts and my eyes close and the intricate colorful patterns of the stained glass are still there, only now exploding in my brain, as Duncan begins to kiss me.

The touch of his mouth on mine is so gentle at first, I feel as though I'm imagining the kiss. Then he parts my lips with his, his tongue tangling in mine in an intimate dance that sends a shivery warmth through me. Almost involuntarily, I press my body into his, and feel his body come alive. *Mmmm.* . .

And then, just as suddenly, he breaks the kiss, his gaze on mine, his eyes lush—even more beautiful now that they are filled with desire. Then he leads me to a quiet corner, where we can finally be alone. . . .

"Remember the last time we were together in a spa situation?" I remark as Jade and I sit side by side in pedicure thrones. We are here for what I call "the overhaul": mani-pedi, body scrub, and all the de rigueur unwanted hair removal procedures from eyebrow to bikini. This ought to be a tax write-off—looking flawless, after all, is my stock-in-trade now. "How freaky was that!" I add with the elated chuckle-sigh that seems to punctuate my every sentence lately.

"See—I told you you'd look back on it and laugh someday."

"I didn't believe you . . . but of course now I know anything is possible." I let out another sigh.

"So . . . how is Mr. Wonderful?"

"Oh . . . wonderful," I answer, remembering what it was like to kiss Duncan. Then I relive the excited shimmer I felt when he breathed an invitation to his place in my ear. Just his breath on my neck alone made me shiver, and I almost succumbed to his request. But I didn't.

His seductive offer *did* make me remember Jade's warning about men in the business being gay or trying hard to prove they are not gay by sleeping with every woman in their sights. Even more frightful are the bisexuals. You can't tell which way they are going to go and I can't imagine sleeping with a guy one night who might want to sleep with my brother the next night.

I don't think that's what's really going on with Duncan, but I just felt that since we waited this long, we could wait a little longer to get to know one another.

What I know so far is absolutely dreamy. I sigh again, then glance at Jade and remember that her love life is not so dreamy at the moment.

"Jade, please." I begin, "I can't sit here carrying on about Duncan when I know something happened between you and Roman. And you haven't even told me what it is."

"Nothing to tell," she says, with an air of indifference I know can't be authentic. "He's just . . . out. I was not, apparently, entitled to an explanation." Sighing, she takes her foot from the tub and lays it in the pedicurist's palm. "You know how stingy guys are when it comes to sharing their feelings. Especially when they haven't got any."

"You mean he didn't say anything at all?"

"You got it. It's as though I never existed."

"But Jade, that's terrible!" I would have thought Roman might have at least given her *some* sort of explanation. Whatever kinder feelings I had about him during our last meeting quickly evaporate.

"Yes. Well. Such things occur."

"And you're . . . not upset?"

"Naturally, I'm upset. But what would hysteria accomplish? I have to move on, be adult about it. I'm managing."

I just hope she's not managing by self-medicating.

"So tell me about Duncan," she says, "You can talk about him—I know you're dying to," she assures me. "Besides, I'm a captive audience."

Well, that's true—we're both up to our shins in suds.

So I tell her. How we spent the rest of the masquerade ball huddled close together on one of the couches. How every moment I looked into his eyes I willed him to kiss me. How he shared some intimate details about his life back in Tennessee. I loved hearing about how close he is to his family. It made me feel more connected to him, since I come from a fairly close-knit family myself. "Do you know he sends back like, *half* of everything he makes to his family in Tennessee? Apparently his family is really close-knit but dirt poor. He only got into modeling so he could give them a better life."

"I'm sure that fancy New York apartment of his and access to the world's most beautiful women have *nothing* to do with it," she says.

Yes, I read about his apartment purchase, too. And I was just as eager to get a look at it when he asked me to come spend the night. But I refuse to give in to Jade's chronic cynicism. If Duncan is as centered as he appears to be, then it makes sense he'd want to set up a home in his adopted city. Everyone needs a place to call home, especially in this business, which takes its toll on a person. "Well, he's very family oriented. Do you know his grandmother died while we were at the European collections? That's why we didn't see him after Paris. He left just after the Versace show. He barely made it back in time for the funeral."

"God forbid he gives up a chance to walk for Versace for dear old grandma's sake."

"Jade, how can you be so harsh?"

She looks at me, eyebrows dropping as she seems to study my face. Then, switching tracks, she says, "Oh, all right. So tell me something else: does kissing Duncan feel like receiving a sacrament—or do Duncan's kisses have that all-important nasty, naughty tang?"

Leave it to Jade to put it that way. By her standards, the intimate contact Duncan and I have shared so far would make a Nick at Nite rerun of *Mayberry RFD* seem risqué. Not that it bothers me, taking it slow. Okay, maybe I'm a *little* bothered. When I turned down his offer to spend the night together, I hadn't thought about the fact that our schedules would get in the way of us getting to know one another for a while longer—a long while longer. It's been two whole weeks since I've seen him, and we've barely had time for more than some texts and the odd phone call. Now aspects of my anatomy are so eager for his touch I find myself lapsing into a woozy stupor at inopportune times, like while sitting in the reception area of Ogilvy & Mather on a go-see for Oil of Olay. There's not much I can do about it, though—our schedules aren't in synch. Modeling's not the kind of normal job where you punch out at 6:00 p.m. so you can get with your significant other. Dating is for, I don't know, stockbrokers and secretaries.

Still, I refuse to let Jade taint what we have—whatever that is—so I think for a moment in order to describe how it feels when Duncan kisses me. "It feels like falling and you can't catch your breath," I explain. "Falling and you can't see straight as the world spins by you. I feel like with him, I have no need for gravity, because I'm safe when he's holding me, touching me. . . ." Goose bumps light up my entire body at the memory. Yes, that's exactly how it feels.

Jade stares at me, her mouth slightly open, and blinks.

"*Whoa!*" is all she says, without a hint of cynicism.

Suddenly I'm embarrassed. "Well, anyway, I haven't seen him since that night," I say quickly. "He's really got to work—he's in demand. He's just . . . I don't know, Jade, there's something about him that goes beyond his looks."

"Oh, clearly," she says. "He's special, your Duncan Shiloh."

Sixteen

When a supe deigns to shoot for the paltry editorial rate magazines pay, she can at least enjoy the ego trip of a ten-page layout all to herself. Plebian up-and-comers like myself don't have it quite so rich. After jumping through hoops—three go-sees! three!—*Vogue* didn't offer me a cover. That honor went to Stella Cheever, who is really hot at the moment, between her Victoria's Secret contract and the other covers she's done. According to Francesca and Renee, I'm on Anna Wintour's radar and it's only a matter of time before I get my own editorial spread there.

In the meantime, *Harper's Bazaar* is dispatching a Pretty Young Thing posse to gorgeous Palm Springs. According to Francesca, sending me there is bound to get Anna Wintour fired up about hiring me for *Vogue*, since the two magazines are in competition. I'm so excited because I get to work and to travel with not only Jade, but Duncan!

It's seems all my waiting for him is about to be rewarded. Though in truth, I'm not sure how much longer I'll be able to hold out with Duncan, once we're together under the hot desert sun.

I'm glad to have some quality time with Jade, too. Ever since Europe, my ambitions have kept me busier than ever. Jade, on the other hand, seems to have lost some of her drive. It's as if with Roman around, she felt she could conquer anything. And now. . . .

Now it's as if she's going through the motions.

I'm hoping Palm Springs turns things around for her.

Apparently, Jade isn't the only one who needs to turn things around in Palm Springs.

Randolf Duke, design darling from a decade ago, is trying to make a huge comeback with his new line—wide-legged calf-length cowboy pants, knotted ruffle shirts, bolero vests, and spring boots. Yup, boots for spring. Sillier trends have been known to happen, and since I'll be touting them in the pages of *Bazaar*, I shouldn't make mock. Only the last thing I want to do at the moment is put them on—it's 110 degrees in the shade, and there isn't any shade.

Still, nothing could wilt my mood. I've never been to California before, and here I am with my best friend *and* my new boyfriend. Okay, maybe it's premature to call Duncan a boyfriend, but something big is happening between us. In fact, as soon as we landed, he came by my room and asked me to meet up with him. We wound up taking a walk together with the desert sunset as a backdrop; he turned those gorgeous green eyes on me and said, "Look, this is probably going to sound crazy to you, Mac, but I've been thinking about it an awful lot and I just have to speak my mind. Even though our lives are crazy and it's so hard to connect, I want you to know that I think about you a lot. It's like I'm with you—even when, I'm not with you, you know?"

Oh, do I ever! Especially when he kisses me. My body heats up immediately, the warmth moving slowly up from my groin, an ache moving through me I need to satisfy. I feel like I'm coming home to something—someone—I've been longing for forever. . . .

"You're dead! You hear me? Dead! Mortuary meat! Dead, dead, dead!"

We're three thousand miles away from New York and it feels as though we're at least that far from November as the Palm Springs sun beats down. Reeve Levine's interpretation of Randolf Duke's collection refracts through the lens of the photographer's own style—a high-strung, chain-smoking study in tattoos and kohl. Call it Goth Gaucho. It took forever in makeup to powder us a ghoulish white and smudge our lids in a way that might be cute to a raccoon. But who am I to argue with a visionary like Reeve Levine?

"I feel like an extra in a Romero-Rodriguez 'collabo,'" Jade snickers, extending her arms and lurching forward. *"From Dusk till Dawn of the Dead."*

"That's it, Jade!" oozes Reeve. "You've got a lust for blood!"

Flora, a DNA girl, and Claudine, who's with Ford, follow Jade's lead, but it's hard for me to get inspired by their stiff-legged stalks and zoned-out stares—I've never felt so happy and alive. The jumpiness and fatigue and flat-out hunger I'd been experiencing vanished once Duncan entered the picture for real—it's as though I can live on his vibe.

"Go! Duncan, go!" Reeve screeches. "Give us your pent-up postapocalyptic passion!"

The man really is nuttier than a can of Planter's. But here

comes Duncan, a cross between Zorro and Dracula, shirtless under a cape, fake (I hope) nipple rings clamped to his chest. He gazes at me with his great green eyes, and at first I go weak—

"That's it, Mac. Swoon with the horror of the restless grave."

But then I blaze back at him—I can be equally fierce and frightening.

"Oh yes!" Reeve paroxysms. "Yes! You're a diva of destruction! You will not crawl back to the crypt till you've laid waste to all in your path."

And so the afternoon goes on, outfit after outfit, mirages appearing in the shimmering heat.

Then: "What? What? WHAT?" Reeve virtually attacks one of his assistants. "I cannot stop! We'll lose the light!"

The assistant meekly ducks and hands off the cell phone. "This had better be good!" Reeve shouts at it, then shuts up. "Ten-minute break, everyone," he calls. "Oh, Mac? It's for you."

Now I'm truly scared. My throat closes as though I just drank a quart of sand. Something awful must have happened to interrupt the shoot—my mom! my dad! Duncan, sweetness personified that he is, comes with me, guiding me toward the air-conditioned motor home we use as a dressing room. "Hello?" I croak.

"Moch, we must talk right now!"

"Renee? Is everything all right?" I almost faint from relief.

"All right, yes, of course. I have wonderful news, but we need to make some quick decisions."

Someone hands me a water bottle, and I gulp thirstily, hold it against my forehead. "Okay."

Renee says two words: "*Sports Illustrated*."

And I think: *Sports Illustrated? What could she possibly mean?* My dreams of *Sports Illustrated* vanished when they told me they would never hire me because I looked too much like Lilly Benedict, which was ridiculous, since her face is rounder than mine and besides, she dyed her hair black this season, but what was I going to say?

Then Renee says, "They want you for the Swimsuit Issue." Oh . . . oh! "Me?" I say.

"You. It is all over the tabloids today: Lilly Benedict is a neo-Nazi."

"Lilly Benedict!" I gasp. But she seemed so nice. . .

"Such a scandal. Terrible, terrible, terrible. Of course, I knew there was something rotten about that girl the first time I laid eyes on her. But that's Bonnouvrier's problem, not mine," Renee says dismissively of the DNA CEO. "You, my dear, are my concern. And since the film *S.I.* shot on Lilly is now worthless except to the most depraved and arcane collector, they must replace her, and I am in the process of convincing them to replace her with you. After all, they do think you two look alike."

Well, I suppose we are sort of similar in the looks department, but I never thought of myself in Lilly's league. "Oh, Renee!"

"It will mean acting quickly. The Swimsuit Issue is out in February; this is all very last minute. Several of your bookings next week would be canceled, including *Elle* and the Saks catalogue, and despite diplomatic finessing we may make some enemies. You would need to come back here right after the shoot tomorrow night. No dilly-dallying."

"Oh, Renee!" I'm like a broken record, but I don't know what else to say.

"Moch, this is a no-brainer. Any model would kill to be in *S.I.* What an opportunity! Never has anything happened like this before. You, Moch, you are perfect for *S.I.* You exude the robust, glowing image the industry needs right now. So I'm advising you to do this instead of your other bookings, and accept whatever slings and arrows Saks and *Elle* may send your way as a result."

This from a woman who a measly five months ago told me I was too fat for fashion. And here I am with a photographer exhorting me to look like I'm next in line for an autopsy. But it is true that the Council of Fashion Designers, in the wake of Veronica Gesso's death, established guidelines to promote healthier behavior and images. It's also true that I've still got about ten pounds on the average model. I'm not a stick, and I'd be proud to carry the torch.

"For you, Moch," Renee continues, "the direction your career is moving in, yes, I recommend that you do this, you take the risk."

I don't even think twice. "Oh, Renee!" I say. "Yes, yes! Of course!"

I turn to Duncan and realize I have just dashed our chances of being together on this trip.

"Is it just me, or is anyone else finding it difficult to *feel*?" Jade puts the question to the lodge at-large. Instead of a posh, modern Palm Springs resort, we're staying off the beaten track at the Esperanza Hacienda, a renovated Spanish adobe place that was a Hollywood hideaway in the '50s. Maybe Marilyn did JFK here. I'm sure *Bazaar* got it gratis, since it will serve as the location for tomorrow's shoot. Tonight, a few of us linger in the lobby bar, still recovering from post-traumatic stress of Reeve Levine.

"What's that supposed to mean, Jade?" asks Flora, slumped in a chair, inhaling lemonade.

"The shoot today—it's left me numb, inside and out." It's cool to be candid—Reeve and his crew flew out as soon as we wrapped.

"I hear that," says Dresden, the plump, punky makeup artist from L.A. "All that death stuff gave me the willies."

"You just don't appreciate what Reeve's trying to convey," says Claudine. Like many models with half a brain, she's compelled to justify the profession, attach a philosophical sensibility to fashion. "See, death is this metaphor for life." I did say she had *half* a brain.

"It's not that I fail to *appreciate* it, Claudine, and I'm sure it will print very arty with all those stark rock formations and twisted Joshua trees," she counters. "I'm just saying it had an effect on me."

"It *was* weird," I say, cuddled up with Duncan on a sofa. "Disturbing. Personally, I had trouble getting into it." I'm trying to be very chill and humble, not carrying on about my call from Renee, even though everyone knows I'll soon be en route to Costa Rica and bikinis and true supermodel stature. I'm enjoying these moments with Duncan and Jade and the other models, and I don't want to spoil the camaraderie I feel with them.

"Well, I had no trouble getting into it," Jade says, "and that's the trouble—I can't get out of it." She walks to where Dresden sits in a club chair, picks up her still untouched Rob Roy, and downs it in one swallow. Dresden beams up at her, impressed. "See? Basically straight whiskey and I feel *nada*."

"Give it a minute," Dresden says. "They sneak up on you."

"No, I'm anesthetized." She holds out her arm. "Pinch me," she says. "Go ahead, pinch me as hard as you can."

"No, Jade!" Dresden protests, so she changes position, proffering her tush and hiking up her shorts.

"Do it, Dresden. Grab hold of some cheek."

"*Um*, I . . . okay, you asked for it."

Dresden does it, with a little more zeal than necessary. But then I suspect Dresden has a thing for Jade so this invitation might be more than she can handle.

"Nothing," Jade declares, standing upright again.

"Well, now, I don't know about all this, Jade," Duncan says, then he turns to me and touches my jaw, shifting my face to kiss me.

"You feel that, angel?" he asks me when our lips part.

"*Ohhh*," I coo. "I'm not sure. Better try again."

"You know what? It's getting hot in here," says Flora. "I think I need to go to my room and call my boyfriend."

Claudine rises with a stretch. "What time is our call tomorrow?"

"Five." Glenn, one of the hair guys, looks up from his magazine. He's older, in his thirties, the veteran of a million shoots. "We all ought to turn in."

"Oh, Glenn, you know what? I have a mother." Dresden leers at Jade amiably. "Come on, Jade, you want to try the same experiment?"

Jade puts a hand on either side of her chair, leans over and gives her a teensy, teasing peck. "Sorry, Drez, still numb as they come." Then she stands up. "I just . . . want to . . . feel . . . ," she sings.

She traipses around the lounge, searching for God knows what. Then she saunters over to an end table beside the sofa no one's sitting in. The lamp with the stitched Western shade is switched off; she puts her hand inside and pulls out the bulb. Then, flipping the switch, she licks her two fingers and shoves them in the socket, letting out a sharp, piercing shriek.

"Jade!" I say, sitting up among a chorus of exclamations from everyone. "Jade! What happened? What did you do?"

"This!" she says, and does it again.

Eventually everyone disperses to their rooms. Even Jade pays heed to our early call tomorrow and turns in before she can fry the rest of her brains out. Either that, or she just got bored with our company once we pulled the plug—literally—on her little display of masochism.

"We should probably go to bed, too," I say, settling anew into marshmallow cushions in the lounge. We are the last to leave and I'm loath to go, as this will be the last night we can spend together. I'm nearly powerless to move; especially with the way Duncan's looking at me now that we're alone.

With the lightest, most sensitive touch, he traces the line of my collarbone, then slowly follows the same path with his lips, the ends of his hair brushing the rise of my breasts. It's agony to remain still as he does this, indescribably gorgeous agony that I withstand until his meandering mouth completes its journey. Then I reach for him, and our kiss is deep, tongues tangling, his hands running through my hair, then down my neck, over my breasts.

"I want you so bad," he says.

I kiss his throat, his chest, trailing back up again to his lips.

"Let's go to your room," he whispers. "Or mine . . ."

My eyes open. "I don't know if that's such a good idea . . . ," I begin, though the throbbing in my body tells me otherwise. I still feel a need to wait, to be sure. "We have to be on the set at five tomorrow and it's already eleven . . ." I smile shyly at him. "I don't want to rush for our first time. I want it to be perfect." Besides, I think, what do we do with our roomates?

He doesn't answer me, kissing me instead.

When his hands move over my breasts, I wish we were in my room. I have an aching urge to be out of these clothes.

Suddenly I feel cool air on my chest and I look down to see that Duncan has slipped the spaghetti straps of my sundress down, his tongue moving over my breasts.

I glance around, acutely aware that we are in the lounge. There's no one around, but still. . .

"Duncan, someone might see . . ."

He's slow to respond, his tongue circling my nipple before he slips my top back over my breasts, his mouth moving over mine once more.

I feel a momentary disappointment, until his big, warm hands slide under my dress, into my panties. . .

As he touches me, I feel his hardness as he pushes against my leg, the urgency of his breath on my face as he shudders and moans. His hands move in me gently, insistently. . .

"Oh God . . . Oh Duncan!" I cry out moments later, every thought of him, every fantasy I've ever had of him, coming to shattering climax.

"Did she really try to electrocute herself?" Flora asks as we sit in hair and makeup the morning after Jade's lightbulb impersonation.

"Of course not, she was just . . . being Jade." I try to play down the replay Dresden decided to share with Flora and Claudine, though the truth is I'm relieved that Jade's fireworks, rather than mine and Duncan's, are the topic du jour. I feel my face getting red even now when I think of what Duncan and I did in the hotel lounge last night! What if anyone had seen!

I try not to imagine what might have happened if I'd let him into my room. . . .

"I heard she stuck her tongue right in the socket," says Claudine, interrupting my woozy thoughts.

"That's ridiculous," I say, "Jade . . . she's like a child sometimes."

"A wild child," says Dresden with blatant admiration as she sweeps foundation onto Flora's face.

"If she's a child, then she's the poster child for birth control," says Glenn, his scorn affecting the way he goes at my head with his curling iron.

"You can stop talking about me in the third person because I'm here," Jade announces, plopping into a chair. "Very much alive and with my sensory organs restored."

We all fall silent. Jade munches a croissant, shrugs at us in the mirror bank. "You guys think I'm some kind of freak, but it's cool," she says flippantly. "I envy your simplicity, I really do. You can't even begin to imagine what it is to be me."

Claudine closes her eyes to oblige Tori, the other makeup artist. "How true, Jade, how true. My simple brain would never entertain the notion of making out with a lamp!"

I sure wish they'd change the subject. Between my little tryst with Duncan in the lounge and my upcoming *S.I.* shoot, I'm on top of the world right now, and Jade looks none the worse for wear. Soon we'll be rocking retro frocks in tropical colors and posing for Elena Blume, whose aesthetic is far less creepy than Reeve Levine's. So enough with the negativity, already. But Claudine is stubborn.

"Why not illuminate us, Jade? If there's a rationale behind sucking a light socket, I'm all ears."

"I don't want to talk about it," Jade snaps. Only her next sentence is, "It's like cutting. You've heard of that, Claudine? Surely someone you know has had relations with a razor blade."

"Yes, I've heard of cutting, but no, I don't know anyone sick enough to do it."

"I do," admits Dresden. "In high school, and even now. Self-injury isn't some teenage thing like everyone thinks, like some kind of fad or phase."

"In boarding school there was this girl who'd pull her hair out," ventures Flora. "Just yank it out in chunks. It was so incredibly sad."

"Oh, she was probably just desperate for attention," says Claudine.

"See, that's your problem." Jade's getting exasperated. "It's not sad or sick, and it's not about saying, 'Look at me, Mommy.' It's a way of getting a grip. Whether you're completely desensitized like I was last night and you need to reconnect, or you're in so much emotional pain you need a physical pain to distract you. It's a perfectly feasible way to take control."

The way Jade breaks it down, it makes sense—but of course it doesn't make sense at all. Jade stuffs the last of the croissant into her mouth, and Dresden pats her lips tenderly with a tissue. "I will say, however, that for a model, cutting isn't a viable option," Jade goes on relentlessly. "Nor is pulling your hair out or burning yourself. No scars, no marks, and certainly no bald spots!"

Listening to her makes me a little queasy, but Jade just laughs. "A model must always look intact—isn't that one of the commandments?" she says. "Thou shalt not self-mutilate. So I believe I had a genuine eureka moment last night. I can't wait to go online and share my epiphany with the modeling world."

I look at her, trying to see what's beneath this tirade, but as usual, Jade hides it all behind her smile.

Lilly Benedict's fall from grace is the talk of the set. That's because Alec Weidenhorn, a square-jawed, überpreppy male model with DNA, has flown out from New York last night and he's the human tabloid.

"At first they thought it was this big hoax, someone cut-and-pasting Lilly's head onto another body on the Internet," Alec regales us as we prance around the Esperanza's patio and pool. "Then one of Lilly's ex-boyfriends came forward with this videotape, and it was indisputably her. Not that it's illegal, this is still America and free speech and all that, but I bet my Rolex that girl never works again."

An enormous old-school beach ball is tossed into our midst.

"I bet she becomes more popular than ever," Jade says.

"Okay, kids, play nice now!" Laidback lens woman Elena Blume is a welcome reprieve from Reeve Levine, except I feel like I'm going blind in the merciless desert sun. Thank goodness for this setup, I get a vintage pair of shades, rhinestones twinkling in the cat's-eye corners—not that anyone's concerned with my retinal welfare, either; the specs simply go with the wasp-waisted, full-skirted spaghetti-strapped Re-becca Taylor I'm wearing.

"Well, did you know *Sports Illustrated*'s sending Mac to Costa Rica in Lilly's place?" Duncan says, as he lofts his ball to me. I smile at him, feeling a little thrill at the pride I hear in his voice, despite the flutter of anxiety I've been feeling around him today. Maybe I'm just nervous seeing him after what we shared last night, but I can't help but notice that ever since Alec arrived, Duncan has revved up the number of PDAs per minute. It makes me remember Jade's warning about straight models out to prove something. I wonder if Duncan is doing this grandstanding for Alec, who no one would ever mistake for a heterosexual. Maybe Duncan wants to make sure Alex— and the rest of us—know he's straight. In retrospect, he did really like the whole public aspect of our lounge moment last night. . . .

"Ooh no, I didn't know that," says Alec, ravenous for the latest tidbit. "Mac, that's fabtastic. Kudos to you." He encir-cles Jade's waist with fastidiously smooth hands, and she leans back against his linen shirtfront, raising a finger to caress his cheek.

"Jade, stop scowling," chides Elena. "Remember, you're having *fun*."

I glance over and see Jade go from a frown to mindless gaiety in a heartbeat, and it seems to satisfy Elena, who starts shooting again.

"Okay, kids, that was too cute," Elena lauds us, and off we troop for yet another change.

"Mac, suck it up a little," the dresser pleads as she struggles to zip me into an Alexander McQueen.

"I *am* sucking it up," I reply, exasperated.

She stops the tugging frenzy going on behind my back. "Goddamn it, the zipper's stuck. I'm going to get some soap. Mac, don't move."

"Yo, hon-bun. What up?" Jade says, gliding into the dressing area as she munches on a doughnut. She and Brynn, the editor for *Bazaar*, seemed to have bonded over their ability to eat endless amounts of food and never gain an ounce. It seems every time I look at them during the shoot today, they're at the catering table, wolfing down cookies or cake and chatting. I've never seen anything like it in a fashion editor—or a model, for that matter.

"Not my zipper," I reply, trying not to begrudge her for her metabolism, which would be pretty easy to do at a moment like this. "Donna's gone for soap—hopefully I won't hyperventilate before she gets back."

"Ah, the old soap trick," she says, circumnavigating me appreciatively. "That dress is awesome on you."

"Half on me, you mean." I squirm.

"Jesus, Mac, be still—your skin's practically caught in the teeth." She comes up behind me. "They ought to fire that woman for leaving you like this. Better let me unzip you before you get bitten; you can't afford to have the slightest nick on your skin. Damaged goods will never do in *S.I.*"

I step out of the dress, exhale fully, inhale deeply. "So that's oxygen," I say. "Thanks, Jade."

Clucking, she examines the garment. "Look at this, here's the problem—there's a tiny thread in the zipper. Let me take it to better light; I'll be right back." Then she disappears, the Alexander McQueen in tow.

* * *

Let's just say I'm pretty mad in pink. Clueless, too. All I know is Donna returns and sheepishly thrusts this horrific froufrou polka-dotted clown suit at me and I'm supposed to put it on. Team player I may be, but I'm hardly pleased when I hit the set to find Jade doing her best Sleeping Beauty routine in *my* Alexander McQueen. Of all the sneaky, bratty, bitchy. . .

Let it go, I tell myself and I try to, except it's hard when I learn that the McQueen is going to be the subject of a two-page horizontal layout. I glance over at Brynn, nibbling on a chocolate-chip cookie as she looks on, obviously pleased with her decision to put Jade in my dress. Clearly, she doesn't feel like she's had a fast one pulled on her. And why would she? Her brain is just as clouded over by sugar as Jade's is by . . . ambition? Envy?

Whatever it is, I'm sick of it.

But, as I watch Elena adjust the drape over the dress and direct Jade to lie back on a settee, I decide that I'm not going to let it get the better of me.

It's just one picture, one dress, and I've got more important things to think about. For instance, how quickly I can pack after this last shot, as I'm taking the red-eye home after we wrap. And if I can sneak some face time with Duncan before I go. I wish I didn't need to leave tonight but *S.I.* needs a fitting and *S.I.* fittings are supposed to be an event in themselves. I heard through the grapevine they try on as many as five hundred suits per girl, looking for the suits that fit best. Some of the models and crew are leaving tonight; I'd much rather be here with Duncan. Tonight could have been our night.

The thought excites me just as much as it scares me. I am in love with him, though—I think . . . maybe. It could still be infatuation. Or a giddy symptom of the atmosphere here in the middle of nowhere.

Whatever it is, it's got me a little crazy.

I'm trying not to be annoyed that I have to leave. Trying to maintain my cool. But when I come upon Claudine and Duncan sitting together in the hotel lounge, I nearly lose it.

I remember the throngs that surrounded him at the shows, how he seemed to lap up the attention. He seems to be enjoying this little tête-à-tête, too.

A little too much for my liking. Maybe it's for the best that I've decided to leave tonight. My career needs to come first right now, not some sweet-faced southern boy who appears to have charmed me—and everyone else in his path, apparently.

Since they don't see me, I stop, slip back behind the curtained entranceway to spy on them.

It's harmless, I realize with relief. No one would characterize their exchange as anything other than friendly.

Yet there's something about it . . . something about Duncan's expression as he gives her the old southern-boy-does-good story, telling her about how he's supporting his parents back home.

And Claudine . . . well, her features go soft as he tells his tale, her expression looking a lot like how I *felt* when Duncan told me the same story.

If I didn't know better, I'd think Duncan was using that story to win favor.

"Well, hey . . . ," he says now when I enter the room finally, not because I'm ready to but because voices behind me—only two busboys, I realized belatedly—startled me out of my hiding place.

The moment I see those eyes, that smile, I forget my reservations. He is the sweetest guy in the whole world. I'm going to have to get used to the fact that I may not be the only woman who adores him.

"Hey, Duncan," I say. "Claudine."

She smiles at me, then gets up from her chair. "I'll leave you two lovebirds alone," she says, glancing up at the clock on the wall. "I need to get ready for dinner."

Once she's gone, Duncan pulls me into his lap. "So, angel, looks like we aren't going to get a full night together after all."

I look into his eyes, and it almost breaks my heart to have to leave him here. We hadn't discussed sex, but what happened between us in the lounge last night made it all but a given for tonight.

Yes, tonight *would have* been our night for sure. Except I've got to fly to New York.

"Much as I want to stay here . . . to be with you . . . I have to go, Duncan. I need to do my fitting for *S.I.* and—"

He pats a finger to my mouth and I stop. I can see a swirl of emotions in his eyes—disappointment mixed with desire mixed with something I don't recognize—anger? No, not anger. Duncan doesn't have an angry bone in his body.

Then he kisses me again, making my regret even greater.

Leaning back, his expression becomes serious. "This shoot is a big deal, Mac. You have to put it first."

I smile then, leaning in to hug him, so grateful for his goodness, his understanding.

Jade was wrong. Dating someone in the business isn't as bad as she made it out to be. Who else but another model would understand?

Seventeen

It's snowing in New York. The first snowfall of the year, a blizzard actually, and earlier than expected. I would have loved to have seen it—I'm a big fan of winter.

Except my flight has been canceled. Now I will have to fly straight to Costa Rica and do a fitting when I arrive.

It feels a little like fate. Like Duncan and I were *meant* to spend this night together.

Which is why I'm giddy in the limousine back to the hotel. I call Renee and she re-books everything for me and breaks the news to Diane Smith, the editor of *S.I.*, that they will have to carry all five hundred suits to location.

Now I can't wait to see Duncan's face when he discovers I'm back for the night!

Racing through the lobby of the Esperanza, I spot Claudine talking to Flora at the hotel bar. "Have you seen Duncan?"

They exchange a look. "Not lately," Claudine says. "You might want to check his room."

I think I hear them laugh together as I walk away, though if there's a joke being told, I'm certainly not in on it.

And I could care less, heading straight to Duncan's room,

knocking on his door and calling his name. No answer. Maybe he turned in early? He did say he was tired from the shoot. I smile at the thought of crawling into bed with him, surprising him.

When they remodeled the Esperanza Hacienda, they didn't modernize it much. The doors don't have security cards, and they don't lock automatically—you have to lock your room from the inside, or use your key as you leave. Hoping he may have forgotten this, my hand reaches for the knob. It turns easily. The door opens.

I don't want to believe what I see: Duncan on the bed, stretched out full, the soles of his feet staring up at me, his face hidden by the girl who straddles him, her tumble of platinum curls tossing with the slow, insistent, rhythmic motion of her body.

Are toe prints like fingerprints, completely unique to the individual? Can you read a sole like a palm—might a man's destiny be encrypted there? Strangely still, I stare at the soles of Duncan's bare feet. Where else can I possibly look? Not at Jade, her hips bucking gently forward and back, the notes of her spine one long arpeggio from base to nape. Another girl wouldn't bother to look; she'd just leap, take a fistful of that pale hair and yank her off him like a rag doll. Only there's no rage in me. All I feel is startled, sad, and confused.

Jade looks over her shoulder, mild and calm, as if somehow, she was expecting me. "Oh, hey, you're back," she says, and with lazy catlike grace makes her dismount. Duncan, at least, has the good grace to pull the sheet over himself, his expression startled, though not as upset as I might have liked. He seems almost proud of himself, as if he's proven something to himself, to all of us.

Leisurely, Jade reaches across his torso for her tank top, pulls it over her head. "Either of you guys see my skirt?"

I simply shake my head—at everything, every single pathetic thing this girl has done since the day I met her.

I look at Duncan, waiting. Finally I do get something that sounds like an apology, though it's not very satisfying. "I'm sorry, Mac." He shrugs. "You know how it gets on these shoots. Downright lonely." Then he gets up, "I'll leave you two to duke it out," he says, as if he was the prize, as if what was at stake was winning him and not losing me.

How could I have been so wrong about him?

"Ah, here it is," Jade says, as Duncan slips into his jeans and out of the room. Wriggling into a slinky jersey, she lets her eyes meet mine—boldly, but briefly.

It's long enough for me to recognize she's on something. Some potent mixture of speed and alcohol would be my guess.

Not that that makes this situation forgivable.

There's a tight, terrible weight in my chest, like I'm wearing a lead corset. But no, it's inside—it's my heavy, heavy heart. And here's Jade, slipping on espadrilles, heading for the door. Will the solid boulder of misery root me to the spot? No—some kind of confrontation is necessary. I'm not going to hit her; I don't have the strength or desire to fight. I only want to understand. So all I say is, "Jade—*why*?"

Instantly she's in my face—it's what she's been waiting to hear. "Why?" Her hands plant on hips, her lips twist into an ugly sneer. "I'll tell you why. Payback."

"Payback?" My face begins to crumble with incomprehension. "For what? What have I done to you? What have I *ever* done to you?"

"Not what you did to me," she says. "Roman. What you did to Roman."

"Roman?"

"What, you thought I'd let you get away with it? I saw you *pawing* him. You took my man—or tried—so I took yours. All's fair in love and war, *n'est pas?*"

Pawing him? What does she . . . ? Oh. That. But please, not even a quivering mass of insecurity like Jade could misconstrue the conversation that took place in a chilly corner of a rock club. Except, of course, that's exactly what she's done. "Jade, you're wrong. There was nothing going on between Roman and me. Nothing. We were just talking." Sentences fall from my mouth like stones.

"Yeah? What about? What could you—you insipid suburban diva of mundane—possibly have to talk about with Roman, all alone in the dark? Only it wasn't totally dark, was it, Mac. You undo a few buttons for him, give him a peek at the goods before sealing the deal? Huh? You let him cop a feel?" Her words are coarse but her tone is light—she's being all blasé, acting like she's over it, without having the vaguest notion how ridiculously and ironically wrong she is, "Not that I care anymore," she goes on. "Seducing Duncan was merely an addendum, my way of achieving closure. Hope it doesn't hurt *too* bad."

The strange thing is it doesn't—not in the way she intended, anyway. "It doesn't hurt, Jade—it doesn't hurt one bit." This gets her; she looks at me sharply. "What does hurt is that you didn't trust me—that you actually believe I would go for Roman, that I'd do that to you. Because here's the thing, Jade: I'm a virgin. That's right, me, jet-setting *Sports Illustrated* supermodel. Do you really think I'd reach the ripe old age of eighteen with my so-called virtue intact just to do something as twisted as waste it on the guy who's in love with you? You want to know what we were talking about, Jade? We were talking about you . . . how to *help* you."

I see this information register on Jade's face. She is clearly struggling with the idea that she just made a terrible blunder. Finally, she folds her arms, defensive. "Help me?" Her eyes are riveted on me now. "Help me with *what*?"

"Oh, just the little matter of your drug problem," I tell her. "Yes, Roman told me, and we were discussing how to keep you from destroying yourself." I shake my head. "Heroin, Jade, Jesus Christ." How had he described her? A human rubbish bin. "What's more, he said you were indiscriminate; you'd take anything. Snort it, smoke it, swallow it—maybe even inject it for all I know. Not that he's any better; he basically admitted that, too. The point is we were worried about you. Roman knew he was a bad influence, he didn't want to drag you down, so we decided it would be for the best if he broke up with you."

There, I've said it. And suddenly I wish I could take it back. The wretched reckoning of betrayal in Jade's amber eyes makes me want to spin back the seconds. But I can't. The truth is out. It's dripping all over Jade as if I'd splashed her with a bucket of paint. It's awful and it's ugly and it's out, and I can't begin to fathom what she's going to do with it.

"That is so funny," she says finally. "You crack me up, Mac."

I shrink a step away from her, averting my eyes.

"You ought to write for Conan or *SNL* or something. Really, I had no idea you were such a wacky, wacky wit." Then, she lets out a cackle that I can hardly describe as laughter. "How brilliant of you to deliberate my fate with my boyfriend. You,

Mac, with all your vast experience and infinite wisdom, took it upon yourself to encourage the man I love to leave me. And why wouldn't you? You're Mac Croft, and everything *you* do is correct and everything I do is corrupt, so how could I possibly be able to lead my own life and make my own choices. And then—this is the truly funny part—as if urging him to break my heart isn't enough, you keep it a secret!"

Jade strides forward, until she's an inch away from me. "So you know what's best for me? You didn't want Roman to fuck me up, drag me down? Well, guess what? I don't need anyone to do that. I can do it all by myself."

Alone in my hotel room, wide awake, watching the ceiling as my mind unravels knots of thoughts like snakes.

The most disturbing thoughts aim their barbs at me, though. Jade's accusations are, of course, right on target. What gave me the right to intrude on her life? Who do I think I am? And look how it all turned out—what a colossal mess. Yet while I want her forgiveness, can *I* forgive *her*? She not only scammed me during the shoot yesterday, she seduced the man I was falling for! Even if Duncan turned out to be just as insecure and in need of affirmation as Jade claimed, that doesn't excuse her actions. She as much as admitted that the seduction was part of her revenge against me for my "seducing" Roman.

Secrets. Stupid, stupid secrets. We keep them because we think they protect us when all they do is set us up. If I'd only told Jade the truth, that I'd never been with a man, "done the deed," or whatever, she'd have known I wouldn't have gone for Roman. It's so silly, my accidental chastity—I've just been too busy for sex. Or too scared. Maybe I was just waiting for the right man. I thought Duncan was that man. What a mistake that would have been. Whatever, if only I'd shared the truth, Jade and I could have laughed about it. Except I feared she'd laugh at me, not with me. Cite me for the suburban yabbo I was and take her friendship and all it afforded away.

Of course, I wasn't the only one with a secret. If she'd been up front about her drug use—well, I can't say I would have sanctioned it, but I think I could have accepted Jade. I know I would have tried. At least I wouldn't have had to pretend I didn't know all about it. There would have been no clandestine conversation between Roman Price and me—and no need for Jade to use Duncan to exact her revenge.

I sigh, blowing out all my sadness and frustration. A few hours ago I was on top of the world, feeling like the luckiest woman ever! In love with the most gorgeous man and about to offer myself to him. Funny how fate can twist like that. Who would have imagined this ending to what was the most wonderful day?

Losing Duncan was one thing. And now that I know he's just as messed up and insecure as the worst of the people in this business, I can't say that I even want him. I'm just glad I found out sooner rather than later.

But losing Jade . . . it's a bit more complicated. As much as she drove me crazy, and even though I wondered if I was insane to keep her in my life, I'd come to rely on her. I'd come to love her. As a best friend. But now . . . now I didn't know what we were to each other.

I awake to a knock on my door.

A mix of surprise and sadness and, yes, anger fills me when I find Duncan on the other side.

"I know I'm the last person you want to see, but I thought you'd want to know . . . Jade is missing."

"Missing?"

"Apparently she borrowed Dresden's car and took off."

My body stiffens and I'm sure my face has gone white, if the way Duncan is looking at me is any indication. "Duncan, Jade is a New Yorker. She couldn't have taken Dresden's car because Jade never bothered to learn how to drive!"

Priorities rearrange like pieces in a puzzle, snapping into place. The concierge hears our concerns, leaves her post, gets her car. Within three miles we see it—the silver and blue discarded candy wrapper that was formerly Dresden's Volkswagen Beetle. Against an inselberg—one of those forbidding rock formations that make the Mojave so otherworldly—the bright metal looks like carelessly strewn litter. Only this litter is smoking. I feel as though I've been shot and grasp onto Duncan's T-shirt, taking the shelter he offers, despite all that has gone down between us. Sirens pierce the morning. *Hurry*, I pray, *dear God, please, please, hurry*. The ambulance, the rescue crew, the Jaws of Life. Could anyone survive a wreck like this?

Even now we don't know for sure. We don't know much of anything. We've spoken to police, doctors, Jade's mother on the phone but we haven't told all we surmise. That on a whim she gulped what was left of her stash, got behind the wheel, figured out the fundamentals but then lost control and went off the road, running headlong into the massive pile of rocks.

Lost. I seize on the word. No way will I accept that she decided, willingly, willfully, threw up her hands and closed her eyes. Jade's life may be a crazy one, but she wanted it. *Wants* it. *Please.* She's in surgery, and they won't reveal much about her condition—we're not family.

"That's not fair; you don't understand," I try to communicate with a nurse, an administrator, anyone with a clipboard or a lab coat. "You *have* to tell me what's going on." My voice breaks. "She's my best friend."

"Sorry, miss, we can't give out that information." The line is delivered politely yet firmly. It's TV dialogue. Brisk motion everywhere. Aside from the hospital staff, everyone is ancient—I guess that's why they call Palm Springs God's Waiting Room. We're in the waiting room of God's Waiting Room. Creepy.

My phone rings. "Oh, Leonora, yes, okay . . ." Jade's mother gives me her estimated time of arrival. Why, I don't know; I guess she needs some semblance of connection. She also tells me Jade's father has been found; he's flying in, too. I try to convince myself that the presence of these two people whose genetic material converges inside my friend will be helpful, healing. But I don't know. It's as though we've all failed Jade.

My parents call, ask if there's anything they can do. Then Renee calls. And Francesca. Then Renee and Francesca, double-teaming me on the speakerphone in Renee's office.

"Moch, darling, I know how you must feel," says Renee.

No you don't, I want to tell her.

"But you've got to keep your eyes on the prize," says Francesca.

Oh. Sure. That's what this is about. Costa Rica. *S.I.* I don't want to even have to think about it, but Francesca and Renee will not let me avoid the facts: I'm on the cusp of something new, the next higher level. If I turn my back on it now. . .

"Moch, are you listening?"

"Yes yes yes," I say. But my heart, soul, and mind are united in denial. *No, no no. . .*

I return to the hotel with Duncan.

"Hey, Mac," he says, when I start to walk away the moment we get out of the cab. I need to get my bags. I need to call a car. I need to keep my distance.

But Duncan reels me back in. "Look, I just want to say that it's not that I didn't—that I don't—care about you."

I look at him. "Remember that time I told you how hard it was to make friends?" he continues. "Well, you were my first friend, Mac. Maybe my only friend. With Jade . . . well, something else was at play there. I don't know. Maybe it was loneliness . . ." He meets my gaze. "Or maybe I just needed a quick fix. You and Jade were so close. Maybe I want to grab onto that somehow. Experience some of that intimacy you both had."

I want to lash out at him. Want to tell him that he doesn't know the first thing about intimacy if he could treat another person the way he treated me. But his words fill me with an ache for all I've lost.

Not with Duncan.

With Jade.

"I'm so sorry, Leonora," I say when she calls me from the cab to LaGuardia as I head to my room alone.

"Mac, thank you, but I'll be fine," she says, her strained voice filled with resolve. "More importantly, Jade will be fine. We must believe that."

Her conviction is a tow rope; I try to hold on. "*Um*, Leonora, there may be this other girl there," I explain. "Dresden—she was on the shoot with us, the makeup artist, and she and Jade made friends. It was . . . it was her car."

A pause. "I see," Leonora says.

"I can pack up Jade's stuff if you'd like." I just want to be of some use.

"Thank you, I'd appreciate that. Have it sent to Le Parker Meridien."

"Okay, I will."

"You're a good girl, Mac," Leonora says, her voice quavering. "A good friend to Jade." *Am I?* I wonder. Abandoning her in a coma, to do whatever it is I do. "Don't worry. We'll all be together in New York soon."

"Okay." I breathe, and hang up, and stare into space. Then I grab whatever things I unpacked last night, stuff it into my suitcase. Jade's stuff won't be so easy. It's like a bomb exploded in Bryant Park, items flung willy-nilly, way too much for a five-day location trip. Wispy Narciso Rodriguez, funky Betsey Johnson, a little Luca Luca, a smattering of Miu Miu, and what's this—I pick up a dress that looks familiar and realize it's the Vivienne Westwood she "shootlifted" from our very first job together.

I sink down on the bed and finally give in to the tears that I've bottled up inside ever since the beginning of this ordeal. Sobs rack my body as I remember Jade that day, how she was the only one who even paid me any mind. How she offered her sage and witty, albeit cynical, advice time and time again. How she opened her home to me and rescued me from whatever pitfalls of the business I fell into. *God, she was even right about male models*, I think, remembering her words of warning about Duncan.

I'm not sure how long I cry, but when the tears finally sub-side, I sigh and snap back into action, gathering her things quickly. No matter how bad I feel, I still have a plane to catch. That thought sends another shot of despair through me. No matter how bad I feel, I still need to go on. Then, I smile sadly, realizing that perhaps Jade might advise the same thing. . . .

I come across the handbag with her essentials—olive green leather, gold hardware, a French label I never heard of, an era I cannot place. When she went on her joyride, she'd left it behind. Refusing to dwell on whether that "means" anything or not, I make sure it's all in order. House keys, Gucci wallet, passport—which of course she carries everywhere, having no driver's license for ID—Altoids, phone. I throw it all back in. Then I freeze. Collecting clothing and accessories isn't help-ing Jade. It's one less thing for her mom to do, maybe, and it's giving me an illusion of being helpful. But it's not doing a damn thing for Jade—touch and go between life and death.

And I want to, need to, do something for *her*. No, *undo* something. Back in her bag, I pull out her phone. The number is still on speed dial. I steel myself, take a breath. It rings and rings and rings.

The spiders are the size of grapefruit. After a while you get used to them. In the rain forest you never know what will fall from the canopy of trees. The birds, the bugs. There's one incredible moment when I'm literally tree hugging and this butterfly lands on my arm. Brilliant blue wings, big as slices of bread, yet completely transparent. Cliff Watts, the photog-rapher, is capturing it all but the camera in my mind is far superior, permanently recording this miracle to memory.

In a way I was dreading the shoot, but nature has curative

powers. I'm submerged in it, like a pool. I haven't worn shoes in four days. The air is so thick with moisture, it gives a glow to my skin that's almost phosphorescent. There's mud in my hair, under my nails. I'd feared the *S.I.* team would have this frat-boy mentality, but everyone seems as awed by the environment as I am. We speak as little as possible—language would feel intrusive here. And while the bathing suits are more than minimal, there's a part of me that would rather wear nothing at all.

Since there are no cries of "fabulous!" and "beautiful!"— encouragements I've grown accustomed to—at first I wonder if I'm doing a good job, if I look okay. Except after a few setups the jungle gets inside me and I know this is the best work I've ever done. My inhibitions vanish. This is the real deal—a full 180 from the fake Eden the Corsican rigged up in his studio. The lush leaves and petals are richer than any velvet or satin; the colors invigorate and excite me. There's no need for Cliff to direct me; I know exactly what to do. Climb, stretch, loop, hang. I'm an animal. I wade into a waterfall, slippery stones and all. . .

Yet as easily as I "go native," every evening I'm brought back to the real world by fax. I'd asked Francesca to check in with Leonora and send updates on Jade. She's conscious. She has nineteen broken bones, one for every year of her life. It will be a long recovery, but she's getting stronger. Her man, Roman, is at her bedside. Her mother wants her moved to Columbia Presbyterian; her father insists on Mount Sinai. She sends me her love. I need this news; it gives me permission to go on. Part of Jade is with me in the wild, and I know she would approve of my savage soul unleashed.

A+

AUTHOR
INSIGHTS,
EXTRAS, &
MORE...

FROM
**CAROL
ALT**
AND
AVON A

Advice from Carol Alt

People often ask me for the best advice I can give a young girl who wants to become a model, and here is what I tell them: "Go straight to the top!" Don't fool around with your hometown agent (unless, of course, your hometown is New York City). Go straight to the people renowned for "making stars."

If that doesn't work, go to the next best agent you can find, and work your way down. If you have potential, why waste time starting at the bottom? This is a business for the "young," so don't waste any time achieving your dreams.

Also, do *not* waste money, sometimes thousands of dollars, and, again, valuable time, on a portfolio. My agents took one look at *me,* at my face, and made the decision right there that I had "it." So, unless you photograph very differently from the way you look in person—and I mean your big nose looks tiny without Photoshop and from every angle—you do not need photos to prove to an agent that you can get out there and work. Remember, they are trained to see potential, and if you have that potential, they'll see it.

Finally, if anyone approaches you at any time, whether you are with an agency or not, always take the card and turn it over to your agent (if you already have one) or your parents. Most predators will shrink at the voice of an adult talking on your behalf!

However, if this is a person with honest motives, one who really wants to give you a helping hand, they will still do so through your parents or your agent. They will respect you for being smart and protective of yourself and your future. No one wants to work with someone reckless—especially not a top modeling agent!

Now, you're probably thinking, "Okay, I know what I should do to find an agent. But what else can I do if I want to be a model?" Keep reading. . . .

The Ten Best Ways to Prepare for Your Meeting with a Modeling Agent

1. Eat raw foods for one month beforehand. Your skin will look healthier. You will look less bloated. If you are overweight, you will lose weight while still looking healthy! And, most important, you will have great energy—a must for any top model today!

2. Go see a professional hairdresser and *do not cut your hair short*. Just trim it neatly so it looks groomed.

3. Get your eyebrows plucked by a pro. You cannot see yourself clearly when you do it yourself. You need an outside observer to do a good job.

4. You don't need fancy clothes. Wear a nice pair of low slung jeans. Pair them with a white T-shirt and a clean tailored jacket to go over it. NO makeup. Let the agent fantasize about what you will look like all dressed up and on a set. Better to be less specific and more all-around clean and good-looking.

5. Instead of that fancy portfolio bring some family photos. If you have potential they will see it just as easily in some family snapshots as in an expensive portfolio. By bringing

the photos, though, you show that you've given this meeting some thought and made some preparation. (Instead of just seeing a sign on a door that says Model Agent and coming in to give it all a try!)

6. Do not look desperate. No one wants to work with someone who is desperate—desperate people can be so annoying.

7. Eat something before you go, because no one looks more desperate than a skinny, hungry model.

8. Carry your own water and go to the bathroom first! It may take some time before the agent is free, she might have fifteen girls ahead of you. You don't want to miss your turn because you left to get a drink or were in the ladies' room.

9. Turn off your phone. Politeness is a great weapon.

10. Don't be in a rush. Remember, patience is not only a virtue, it can also be the key that opens up a multi-million-dollar door for some lucky girl. So stay cool while you're waiting; your turn will come.

Five Questions for Carol

1. **If you had a daughter would you let her get into the modeling business?** Absolutely! It is one of the only businesses where a woman makes more money than a man, and in which a young girl can achieve financial stability, meet great people, and travel the world—all while becoming famous and securing her future.

2. **Were you really discovered waiting tables in your hometown?** I sure was. I was working at the Steer Barn on Long Island. And I really had forgotten that the photographer had given his card to me—and I did put it through the wash!

3. **You were traveling all around the world, and seeing some pretty wild stuff, while you were quite young. How did you manage to keep your head on your shoulders?** I had a good family behind me. My parents always said I could come home at any time, no questions asked, and they would not consider it to be "failure." So, knowing that I always had a place to go made me less desperate.

    Also, because my parents were strong and tough on me when I was a kid, I knew quite decisively what was right and what was wrong and I never deviated from what they had taught me.

4. **What's the craziest thing you've ever been asked to do while on a shoot?** Hang from the Brooklyn Bridge! While the cars were still passing below, mind you!

5. **You are a huge proponent of the raw-food diet. How did you get involved in it, and how has it changed your life?** I got involved with raw foods because so much dieting was killing me—literally! So I had to do something to save my career and save my life. And in fact, I wonder what kind of major changes there would have been to my destiny/ career—for the better, I am sure—if I had found raw foods sooner. If someone had told ME what I am telling YOU.

Carol Alt

For more than two decades, **CAROL ALT** has been one of the world's most recognizable names and faces. In addition to gracing the cover of more than seven hundred magazines, she has made calendars, posters, and exercise videos, all of which have sold millions of copies. An accomplished spokesperson, frequent guest on talk shows, and a contestant on this year's *Celebrity Apprentice*, she has acted on stage and television and in more than sixty-five movies. Carol is also the author of two raw-food lifestyle books, *The Raw 50* and *USA Today* bestseller *Eating in the Raw*.

ARE YOU
NEXT YEAR'S MODEL?

And between the ages of 16 and 25?

If so, you can **ENTER FOR A CHANCE TO APPEAR ON THE COVER** of Carol Alt's next novel from Avon A!

The winner will also receive a **trip for two to NEW YORK CITY** to participate in a professional photo shoot.

And a **$500 shopping spree** from Lord & Taylor!

And the opportunity to have an **agency "meet and greet"**!

Supermodel Carol Alt and a panel of judges will help to select our winner!

**Go to our website
http://harpercollins.com/nextyearsmodel
for official rules and details.**

AVON

This contest runs from 8/26/2008 through 11/20/2008.
Open to US residents only. No Purchase Necessary.

TYM 0908